The Gift of Shame

'If you are to be taken like a man, then you will dress like one,' said Jeffrey. 'You have one hour before I greet your identical twin brother.'

Turning, he left her alone with a heart-pounding dread at what she had asked for. Damn him, she thought. Why couldn't he have just taken her? Why force her into this humiliating ritual and make her responsible for her own madness? If she did as he asked there was no escape, no turning back, no excuses she could make to herself. Finding a full-length mirror she questioned her reflection.

'Shall you be his whore?'

After a moment's pause the image in the mirror, eyes wild with light, smiled and nodded.

By the same author:

Unfinished Business

The Gift of Shame

Sarah Hope-Walker

BL

This book is a work of fiction.
In real life, make sure you practise safe, sane and consensual sex.

First published by Black Lace 1994
2 4 6 8 10 9 7 5 3 1

This edition published in Great Britain in 2008 by
Black Lace
Virgin Books
Random House,
20 Vauxhall Bridge Road,
London SW1V 2SA

www.rbooks.co.uk

Addresses for companies within The Random House Group Limited can be found at:
www.randomhouse.co.uk/offices.htm

The Random House Group Limited Reg. No. 954009

Distributed in the USA by Macmillan, 175 Fifth Avenue, New York, NY 10010, USA

A CIP catalogue record for this book is available from the British Library

ISBN 9780352342027

The Random House Group Limited supports The Forest Stewardship Council (FSC), the leading international forest certification organisation. All our titles that are printed on Greenpeace approved FSC certified paper carry the FSC logo.
Our paper procurement policy can be found at www.rbooks.co.uk/environment

Typeset by Palimpsest Book Production Limited, Grangemouth, Stirlingshire

Printed and bound in Great Britain by CPI Bookmarque Ltd, Croydon, Surrey

1

Helen lay her head on this stranger's belly and contemplated the source of her pleasure.

His cock, in repose, she decided, was quite beautiful. Much more complicated and intricately worked than she had ever before noticed. Thick veins ran their complicated patterns under its fleshy surface. The skin shone with the buffing of its recent exertions. Exertions which still burned deep in her belly. Taking it delicately between the tips of her fingers she lifted it to feel its dead weight and then, moving her head, probed it with her tongue. It moved like the live thing it was, and she could feel it tensing in expectation. An answering response came from deep inside herself and, reaching just an inch or two more she took him, limp still but already stirring, between her lips. She savoured him for a moment before taking him wholly into her mouth.

His body flinched and he moaned, but all she cared for was the stirring in her mouth. With rising excitement she felt him growing, hardening, and she raised herself slightly so that the downward thrusts of her lips could become whole-hearted engulfments. As she felt him reaching down to caress her head she knew she wanted to swallow him whole. She pounded him against the back of her throat and only wished she could reach further and deeper to take him in completely.

He called out and broke the mood but the Devil rose in her. She resented his intrusion on her private pleasure. She didn't want him involved in this. Didn't want his voice, his needs, to interfere with her own pleasure. For hours she had submitted to his demands, but this, she was determined, would be hers alone. She wanted this pleasure for herself – he was a necessary accomplice but she didn't want him interfering.

Taking her mouth from him she whispered urgently. 'Be still!' She saw that his own pleasure had caused him to thrash his head from side to side. Raising herself up, she swung her thighs across his fully roused cock. 'I'm going to have *you*,' she told him. 'This has nothing to do with you. Be still.'

Tucking his huge arousal inside herself, she looked down on his closed eyes, clenched teeth, and knew that this was difficult for him. It was his initial assertiveness that had brought them to this pass in less than twenty-four hours from meeting. She was as astonished as he that she was taking the initiative – asserting herself in a way she had never done before.

Her hands pressing down on his hips allowed her to more precisely control her own body's movement. As she did so she tried to, objectively, study her body's pleasure. Outside of this room, beyond this bed, she knew there was a world resounding with sophistication, constructed to man's own arrogant pleasures but here, at the junction of her loins with his, was the oldest, most exquisite pleasure known to human-kind. Needing no artifice or machines, it was a lust unchanged from beyond the birth of civilisation and one she intended to have in full measure.

Her head flung back as she ground slowly down onto him, the fire licking deep into her belly, his hands on her breasts. 'No!' she admonished him. 'Don't touch me! This is mine!'

Still moving with a smooth, slow, rhythm, refusing to respond to her body's increasing urgency, she swayed herself into a circular motion and reflected on how this exquisite moment had come about.

This man had found her out. Less than twenty-four hours previously she would have been offended if anyone had thought of her as anything other than a virtuous widow.

Kenneth had died ninety feet under the Caribbean. His air tanks, they told her, had become entangled with the loose hawsers of the wreck he had been diving on. She should have been with him. Regulations insisted that divers go down in pairs. Kenneth had been the expert, she his novice diving 'buddy' but, suddenly appalled at the weight of water surrounding them, she had panicked and surfaced.

The Diving Master had told her not to worry. It happened to novice divers. She would do better next time. Reassured, and quite proud of how she had managed the surfacing drill alone, she lay down on the deck to work on her tan. She had forgotten to report that Kenneth was now alone. Had she done so she would have saved his life because Kenneth, his air tanks holed and running out, was at that moment fighting for his life. His diving 'buddy', who should have been there to seek assistance, was instead contemplating that night's renewal of their sexual revels.

No one but herself had blamed her for Kenneth's death and she had told no one of the guilt she felt, so no one understood why she had gone into such social seclusion.

'You'll have to start going out sometime, Helen, darling,' Millie had insisted. 'Either that or join a religious order. Besides, there's someone I want you to meet.'

So, after six months of grieving she had forced herself to accept the relentless invitations and gone to the pre-Christmas party.

The moment she'd arrived she'd known it had been a mistake. Too many sidelong glances at the woman who had returned from her honeymoon alone.

Jeffrey had come out of the mix of faces and she'd known at once that this was the one Millie had meant her to meet. Guiltily, she realised that Millie had been right. As she chatted to this tall, quietly spoken man she found herself thinking the unthinkable. By sitting and talking with this stranger she felt as obvious as a whore sitting in an Amsterdam window.

'Are you all right?' he had asked.

His tender enquiry broke her. She knew if she didn't leave now she was lost. Rushing away she went to find her coat, intending to leave.

Millie caught up with her as she searched among the piled coats. 'Helen! Whatever's the matter?'

'I'm sorry Millie. It's just – I just can't do this. I have to go.'

'What happened?'

'Nothing happened. I shouldn't have come. It's too soon.'

It was then that Jeffrey caught her arm. 'I'll drive you home,' he'd said. 'St John's Wood, isn't it?'

Looking into his eyes, so full of real concern, she knew she was defeated.

She waited with embarrassing docility as he found his own coat and then, taking her firmly by the arm, had led her out to his car.

It was a long-slung Continental sports coupé of a kind she had never seen before. The seat into which she sank was so low that her legs were forced flat out along a luxurious carpet. This was a car totally out of tune with her mood.

As he drove she looked across at his profile. Somewhere deep inside her there had been a gear-shift of emotions. The empty guilt she had felt at the party fell away to leave, in its place, an emotion so powerful and direct that she felt instant shame.

With a feeling of growing unreality, an internal denial that this was really happening, she had let him escort her to her door.

As she fitted her key she had meant to say. 'Please *don't* come in,' but somewhere between her brain and her tongue the negative had got lost and came out sounding like a brazen invitation.

For a long, agonising moment he had looked directly into her eyes. 'I don't think you mean it,' he said. 'I'll call you and we'll meet when you're less upset.'

Then he had gone, leaving her with a perverse feeling of rejection.

Miserably, she went to bed feeling shame tighten round her like an instrument of torture. She felt hollow inside while her outer shell became rigid with the horror she had been about to perpetrate. She told herself she might as well have gone to the cemetery and squatted over Kenneth's grave.

Helen woke from a fitful sleep to the sound of the telephone. It was an anxious Millie.

'What happened?'

Wearily she tried to read the face of the bedside clock which always eluded her. 'Millie! What time is it?'

'Good God, girl, it's nearly noon.' Millie took in a long, pretend shocked breath. 'Don't tell me he's still there?'

'Who? What are you talking about?'

'When I saw the way he whisked you off last night I was certain – well, that there would be *developments* . . . ?'

She knew precisely what Millie meant and she was ashamed that, but for Jeffrey's understanding, it would have been true. She hated being that transparent before her friends and so, perversely, continued to play at confused virtue.

'Millie? Are you talking in riddles or what? I haven't the faintest idea of what you're talking about.'

'Jeffrey . . . !' prompted Millie. 'Don't pretend you don't remember!'

'Oh. Him. Yes, well he just drove me home. That's all.'

'Not even a late night coffee?'

'Nothing. I told you.'

Millie drew in a long, exasperated breath. 'I really don't know what we're going to do with you.'

'Nothing. You don't have to do anything with me. I'm quite happy as I am. But, Millie, could we talk about this later? I've just woken up and have to run to the bathroom.'

'All right, but be sure and call me back for a long gossip.'

'About what, Millie? I told you nothing happened.'

'So *you* say!' said Millie, and hung up.

Almost immediately the telephone rang again. It was her mother. She felt trapped. It had been accepted and, she had agreed as always, to spend Christmas with her parents. She was meant to be travelling down to the coast that very afternoon. She was being reminded of her promise to bring liqueurs as her contribution to the festivities.

What once had seemed the commonplace of family courtesies was, suddenly, an intolerable burden.

'So you won't forget them, darling?'

'No, mother. I promise.'

Her mother took one of her long pregnant pauses before repeating what was, these days, a constant theme.

'Perhaps you'll find the idea of living at home again a little more appealing after you've spent some time with us. It'd be for the best, you know.'

'Mother – we've been through this so many times ...'

'I know,' said her mother in that familiar dismissive tone, 'but I'm your mother and I worry about you. Kenneth's gone and there's nothing we can do to bring him back. I worry about you, alone in that flat with all those memories. I really believe you would do better to come home.'

She wanted to tell her mother that, in her mind, she *was* home but where could she find the words to soften the ultimate rejection? Her mother had thought of her leaving home – even for marriage – as a temporary condition which, by a twist of fate, was now capable of remedy.

Mother loses daughter to husband, daughter loses husband, ergo, mother regains daughter. The logic of it, seen from her mother's perspective, was flawless.

How could she explain that she didn't see it quite so simply? How to explain the agony of the guilt she felt about Kenneth's death? A guilt as yet unexpiated, since no one but herself had ever laid it at her door? Far less could she hope to explain the crushing burden of having contemplated adding sexual betrayal to her list of crimes.

She took her nagging guilt with her to the shower. There – never having learnt the trick – she couldn't avoid getting her hair soaked and so had to hunt the hairdryer out from where it had, inevitably, hidden itself.

She sat on the base of the bed and watched herself drying her hair in the mirrored closet doors.

She remembered going with Kenneth to buy them, both feeling wicked because they reflected the full length of the bed and the erotic possibilities they offered. She remembered those images and, bitterly, the images they would never show.

Switching off the dryer she had the feeling that the telephone had been ringing for some time. Thinking it would surely be her mother with some more last minute instructions she lay across the bed to reach for it and spoke her 'hello' a little wearily.

'I didn't wake you did I?' Jeffrey asked.

Startled, she sat up, reaching for a bath-robe to cover her otherwise naked body. 'No. I just didn't hear the telephone, that's all. My hair got wet and I was just drying it. I've got a very noisy dryer.'

She cursed herself, even as she spoke, for this overlong

explanation. Why hadn't she told him she was naked? She'd mentioned everything else!

'I was wondering, somewhat forlornly perhaps – it being Christmas Eve – if you would be free for dinner tonight?'

'No. I'm sorry. No. I'm going down to Eastbourne tonight.'

'Tonight? What time?'

'Well. Usually I like to drive down and get there before dark but I overslept so that isn't possible.' Why was she going on at such length like this?

'Suppose we met for an early dinner?'

'No. I really would like to get away as early as possible. I hate driving at night.'

'I could drive you down there.'

Suddenly she was vulnerable. He was pushing too hard and she felt she ought to mind but found she didn't.

'To Eastbourne? No. That would be ridiculous. Besides I need my car down there.'

'I could drive your car.'

'And what would you do then?'

'Take a train back.'

'They stop running early on Christmas Eve. There aren't any on Christmas Day.'

'Then I could take a cab.'

'From Eastbourne to London? You must be mad.'

He paused and she found herself hoping he could think of something more acceptable.

'Look,' he finally said, 'I'm only about ten minutes from your place. Why don't I come round. I really would like to see you before you go away.'

Aware of the unmade bed, her own nakedness and wrecked hair she tried to put him off.

'I'll only be gone three days. We could meet when I come back.'

'No,' he said decisively. 'I'll give you half an hour.'

She laid down the phone and stared at it. Was she really going to allow this? What was the point? What time would they have? None. An hour at the most and then she would have to leave. This was insanity. This time yesterday she didn't know of his existence and now he was making assumptions and invading her life.

Hurrying back to the bathroom she stared at herself in the mirror. What would she wear? How could she get her hair into some semblance of order? Should she try and rush to make up her face?

Settling for a vigorous brushing, a smear of foundation and a sweater and jeans, she was still feeling harassed when he rang the bell.

'I really don't have time for this,' she told him as she opened the apartment door to him.

'I've been up most of the night thinking about you,' he told her.

'Me?'

He came to stand intimidatingly within her space. 'You needed me last night and I walked out on you.'

'"Needed" you ... ?'

'I'm sorry,' he said and, reaching, made his arms into an embracing arc and brought her tight against his body. The move had been so sudden, even if half anticipated, that she made no protest.

That first real kiss had unnerved her. Swept along, without thought or protest, she had come to be naked under him, feverishly rising to meet his every harsh, cruel, thrust.

Her brain, protesting her libidinous body's betrayal, had sought to transmute pleasure into punishment. His powerful thrusting had caused her to thrash helplessly from side to side, blocking protest, preventing contrition, denying resistance.

That first time her eyes had been tight shut to block out the contempt she was sure he must feel for the abandoned person under him. A woman now so crazed and out of control that she heard her own voice begging for pain, then sobbing and screaming as his fingers responded, digging deeply, painfully, into her buttocks. It had hurt and it had been punishing, but it had also thrilled and intensified her pleasure.

Then came the moment of her body's final betrayal as she felt the clenching throb of her own orgasm against his. It was a mutuality she had never achieved with Kenneth in a thousand tries, but which had ceded to this man on his first assault.

When he had exhausted himself she had not resisted the downward pressure on her head but had gone to greet the fallen, sullied, warrior with an enthused mouth that sought only to bring him back to full erection so that he might plunge into her again.

And he had.

And she wanted to die of shame.

Now, barely minutes later, she lay listening to him in the shower and wondered how she could face him. He must have known, Millie would have gossiped about her, that he had made her change from resolutely virtuous widow to voracious wanton in less than a day. Could any man respect such a creature? How was she going to bear the lash of his contempt? She lay in wretchedness, a hollowed, empty victim awaiting the inevitable humiliation.

When he finally emerged, smiling, naked and even half erect, she wanted to hide. Certain of his scorn, she was even more shamed when he took a firm hold on the pillow with which she had covered her face and, looking down into her wide, defensive eyes, had gently kissed her full on the lips.

'That was marvellous.'

She braced against his contempt, lay still and frozen. She had heard only the words she had expected and not those he had spoken.

Looking down at her widened eyes, and still lips, he was puzzled. 'Something wrong?' he asked.

'Please go.'

His brow furrowed even deeper. 'Go? I thought we'd agreed I'd drive you to Bournemouth?'

'Eastbourne,' she corrected him.

'Wherever. Didn't we?'

'It's not a good idea.'

'I think it's an excellent idea,' he said, and his hand sought out her traitorous loins that both burned and flinched at his touch. 'I have lots of excellent ideas.'

Summoning the will to move she thrust aside his hand, swung her feet to the floor and raced to the bathroom. She would have closed and barred it to him but he was already there gently preventing its closure.

'You don't regret what just happened, do you?'

'No. But please leave the door . . .'

He pushed against it even more firmly. 'No. I want to watch you shower. I haven't seen you properly naked yet, you know.'

Now close to tears she turned to begging him to leave her alone, and he, looking wounded and puzzled, finally relented and let her close the door on him.

Feeling safe for the moment she turned to confront herself in the full-length mirror which Kenneth had installed so he could watch her face while he took her, fresh from the bath, from behind. Now she could only beg its forgiveness.

Standing in the shower she felt her legs weaken and had to hold onto the pipes to allow the water to do its best to wash away the dirt and the guilt. Guilt that rose not so much from what she had done but from recognising just how thoroughly it had excited her.

She was still there when she became aware of the hammering on the door. Turning off the water, she called out angrily.

'It's the telephone,' he called through the door. 'It just keeps on ringing and I thought I'd better not answer it.'

Illogically angry at him, Helen wrapped herself in a towel and opened the door to hear the phone still ringing. He stood back to make a respectful space as she crossed the room to answer it.

'Darling!' cried Millie. 'I was sure you'd gone off without thinking to call me back!'

'Not now, Millie. I'm all in a rush. I'll call you from my mother's.'

She hung up, careless that Millie would be offended. The call had brought her out of hiding and now she was face to face with him, with nowhere to hide.

'What are you so guilty about?' he asked.

'It shouldn't have happened. I shouldn't have let it happen.'

'I'm sorry.'

Had he said any more she might have been able to summon up anger, but he hadn't. She cursed silently as she felt herself weakening towards tears. Without warning they engulfed her and she found herself wrapped tight against him, begging for comfort.

She cried herself out for some minutes, pleased to be within his warm embrace but hating herself for seeking this unsafe and dangerous sanctuary.

'Do you want me to punish you?' he asked in a soft, gentle tone that belied the enormity of his words.

Thrusting herself away from his body, made suddenly chill, she stared at him.

'What did you say?'

'I asked if you wanted me to punish you,' he said again in patient, even tones.

The words were plain but their meaning, to her at that moment, obscure.

'What for?' she finally asked.

'Whatever is haunting you.'

'Are you mad?' she asked, throwing out one last desperate lifeline towards sanity.

'Not at all. You seem upset about something. Guilty, even. Guilt left unpunished can fester.'

She stared at him, not wanting to believe what she had heard. There was only one possibility – of the many which raced through her mind – he was insane.

'I think you'd better go now,' she said as evenly as she could manage.

'No,' he said. 'I'm driving you to Eastbourne.'

Aware that the towel was the only thing between them she felt suddenly vulnerable and went to walk round him to the relative safety of the bathroom. She didn't make it. He caught her arm, reached for the towel, stripped it from her and threw it aside. In an attempt to minimise the feeling of vulnerability that now consumed her, she sat down on the bed, staring up at him through tear-stained eyes.

He reached for her, turned her naked body onto its stomach and, holding her down firmly, slapped her repeatedly on the soft flesh of her buttocks.

Wriggling for freedom from his firm grasp, yelling to be let up, she felt the heat from the blows suffusing her entire body.

Still angry, she was flipped onto her back as easily as if she were a pancake on a hotplate, and looked up at him in fear as he loosed the belt from the loops of his trousers.

'What do you think you're doing?'

'Something you need badly,' he told her.

She watched mesmerised as the belt was flipped up into the air and then brought down across the bed within millimetres of her tender flesh. Yelping with sudden fear she dived from the bed and made for the bathroom. He caught her wrist and lashed at her calves and buttocks – anything that was presented to him.

Now she was yelling, sobbing and protesting all at the same time. Next she felt her burning, outraged body thrown to the bed, where she could do nothing to prevent further invasion of her spreadeagled self.

The fire that had played about her buttocks and loins was now being pressed deep inside her. He felt huge against her inner flesh, as, desperately hating herself, she found her nails digging into his back which he answered with sharp digs into her buttocks. Effortlessly he held her hips high as he drove even deeper into her again and again.

She felt flames licking her every nerve as she abandoned herself to the inevitable orgasmic climax.

He knew. Oh, how humiliatingly well, he knew how abandoned and lost she was. How easily her wanton body dismissed her protesting reason, how readily her thighs rose to answer his every sortie with greedy, clenching attack. She had surrendered everything of herself and now only regretted she could find nothing more to give.

They lay exhausted on the bed for a long moment before she could bring herself to articulate the one word that had resounded in her head since her climax.

'Bastard!' she breathed with an intensity born of real hatred.

He had smiled, she had lain her head down on his belly and, with the heat of the beating still burning on her flesh, felt the need to assert herself.

* * *

'Now I'm going to screw you,' Helen had said and then, as she sat astride this man, almost still a stranger, she knew she was venting months of guilt and frustration on his body but, also, that it was directed mainly into her own soul.

Assertive and positive he might have been, but now he was passively submitting to the slow tortuous pleasure she wrought out of him. He had even, at her urging, placed his hands behind his head while she used him.

Then something snapped inside and she realised she was losing control. Her body was taking over, insisting she increase the pace and its pleasure. Violently now, she started to move on him, beating her pelvis into him with punishing force, finding she could no longer protest when his hands reached for her, dragged her down and forced her to receive his gushing tribute, spread helplessly on her back. 'Yes!' they screamed in unison and knew that this was right.

There was an appalled silence during which it seemed even the walls of her bedroom held their breath, until, raising himself on one elbow to look deeply into her vulnerable eyes, he spoke. 'I have no intention of letting you go,' he said. 'You're mine. I've claimed you.'

'I have to go to my mother's,' she said, hating the intrusion of a little girl's tone into her voice.

He nodded. 'But afterwards ...' he said.

'Afterwards,' she agreed, and felt inside her the first real happiness she had known since that soporific afternoon in the Caribbean.

They were half way to Eastbourne before she noticed the car following them.

'Isn't that *your* car?' she asked.

He nodded.

'Luckily I managed to get Turner at home and he agreed to follow us so that I'll have my car for the return journey.'

'Who's Turner?'

'My chauffeur.'

'You have a chauffeur? I'm impressed.'

'Strictly speaking he's employed by my company. He usually drives the company car but he's been dying to have a go in the Maserati. It was that that lured him out tonight.'

It was another reminder of how little she knew of the man who had so comprehensively invaded her life and her body.

'What do you do?'

'I've got some property.'

She lapsed into silence. Kenneth had hated people who created paper profits and produced nothing. 'Economic leeches,' he had called them. She had, with Kenneth, developed some radical attitudes of her own. Now she was consorting with one of 'them'. Yet another betrayal – the third or fourth – she was rapidly losing track.

Helen spoke defensively as if he had been listening in on her silent thoughts. 'You must have a very low opinion of me.'

'What brought that on? Have I offended you in some way?'

'Not you. Me.' She looked across at him behind the wheel and saw him smiling. 'I'm not usually like "that",' she added quietly.

'Of course not. I think you're a very special lady and I intend to cherish you.'

'Is that why you thrashed me?'

'I thought that was what you needed.'

'It won't happen again.'

'Didn't it excite you? At one point you asked me to hurt you some more.'

'It's very bad taste to repeat things said in the throes of orgasm.'

'Did you?'

'What?'

'Orgasm.'

'You know I did.'

'I'm one of those men that is never sure. I'm glad.'

She fought down an impulse to say 'So am I' and reached out a hand to lay on his forearm.

He acknowledged it by looking down and smiling. Feeling that his smile meant he was patronising her, she withdrew her arm. Arrogant bastard, she thought, he thinks he's got me precisely where he wants me.

'I have an unfulfilled fantasy,' he said so suddenly that, at first, she wildly thought he must be speaking to someone else.

'Haven't we all?' she asked.

'You have unfulfilled fantasies?' he asked, sounding genuinely interested. 'I'd love to help you fulfil them.'

She laughed. 'You'd need a limitless resource.'

'I have a limitless resource,' he said, very soberly.

Looking across she could see no trace of a self-deprecating smile or laugh. 'So what is this unfulfilled fantasy?' she asked.

'I want a girl to go down on me while I'm driving. It's never happened to me.'

'I've news for you,' she said. 'Nothing's changed.'

'You won't do it?'

She looked directly at him but his eyes never left the road. 'Do you seriously think I would? We've known each other for barely twenty-four hours.'

'You did it in the bedroom. What's the difference?'

She stared out the side window. Resentment, she neither wanted nor could cope with, was rising rapidly in her.

This man was supposing too much, too readily assuming

that she was *his* creature, willing to devote herself to *his* pleasure.

There rose a need to assert herself. To establish that she was an independent being, not some appendage he'd taken from a dusty shelf. She might have done so then and there but for her crippling guilt.

Her mistake, she thought, had been to allow him to drive her down to the coast. She wanted him to stop the car and let her out, before reminding herself that this was her car and that his was following behind.

So there was the solution! He could simply step into his own car, turn round and return to London. She need never see him again.

He broke in on her thoughts. 'Do it for me and I promise I'll fulfil any fantasy of yours. Absolute promise.'

'Now you're treating me like a casual pick-up.'

'I love whorish women,' he murmured, almost to himself.

'Then I've an idea,' she told him. 'Why don't you stop the car, get into your own and drive back to London? You might even be in time to catch some tired prostitute on her way home. I'm sure, given the right incentive, she would happily oblige.'

He laughed out loud for nearly a minute. 'Not the same thing,' he said when he finally finished. 'I want a whorish woman – not a whore. There is a very big difference. Of course it would be perfect with someone who loves me.'

Helen reached deep down inside for all the scorn she could muster. 'You don't imagine I'm in love with you, do you?'

'I'm determined that you will be.'

Now it was her turn to laugh.

'Too late now,' he was saying. 'We're nearly there.'

In the context she thought, at first, the remark had been directed at their relationship but, looking up, she was surprised to see the first of the town's signs. The time had flown, the mileage dissolved. It was the most painless drive from London to Eastbourne she could ever remember

She directed him to her parents' home, conscious that it was much later than they would have been expecting her. A further problem was that she could see no way of avoiding inviting him in to meet them.

Perhaps his generosity would ease the inevitable tension this would cause. As they were driving through the London suburbs she had remembered her promise to provide the cursed liqueurs, without which her Mother didn't consider it to be Christmas. She had asked him to stop at a store and, when he understood why, he had insisted on buying a bottle of every kind they had.

Now, in the trunk of the car were bottles of liqueurs she had never even heard of, supplemented by a huge mixed box of every conceivable kind of liqueur chocolate ever created. Her mother was going to love this man!

In the event, her optimism proved false. Her mother's smile of greeting froze the moment she saw Jeffrey following Helen into the house burdened by the bottles of liqueurs.

The display of abundance did nothing to diminish the chilly reception. She could see her mother's intuition had sight read the situation. Her only consolation was that her mother couldn't possibly guess at the depth of her daughter's debauch.

Jeffrey stayed just long enough to drink a cup of begrudgingly offered coffee before departing.

The only positive response to his visit came from her father, who was impressed by the expensive sports car parked outside the house. Her mother had dismissed it as a ridiculous extravagance.

That night Helen thought about the past twenty-four hours. She remembered the guilt, but also the thrill in her total surrender of self and inhibition. Before sleeping she had recalled his every word and conjured up his every gesture; probing them, turning them this way and that, in a search for hidden meanings.

She decided that there were none, or room for very few. He had a directness about him which was disconcerting but, in its honesty, attractive.

Most particularly, she recalled his fantasy in the car and knew for certain that, one day, she was going to do that – and much else – for this uniquely demanding man.

Christmas Day was, as always, disappointing. Some distant relatives turned up. Her mother fussed over the strewn wrapping papers, lunch was late and the turkey overdone. Her parents got irritable with each other and, when all the 'outsiders' had departed, rounded off the festive day with a row.

In need of some time alone she walked through the early night streets and found herself thinking about Jeffrey, tempered only by the memory of the previous Christmas when she and Kenneth had been here together.

She remembered Kenneth's tentative experiments with her body. Last Christmas, slightly drunk, he had wanted to sodomise her. She had refused when his clumsiness had caused her too much pain.

She wasn't sure about Jeffrey. Somehow she suspected she would feel no pain.

It wasn't until she was almost on the point of leaving that her mother mentioned Jeffrey.

'Who is he?' she had asked suspiciously. 'I don't like him. Not one little bit.'

'He's someone I hardly know. He offered to drive me down, that's all. You know how I hate to drive after dark.'

'Long way for someone to come who hardly knows you.'

'I think he was going to his own parents' house. They live along the coast somewhere.'

The lie hadn't convinced her mother. Mothers know their daughters too well, she concluded, because they were once daughters themselves.

2

The return to London was an unexpected anticlimax. What she had expected, she couldn't imagine. Jeffrey on the doorstep, perhaps? How could he be when he could have no idea when she was coming back?

Wandering around the empty apartment she felt unutterably lonely. With the holiday season still in full swing to call Millie or anyone would seem to be begging for an invitation. Instead, she consoled herself with a bottle of whisky and the endless stream of movies pouring out on every TV channel.

At some point she must have dozed off and was quite shocked on waking to find her first memories were of Jeffrey. She had, in those first unwary wakening moments, for the first time, found it difficult to summon up Kenneth's smiling face.

She dragged herself to bed – to sleep and hope for better things from the following day.

It was close to three in the morning when she woke to the frightening sound of voices in the other room. Fear paralysed her until her more rational mind told her it was the sound of her own voice on the answering machine. Someone was calling her at this unbelievable hour.

Cursing herself for having forgotten to switch off the call monitor she got out of bed, eased open the door and listened, uneasily feeling that she was intruding on herself.

Her own announcement ended, she waited with bated breath to see if the caller would dare leave a message.

'Hello. This is Jeffrey. It's just past midnight ...'

Liar! ...

'... and I wanted you to know I was thinking of you. Please call me the moment you get back. Speak to you soon!'

Listening to the machine re-set itself she wondered why he had bothered to lie about so apparently insignificant a detail.

Puzzled, she rewound the tape to hear the message through again. Had he forgotten that answering machines recorded the time and date of the call?

Even supposing he didn't know, was he so unworldly that he had not even allowed for there to have been an intervening call which would have also exposed his lie?

She found herself having her first real doubts about the true nature of the man who had assumed so much over her.

It was then she realised that she had overlooked the most illuminating facet of the call. Had Jeffrey been lying awake at three a.m. thinking about her? Thinking so deeply that he had been moved to call her with no expectation that she would be there? Then, having done so, been too coy to admit that he had called at such an ungodly hour?

Of course, he might simply have been returning from a night out and had thought to impress her with his devotion. But for what reason?

She replayed the tape, listening carefully for any signs of slurred speech which might have indicated a drink-inspired call. There was none. He sounded endearingly sincere and, but for his lie about the time, she might have, there and then, called him right back.

Instead, she turned off the call monitor and went back to bed.

Some hours later she woke in a state of confusion. This had happened to her several times in her life and more especially since Kenneth's death, but this morning was something different, something more intense and frightening.

Nothing seemed to make sense and nothing was as it should be. Rationally she knew where she was but the images that haunted her dreams remained hovering, undefined, on the edge of her waking mind. Something was bothering her. A problem that her dreams had left unresolved.

The feeling grew and no amount of coffee could drive the apprehension away. Something out there in the mists of the future was lurking, waiting in ambush. She would have liked to call somebody but there was no one.

Millie was her closest friend but she already knew that talking to her would be met with a frown and the admonishment to 'pull yourself together'.

Something more stopped her calling Millie. It was the knowledge that, no matter how great her resolve, she would, in minutes, have confessed everything that had passed between her and Jeffrey. That was a shame she wasn't yet ready to share. Not even with Millie, whose own answer to depression was a romp in bed with someone new.

Millie was without doubt the most outrageous woman she knew. Flagrantly unfaithful to her adoring husband, drooling to know the details of everyone else's sex life, and scornful of anyone that espoused the slightest regret no matter how outrageous their behaviour, Millie had once said: 'In life you should only regret the things you *didn't* do.' No. On this precipitous edge Millie was not the person to confide in.

Trying to distract herself by tidying up the apartment she came face to face with an echo of her own debauch. Lying half concealed under the bedcover was the belt he had used to beat her. Seeing it, she had involuntarily reached out to pick it up but then hesitated as if it had become a venomous snake. All her unsettling images suddenly resolved themselves into one.

Jeffrey. He was the serpent gnawing at her mind. A cancer that needed immediate surgery. Going to the telephone she dialled rapidly, anxious to put her impulse into effect.

'Hello? Jeffrey?'

He sounded excited. 'Where are you? Are you in London?'

'Yes. At the apartment . . .'

'I'll be right there!'

'No!' she yelled into the phone, but her voice bounced back off the already dead microphone.

Infuriated, needing to stop him at all costs, she dialled his number again. His answering machine came on. He couldn't possibly have left immediately, so when the tone came she spoke urgently hoping that he had also left his monitor switched on.

'Jeffrey, please pick up the phone. I have to speak to you. I can't possibly see you. Not today.' She waited a moment more before the answering machine clicked off and returned her to the baleful dialling tone.

Putting the telephone down she found herself in confusion. What did he want of her? Why this instant response to her call? Why had she told him she was home? Why hadn't she told him she was still in Eastbourne?

It was then that she discovered the leather belt was still in her hand. She stared at it. When had she picked that up?

His imminent arrival left little time to tidy herself or the apartment. Refusing to listen to the inner voice which plaintively reminded her that she had intended telling him she didn't want to see him, she flew about the flat and made some attempt at presentability.

The street door buzzed and, picking up the entryphone, she saw his monotone image, making him look like something from an old newsreel. If she were going to turn him away then this was the moment to do it. All she had to do was tell him he wasn't coming in and then not open the door. She was about to do just that when he spotted the monitor lens and, sticking out his tongue, smiled broadly into it.

Unable to resist this childish behaviour she pressed the door-lock release and watched as he disappeared from the video screen.

Opening the apartment door to him she was still intending to make a token protest, but was greeted with a doorway filled with flowers through which poked a magnum of champagne. From behind the floral screen came his voice.

'Don't say a word!'

She stepped back as the flowers advanced on her. His face appeared grinning impishly over them.

'You are forbidden to speak!' he told her. 'I'm here to look.'

'Look?' she gasped.

The champagne was thrust into her hands – it was chilled – and a silencing finger laid lightly on her parted, protesting, lips.

'Not a word! Not one! Nothing. You are sentenced to be silent.'

Having freed one hand, he reached back into the hallway and dragged in a huge white box tied all over with golden ribbon. Saying nothing about the box he swept by her into the kitchen, leaving her to hold the champagne. He was back in a moment carrying a huge vase – he'd found an unwanted wedding present she couldn't have found if her life had depended on it.

He arranged the flowers – which only now did she register as predominantly, unseasonal, roses – while humming a joyous tune to himself.

'But—' she started to say before the finger again pressed her to silence.

She sighed and turned away, wondering exactly how drunk

he might be. On the other hand it was refreshing to find a grown man – who, she thought, knew how to behave and was prepared to play games at this level.

Having placed the flowers precisely where she would have put them herself, he turned his attention to the champagne. Keeping to the rules she stayed silent as he flushed out yet another wedding present – fluted champagne glasses.

Beginning to warm to the atmosphere she held the glasses as he opened the bottle – without any explosive overflow – and poured repeatedly until, the bubbles subsiding, they were filled.

In the manner of a Head Waiter she was guided to her own couch and invited to sit down. The glasses touched and they drank.

He settled on the matching couch opposite and smiled at her.

'You are the most lovely lady I know,' he told her, and then, as she opened her mouth to deflect the outrageous compliment, he again held up his finger. 'Please!' he said. 'The things I have to say will be much more easily voiced if you say nothing.'

Intrigued, she saluted him with her glass, sipped, smiled and looked expectantly at him for him to begin his promised monologue.

She was disappointed. He simply sat opposite her, smiling and looking at her. Twice during the long minutes he spent at this, she opened her mouth to speak and twice he raised his admonishing finger to stop her.

Deciding the only dignified way to support his game was to pretend to ignore him, she sat back and did her best imitation of a silent movie vamp.

He clapped his hands in delight. 'Perfect!' he cried. 'Listen, I could just sit here all day drinking with you but – I wonder – would you do something else for me?'

Staying in character, she swept a hand through the air in a regally dismissive arc.

He leapt to his feet, went to the door, picked up the huge white box in one hand and came back to hand it to her across the coffee table.

'Wear this for me,' he said.

Taking the box she saw the famous designer name discreetly engraved in gold in one corner and, instinctively, although only half-heartedly, opened her mouth to protest – but again that finger was there, readied and threatening.

This created a dilemma. Should she open it here or take it into the bedroom? What if it were something she wouldn't be seen dead in? Could the contents, given the name on the box, possibly be construed as a Christmas gift between friends or was there something inside that would create an obligation or, at least, an expectation.

He settled her internal argument by reaching down to pull at the gold ribbon bows himself.

Under layers of silky white tissue she found a gown of very fine black silk that looked, in the hand, to be practically shapeless. She looked across at him and wondered why he had brought this to her and puzzled over whom it could have been bought for. Certainly not her – couturiers didn't work over Christmas and they would not, anyway, sell such an item without fittings.

'Put it on,' he enthused. 'If there's anything to be done to it we can fly to Paris and have them fit it properly.'

Feeling slightly light-headed and thinking she might have, like Alice, fallen down some mythical rabbit hole, she stood and held the dress against her – it still had little form or even shape. 'Please,' he was saying. 'Try it on. If you don't like it we can change it.'

Allowing herself a deep sigh, she turned past him, went into the bedroom and firmly closed the door.

Hurrying to the mirror she again held the gown in front of her and was undecided what to do. Was she going to join in this 'game'? What if the dress looked as awful on as in the hand? Could this be some kind of fetish of his? Distantly, she heard his voice calling out asking her not to be too long.

Consciously thinking that this was ridiculous, her hands were already unbuttoning the denim shirt she had worn to greet him. She pulled off cotton leggings, and shed her brassiere, unwearable since the top of the gown consisted only of two panels held by buttons at the shoulders. It took a few attempts before she got the dress on and, when she turned towards the full-length mirror, she got a tremendous shock. The fine silk had immediately clung to the warmth of her body. What had seemed shapeless had now taken form – her form! The material, clinging to every nook and cranny of her body, delineated the thrust of her nipples which, she observed, had gone into instant erection. The effect was breathtaking. She saw herself as transformed and, although she had never thought of herself as any more narcissistic than the next girl, exciting. To wear a dress like this was not only to proclaim the naked body beneath but to advertise to the world that the woman inside was ready for sex.

Responding to his further warning not to take too long she searched out a pair of high-heeled shoes – Kenneth had called them her 'tarty' shoes – and slipped into them. She would have liked to do something more with her hair, but settled for a spray of perfume before taking a careful, assessing, look at herself.

There was only one flaw in the reflected image and that was the way in which the silk, now thoroughly warmed to her body, and clinging ever closer, outlined her panties.

With a tingling sense of daring she raised the flowing skirt and, hooking her thumbs into her briefs, pulled them down and stepped out of them.

Looking at herself she became shocked and aware that her breasts were thrusting hard against the silk and her nipples ached – a sure sign of arousal. 'Cocktails are ready!' he called through the door.

With one last regret at not having more time to do anything with her hair, she moved to the door, took a long breath, and stepped out.

He was clear across the room holding two tall, stemmed glasses filled with some kind of champagne cocktail.

'Stunning!' he said.

She got as far as saying 'I—' before he again intervened.

'Rule still applies!' he told her, coming forwards to hand her a glass with one hand and, catching her other hand, raised it to his lips.

'You can only wear it for me,' he said. 'I mean, you look gorgeous and all but I think something a little more subtle, more understated, would ensure you didn't get ravished the instant men saw you. Model it for me. Let me see the full effect!'

Tingling from head to toe, she did her best impression of all the catwalk models she had ever seen.

'Superb!' he called, along with other compliments. 'Again!'

Turning, she swished and sashayed as best she could on the high heels that had suddenly started to pinch, before coming back to accept the drink he had been holding out all this time.

'Who was the gown made for?' she asked.

'For you,' he said.

Her laugh was short and scornful. 'And how did you get a dress made over Christmas?'

He looked bashful. 'The truth is I saw the dress on a model many years ago and loved it so much that I bought it. I didn't have anyone to wear it for me, then or since – until I met you.

I knew immediately that this dress had been made for a body like yours. I was right.'

'True?'

'I promise you. We might have only just met but I've been searching for you a long time.'

Enormously aroused, she found her apprehension growing. This man was different. He had mistaken her for someone she was not but, as she stood there, she knew that she wanted desperately to become that woman.

'There's something else about this dress,' he told her. 'But before I show you what it is you have to promise something.'

'What?' Now she was fully aroused. Secrets and promises were like aphrodisiacs to her. She only wondered how he knew.

'You have to promise me that whatever happens to that dress in the next five seconds you will not interfere.'

She was puzzled. Did the dress dissolve or what? 'I don't understand,' she said.

'But do I have your promise?'

She nodded and he reached out to the top fastening buttons, tweaked them and the dress slid, like a caress, to the floor, leaving her completely naked before him.

Four days – or was it a century? – ago, before she knew him, she might have instinctively grabbed at the dress to stop its downward slide, but something about this man made her trust him and his judgement completely. She was proud to be naked for him and willed herself to be as still as a statue as he looked at her.

'Breathtaking,' he said. 'I knew I was right. You're perfect in or out of that dress. We'll have more of them made. It'll be exciting to know I can have you naked in seconds.'

Trembling before him she realised that he was as aroused as she was and, as she fought for breath, she brought her uncertain eyes to his and read in them that he knew. In that moment there was nothing more important to her than that this man should be sexually satisfied. And then she found she had fallen to her knees.

He was standing over her.

'Incredible. Beautiful!' he was saying as he tried to reach down and lift her to her feet, but she didn't want that. In close proximity lay his cock, veiled only by the thin material of his trousers. It was that fleshly pleasure she wanted and eagerly she reached for it. He had to help her trembling hands seek him out, but the moment his cock was free she sank her mouth down on to it like an eager calf at the teat.

Greedy now, insatiable even, choked by his growing erection, she tried to cry out and let him know what she was feeling, but his penis gagged her. Her mouth clung to him, worked him, fearing that if she let go, took her mouth from him, she would fall backwards into an abyss. This cock and its coming gift were, in that moment, her entire life. She was greedy for the taste of him, wanting him to fill her, choke her, punish her. Then, as she felt him start to throb, she found her own release as she redoubled her efforts to suckle from him. Suddenly, without any seeming transition, she was on her own bed and he was burying himself deep inside her. She felt another wave starting as he moved against her. It came, and she knew another was close behind. This was impossible. Sensation was crowding in on her, confusing her, leaving no room for thoughts beyond satiating her body's needs. There came only one other sensation – a sudden pain on her nipples.

'Yes!' she screamed. 'More of that! Hurt me! Punish me!'

His words started then in an excited stream. Words that assured her she would feel his pain, feel his come, feel his cock and at each teeth-clenched imprecation she yelled back him, 'Yes!'

When did it stop, she wondered? She was lying flat on her stomach, streaked with sweat from his and her own overheated bodies, knowing only that somehow it must have stopped since she now lay in a velvety haze that held her swaying in the most comfortable position she had ever known.

She moved gently so as not to dislodge him, only to find that he was lying turned away from her. What she had thought was his risen flesh inside her was only the bruised, happy memory.

Turning her head she could see the tendons raised on his strained neck where it pulsed with life. Fascinated, she watched the flesh vibrating. Somehow she wanted to match the rhythm of it, feel his urgency inside herself.

Reaching down she cupped herself in both hands, not caring that this spread her naked thighs obscenely. There was only him to see and she already knew that nothing she did would ever be obscene to him. Watching his neck pulse she imagined that it beat deep inside her. Matching her self-caress to his pulse she could fantasise a situation where the throb would be constant, never ceasing, just a constant never-ending drip of infinite sexual arousal.

Never had she felt like this. Now she knew the meaning of insatiability. As her own libido sang she had to resist her body's demand to increase the tempo of her searching, teasing finger. Instead she forced herself to endure this self-inflicted arousal as a regiment of men looked down on her spread thighs and waited their turn with her. Yes! Now she was a cheap whore – the brothel girl who would do anything, satisfy any man's craving. She was the dirty bitch that would crawl to them, beg them for their cocks and cry with gratitude when one deigned to put his cock in her ...

She came gently enough but lay gasping for breath as she fought for control of her own thumping heart. As her more rational mind took over from the wanton that lived inside her, she marvelled at what this man had done to her. He must have known at a glance what she was – what she craved. He had even known she wanted to be beaten. She would have been appalled if anyone had suggested it instead of, like him, just done it. She was startled to realise that, since meeting him, she had been in a constant state of arousal. Even in Eastbourne she had known that, deep inside, it had been still simmering, unacknowledged, within her.

Just seeing him brought that simmer to the boil. If any man could take her by the hand and lead her to paradise then it was this man. A man she must cherish and satisfy, no matter what the cost, for fear of losing him.

Her secret fantasies had always been extreme. Here was a man that would drag those fantasies from her subconscious and uncritically watch her play them out in life.

The thought liberated her. She had beside her a man who had taken her beyond anything she had ever before imagined and, she knew, would take her even further. She only needed the determination, and the courage, to go with him.

She imagined herself standing beside him on some formal occasion wearing the gown as she had today and knowing that at any moment he could reach out, tweak those buttons, and leave her naked. She trembled at the thought of so delivering herself into his hands knowing she would never be able to refuse him anything.

Nothing was impossible – no fantasy beyond his imagination or their mutual exploration. She was free of constraint, of the need to pretend that she was anything other than a newly liberated, decadent, totally filthy-minded wanton – something which, until now, she had only ever admitted to herself in fantasy.

He was a fantasy made real and the thought frightened her a little.

Finally, she reached up and drew the top light cover gently over them both and immediately felt secure.

If she felt herself precariously on the edge of an abyss she also knew that, should she fall, she could be confident he would be there to catch her before she hit the rocks.

Smiling with contentment, she finally slept.

3

She had woken early and stood at the foot of the bed looking down on his sleeping face, filled with a sense of wonder.

He looked so vulnerable in repose. No sign of that energy that could prompt searing orgasm in her. She had never imagined such intensity of feeling existed. With Kenneth their love-making had been tender, only pretend daring and adventurous but always neatly compartmentalised, tagged as something the mind turned to at bedtime. Never had she imagined that there could be a passion so all-consuming that she wouldn't be able to rid herself of it even when asleep.

Acknowledging that her abstinence since Kenneth's traumatic death had created an almost unbearable pressure, she knew that this was more than the sudden, and finite, the release of a bursting dam. Jeffrey had, she suspected, tapped a deep resource and opened her to a continuing, renewable flow.

As she watched him sleep she was afraid that he might wake and find her wanting. What he had to give was so precious it should be given as a tribute to perfection and that, she knew, she was not. What she needed was artifice and the good luck not be found out too soon.

It was as if all that had gone before had been simple preparation. In his presence she had found a fierce pride in her body. Until now it had been appreciated, tenderly kissed and caressed, but never before had she felt it so openly worshipped. With this man she could go confidently naked. With this man she could be openly wanton.

Then, aware that his eyes were open and watching her, she straightened her back, put back her shoulders, and made the best of her pose.

'Come,' he said, throwing back the covers to show his risen flesh.

Like a supplicant approaching a holy relic she crawled onto the bed and gratefully did as he wanted.

First she licked, nuzzled and kissed him, and then, carefully, alert to any contrary instruction he might give her, raised herself to straddle him and, reaching down, guided him into herself.

His intake of breath was all the encouragement she needed. Now he must be ridden like the thoroughbred he was. First the trot, then the canter and finally the gallop.

It wasn't until he cried out and grasped her that she realised the flame that had been heating her had come as much from his hands, rhythmically slapping her buttocks, as from the reliquary buried deep between her thighs.

Feeling him gone from the field she lay beside him and wished away the time that would pass before his next arousal.

'What am I to do with you?'

'Anything you want,' she told him.

'You know that I can't let you go?'

'I've nowhere I want to go.'

They lay silently exchanging caresses for a moment before she found the agony of him not being inside her more than she could bear. 'Shall I make some coffee?' she asked.

'I insist,' he said softly, and added a kiss to the breast closest to his mouth.

She reached for his head as tiny darts of flame came from his lips through her nipples to the pleasure places in her brain.

'Coffee,' he said bringing her from her tantalising fantasies.

Reluctantly, she rose from the bed and, in a reflex born of custom, reached for her robe.

'No,' he told her. 'I want you naked.'

She felt inclined to tease him. 'I was always told a woman's body looked better if she was wearing a little something.'

'A man would have to be mad to acquire a perfect Ming vase and then want to cover it with a cloth wouldn't he?'

'Am I your "Ming"?'

'You are exquisite and very precious and beside you Ming is commonplace.'

She felt liquid with the release from months of remorse and self-denial. She wanted to rush at him and re-pledge herself but, instead, feeling that she was exercising super-human control, she turned away from the extravagance of his compliment and went into the kitchen.

As she went through the mindless ritual of coffee-making she wished she had something more exotic, something undreamt of, to offer him. But, she wistfully understood, there was only herself – and that, too, was soon to be found out. She had an uneasy feeling that they had started too quickly and, too soon, gone too far. She feared that anything travelling at this velocity must surely come off the rails at the first curve.

Towards noon he was to surprise her yet again.

Ordering her to stay as she was, he produced a pencil and a pad of notepaper and started sketching her. At first she was happy enough to have a reason to stay still for a moment and expected his sketches to be no more than amateur crudities. So she was pleasantly surprised, when he handed them to her, to see a vibrant, naked young woman – one who just happened to have her face – drawn with great economy and directness.

'You're an artist?'

'An early ambition, quickly squashed.'

'What happened?'

'My father. I wanted to go to art school but he insisted that I should study something more vocational. The closest to art he would allow was architecture.'

He placed her in another pose and, as he worked, she thought she had found the first weak spot in his until now apparently impregnable armour.

'Isn't it a little unusual to give up art to become a property tycoon?'

'In the first place, I haven't given up art. Secondly, I became – what you are pleased to call – a "property tycoon" by accident. The same father that denied me my earlier ambitions left me a seedy, run down, rambling apartment block whose only asset was a good address. I used my newly acquired architectural skills to refurbish it. Everyone told me I was crazy and that it didn't make economic sense, but I couldn't stand owning anything that was that shabby and that ugly. Then the controlled rent laws were changed. I had moved it up market and it became the collateral asset from which I spread upward and outward.'

'And what happened to the art?'

He shrugged off the question and only the sound of his pencil spoilt the absolute silence until he heaved a huge sigh.

'It's time you knew about me,' he said.

Allowing her only a raincoat and a pair of shoes, she found herself being hustled out of her apartment to feel the chilly December wind invading parts she would never have normally exposed to the winter chill.

'Where are we going?'

'To my place.'

They got to a street corner and he hesitated. She didn't notice his concern at first. She was too busy eagerly scanning the faces of passers-by trying to judge whether or not they could sense she was naked under the coat. She found it particularly thrilling when she understood that no one was noticing. Either that or they just didn't give a damn!

His cursing brought her back to the present reality.

'The bloody car's gone!' he exploded. 'I wasn't sure at first but now I distinctly remember parking it there outside that shop.'

'Stolen?' she asked.

'What else? Come on, we'll have to get a cab.'

He was one of those people for whom taxis miraculously appeared on cue. It was in the cab that she was reminded that he loved to play erotic games.

He urged her to move from the rear seat to the jump seat directly in front of him. Aware of the taxi driver just a foot from her back, she understood the point of the game and moved her thighs apart, allowing the coat to fall away from her legs, fully exposing herself to him.

He mouthed to her that she should play with herself and, for the first time in his presence, she hesitated. The cab driver couldn't see but she feared other passing drivers – especially those sitting high in trucks or buses – might.

'Do it!' he said in a loud authoritative voice that made the cab driver think his words had been intended for him.

'Not you, driver!' he yelled back. 'I was talking to my whore!'

The cab driver chuckled but she was mortally offended. Snapping her legs together she carefully drew the coat back over her thighs to cover herself. She found she couldn't look at him.

'That . . .' he said in a soft even voice, '. . . was very naughty of you.'

Still refusing to look at him, she stared instead out of the side window.

Minutes later the cab drew up in front of the prestigious address that was his flagship property and she sat tight, undecided whether by going home directly she would be punishing herself more than him. It was then she realised her predicament. If she took the cab home she would have nothing to pay the man with and, then again, wouldn't it be silly to take the one cab driver in London who might guess at her condition and lead him to her home so he would know where she lived?

When Jeffrey turned to offer a hand out from the rear of the cab, she took it, telling herself she had no choice.

She still didn't feel like talking to him but was, despite herself, impressed as they crossed the refurbished, somewhat kitsch, lobby towards the elevators.

The receptionist called out a greeting, as did the man in a porter's uniform who hurried from some back room as if anxious to look alert in his employer's eyes.

Once inside the elevator she couldn't help noticing the Yale key he used to unlock the mechanism before it would respond to the PENTHOUSE button. She noted she was with a man who valued his security.

The elevator moved swiftly up but she kept a hurt distance. She felt pained that he made no attempt to break the silence and ask her what was wrong. She knew he didn't have to – that he already knew precisely at which moment the deep freeze had set in and why.

The doors opened onto a small lobby and he had to use a magnetic key on a second set of heavy double doors before they would open.

When they did she was treated to an apartment of, literally, breath taking proportions. It had the dimensions of a hotel lobby but there was little evidence of the over-zealous symmetry which some interior designers imposed. Instead, the main living room was split into groupings of furniture with a profusion of potted, semi-tropical plants that reduced the vast expanse to human proportions.

There were several messages on his answerphone so, in response to his invitation to have a look round, she started on a self-conducted tour.

Everywhere she looked there was evidence of abundant affluence. Its corollary – bad taste – was totally absent. Jeffrey had managed to make a display that avoided vulgarity and ostentation. Although it was demonstrably impossible she got the feeling that this apartment had been here for some long time. There was no questioning its modernity but he had gifted it permanence.

She remembered being told how an aristocrat had made a 'put down' remark about someone he considered a parvenu. 'He's the sort of chap that buys his own furniture.'

Jeffrey had done that but avoided being too precise, too matching. She couldn't help noticing that the bed would accommodate four people with comfort. She wondered how many times it had.

When she returned to the living area she heard him telling a girl, his secretary, surely, about the stolen car and asking her to make the necessary steps, including informing the police. Did this man do nothing for himself?

When he laid the phone down he turned to her.

'It's a beautiful apartment,' she said.

'So! You've found your voice again!'

'You shouldn't have called me a whore!'

'I didn't,' he said, 'call you "a" whore. I called you "my" whore. There's a difference.'

'Well I'm not.'

He shrugged. 'You're free to leave,' he said.

She was standing in front of him, separated from the desk by two metres of velvety carpet. His words had stunned her. She even felt tears beginning to threaten her composure.

'Are you tired of me, then?' she said.

'No, but if you want to play then you play my rules.'

'Don't I get any choice?'

'Only when to stay and when to go. Do you want to go?'

'You know I don't.'

He nodded, stood up, and closed the space between them to stand directly in front of her.

'Get rid of that coat and bend over the desk.'

Angry at him and herself for knowing that she would accept this humiliation, she tried to protest, but he cut her short by grabbing her, turning her and almost literally ripping the coat from her body. As she yelled desperately at him he propelled her forward to the desk and forced her face down to crush her nose into the smell of polished leather.

She opened her mouth to protest again at this treatment, but the word became a cry; then she felt him firmly entering her. Suddenly all protest seemed superfluous. Anger turned to excitement as his words battered her ears.

'You disobeyed me in the cab, didn't you?'

'Yes!' she yelled.

'Are you sorry?'

'Yes!'

'Are you going to be my whore?'

'Yes!'

'What happens to disobedient whores?'

'They get fucked over desks!'

'Wrong!' his words seething into her ears like liquid lava. 'They get punished!'

'Yes! Punish me, screw me! Do anything you like to me!'

And then, in unison, they came.

Later that evening she stood tied loosely between two posts. Her feet firmly on the ground and though not strained she was, nevertheless, tethered, as immobile and fearful as any creature awaiting an unknown fate.

He had come to her and, without explanation, tied her wrists together with a silken cord. Then, leading her to stand between the posts, had first tied her and then gently fed a knotted bandana into her mouth to silence her.

Without a word of explanation, not a look, nor a backward glance, he had left her among the ornamental plants that crowded for space in his heated solarium as if she were just another passive ornament among the many. The worst moment came when he turned off the lights in the solarium, leaving her with only the incidental light escaping from the living area.

She had been there for what seemed to her an eternity. Her thoughts were confused by the dull ache that had started in her raised arms but one message repeated and repeated until she was sure it would become engraved on her throat. She hated him. Hated this. The moment she was released, it was over. How dare he do this to her? How dare he assume that there could possibly be any pleasure for her in such humiliation?

If he had stayed, if he had watched her, it might have become marginally supportable, interesting even, but she could hear him somewhere in the apartment making phone calls – arranging to go to a New Year's Eve party – and then, worst of all she could hear the drone of the TV.

Deep in her discomfort she tortured herself with the thought that she knew very little of this man ... that wealth did not prevent someone being mad – only from being locked up. Suppose he was a maniac and intended to kill her? There was nothing she could do about it!

Hate him! Hate this! It's over between us!

She saw him coming and watched, her face muscles tensing, her vocal cords rehearsing the invective she intended showering on him. Punishment? He didn't know the meaning of the word.

'So, are you suitably chastened?'

His fingertips reached out and gently touched her nipples. It was as if he had touched her with heated needles.

The hands moved outward and encircled her breasts. His lips nestled to her throat, a clinch from which she couldn't escape. His hands circled her belly and then, gently, with the subtlety of a soldering iron, touched her most vulnerable bud of flesh.

Then a switch was thrown and a gear moved in her body. She found herself moaning, pressing herself against his caresses, and desperately wanting him. But please, God, she thought first, please, set me free!

'I love you like this.'

God. No. Not like this! Please don't let me come!

His fingers returned to her nipples, now extended and sensitive. Gently at first he tweaked them then, increasing the pressure, he bit his nails into her tender flesh.

Using one hand he reached up and loosened the silk gag, and threw it from them.

'I want to see you smile,' he said, increasing the nail-given pain.

She was breathing too hard, her throat too constricted to say anything.

'If you smile for me and tell me you love me then I'll set you free.'

Her uncertain eyes managed to still his swimming image

and she saw his eyes – those eyes! Then, straining every muscle in her face, she managed to smile. 'I love you,' she said.

It was late evening before they spoke of anything other than their pleasure.

'Why did you do that to me?'

'You deserved it.'

'Why did you just leave me there and walk away?'

'I had things to do.'

'I hated you. You know that, don't you?'

He smiled to himself and, by so doing rekindled the anger he had washed away with a gesture.

'I think I still hate you.'

'That's healthy. Hate is closer to love than any other emotion.'

Earlier he had shown her the tanning lamps built into the solarium to bring a touch of summer to even the dreariest winter's day.

They now lay side by side enjoying the counterfeit sun.

'Are you frightened?' he asked her.

'I'm not sure. I think I am but it's like a recurring nightmare. You know it will come at you in the night but it doesn't stop you wanting to go to sleep.'

'I have a technique for destroying nightmares. What you do is turn and face them. Stops the pursuing horror dead in its tracks. When you know your fear you can face it.'

'That's how I feel about you. Unknown. And yes, that frightens me.'

'Sure it isn't yourself that frightens you? Haven't you found out things about yourself you never knew?'

'Also.'

Even as she spoke she discovered something new about herself. She could lie here next to him and calmly, objectively, discuss things which would have, previously, shamed her in any context other than the throes of passion. Of course, the protective eye shields they were wearing helped. The past few days had taught her that direct eye contact can be the most excoriating experience between two people.

Warmed by the lamps, confident to be naked yet masked from the world, she felt totally relaxed.

'What do you want of me?' she asked him out of a lengthening silence.

'To be allowed to worship.'

'Worship what?'

'You.'

'Is that what you think you were doing when you tied me up in the solarium?'

In truth, she still harboured a hate of what he had done to her but also recognised there was emerging a perverse recognition that the price was worth it for the joyous aftermath. When he had finally released her, the pain, if anything, had increased. The blood rushing back into her veins had seemed loaded with liquid fire rendering her totally helpless – and therefore without responsibility – for what had followed – an unfathomable depth of pleasure.

He had stayed silent for a long moment. 'Do you know how incredibly beautiful you looked?'

'How could I?' she asked with a degree of asperity.

'You're right,' he said. 'There should have been a mirror. Selfish of me. Next time. Promise.'

'What makes you think there'll be a next time?'

'There won't,' he said. 'Unless you want it.'

This struck her as a bizarre remark and left her feeling curiously bereft. Must she be forced to ask him to torture her? Did he imagine she ever would?

At that moment the timer that controlled the ultraviolet dosage clicked off and broke the mood.

Lifting the shields from their eyes they looked at each other as if for the very first time. Curiously, she even felt a little shy.

'Say it,' he said. 'Say the words you have often thought but have never dared say to a lover.'

The challenge struck her to the core. The words were there instantly, known to her since puberty and although never spoken they were now brazenly echoing in her mind and insisting she give them life. Words that, if she spoke them, would be the most terrible of all her betrayals of Kenneth. Fight as she might she couldn't stop them as they leapt into life from her lips.

'Fuck me in the arse,' she said and, unable to take breath until he answered, she listened, horrified, to the dying echo of the words.

Had he laughed, had he leapt on her and taken her cruelly in that place where she knew she would suffer, she might have been able to plead a moment of madness, but he didn't. Instead he held her eyes for a whole heart-stopping minute then, standing, he reached down a hand to help her to her feet. 'Come with me,' he said softly.

Now quite frightened by what she might have started she padded beside him across the wide carpet and into his bedroom.

Throwing open his closets he indicated the rank upon rank of suits, shirts, ties and underwear.

'If you are to be taken like a man then you will dress like one. You have one hour before I greet your identical twin brother.'

Turning, he left her alone with a heart-pounding dread at what she had done. Damn him, she thought. Why couldn't he have just taken her? Why force her into this humiliating ritual and make her responsible for her own madness?

If she did as he asked there was no escape, no turning back, no excuses she could make to herself in some future sleepless night. She was alone with her own wantonness.

Finding a full-length mirror she questioned her reflection. 'Shall you be his whore?'

After a moment's pause the image in the mirror, eyes wild with light, smiled and nodded.

4

Confusion.

Her mind was racing and outstripping her brain's capacity to process the bombarding stream of thought.

His clothes. Where did she start? Choosing her own clothes for any occasion was stressful enough but deciding what to wear for her imminent sodomisation, with her immolator impatiently waiting, was the very stuff of which panic attacks are made.

Very few useful ideas were getting through to her oppressed brain.

Her body was not much help either. Her heart was pumping blood at a rapid rate. Her hands shook as they fluttered over the serried ranks of shirts and sweaters, while her breathing was audibly hoarse.

She was in no shape to go shopping!

Feeling the task had overwhelmed her, she turned away from the closets to sit down heavily on the huge bed, almost ready to let the threatening sobs break through and, head in hands, simply give up.

Either that or run away and hide.

What a good idea! Where would she go? Home? What would she use for clothes or money? Her decision had been made – forced on her – when she got out of the taxi. What would she do now? Put time on rewind and delete that decision?

Damn him!

Why couldn't he have just done it?

Why put her through this hell?

Because he liked it, that's why.

In retrospect she saw her predicament as the result of a carefully engineered plan.

Bringing her to his apartment wearing only a coat and shoes, he had ensured that she was his captive as surely as if he had bound and chained her. What initially seemed a spontaneous, mad caprice, she now realised was the first move in a diabolical plot!

Testing her, that's what he was doing. Even now he was probably gleefully chortling at the prospect of her tear-stained appearance before him to admit defeat.

It then came to her that he might be expecting her not to go through with it. That would explain why he hadn't just done it. He was counting on her cowardice! It was entirely possible, she thought, that his plot had extended that far.

Well, to hell with him!

Picturing him, confidently waiting for her capitulation, angered her. Out of anger was born resolution. She'd damn well show him she was not going to play his 'little woman'. Now she was determined to call his bluff.

Returning to the closets she found her anger had calmed her. This was, after all, a simple, if unfamiliar task. Take it a step at a time and anything was possible.

First, imagine what her identical twin brother would have looked like. No problem. Exactly like her. Except, of course, for the hair.

Solution? Obvious. Find a hat!

She looked but there were no hats. A cap, then? Sports clothes. Not this closet. Try the next. No. Maybe he kept his sports gear, supposing he had any, in a different closet.

Looking round she could see none that weren't already open.

Intending to look in the bathroom, she had started towards it when she noticed a closet standing between the bedroom and bathroom doors. In there she hit pay dirt.

Rackets for squash, tennis and a curious basket-like glove. Caps? Top shelf. Bingo! Baseball caps in profusion, a multi-coloured curiosity with a gold tassel on it, cricket caps, and then she saw it – a wide-brimmed panama. Perfect!

Going to one of the many mirrors, she piled up her hair and placed the panama on top. Untidy wisps showed through. She needed to wind her hair onto the top of her head and then find something to keep it there. Dismissing the possibility of finding any hair grips, she spotted a pair of his shoes. The lace from one of them would have to do.

Her hair bound into a bun, secured by the lace, wasn't the perfect solution but it would do. Slamming the hat down over the piled-up mess, she smiled. Great! Next, a shirt.

She didn't waste time on it. She took down the first silk shirt she could find. There was a momentary confusion with the left to right buttoning, but she finally got her clumsy fingers to work that out. Oversize and looking ridiculous but, with the sleeves folded back and a jacket on top, she thought it would be acceptable.

Underpants? Why not. In a bottom drawer she found some pretty exotic ones – not a whole lot unlike panties. An unworthy thought came into her head but, considering the determined stamina he'd shown in administering to her, it was immediately dismissed. However, some of his under-pants were little more than posing pouches. It was possible they were unwanted Christmas presents. Whatever they were they fitted snugly round her waist and hips. God knows what they did to him!

Now, trousers. This was an immediate problem. All his seemed to have been made to accommodate two of her, and there was no way her waist and hips could keep them up. She didn't want her own brother to look like a baggy-pants comic.

Skis! She remembered seeing skis stacked in his 'sporting' closet, where there were skis there would be ski-pants. Tight, clinging ski-pants. Perfect!

After a moment's search she found them folded neatly in a drawer. Pulling a pair over his suspect posing pouch she saw that they fitted well enough except for the inordinate length of the legs. Sitting down she found that by pulling and stretching she could fold the excess length up and into the bottom of the pants.

They were loose under the crotch but she took up that surplus by rolling the waistband in on itself.

How did she check out so far? Not too bad. She needed a sweater, loose but not too much, a windcheater, also loose, on top of that and things were taking shape. Socks obscured the bulge where she had rolled in the leg length of the pants. Shoes? Despair gripped her. There was no chance she could find shoes to fit.

Her own shoes! They were only medium heeled. They would do but the trouble was she had lost them while being taken over the desk. How could she retrieve them without risking him seeing her before she was ready?

Simple. Let him do something for once.

Crossing to the bedroom door she opened it a few inches and called, 'Hello!?'

No answer. She opened it a few inches more and put her head out. She could hear his voice murmuring somewhere off in the distance. Cautiously, she slipped into the living room, darting from potted plant to potted plant, peering round them to make sure she wasn't spotted.

As she got closer to his voice she could hear that he was on the telephone but, fortunately for her, at the far end of the apartment and not at his desk.

She found one shoe lying where she would have expected it, but no sign of the other. Thinking it couldn't be far she started anxiously looking round. She had just spotted it partially obscured by the valance of one of the couches when his end of the telephone conversation impinged on her.

'Yes, he's quite young and inexperienced. I want the young lady to, you know, give him something to remember when he goes back to school.'

She listened, mouth open, and horrified. What was he plotting now? She had no doubt that the 'he' of the 'inexperienced' was meant to be her. She couldn't believe he was hiring some kind of call girl.

She heard him winding up the call. 'You can? Oh, excellent. Straight away? Fine. Yes, here's the address.'

She listened, her mouth so wide open that it became dry, and as he gave his address she wondered what he was playing at.

Realising the conversation was coming to an end she scuttled back to the bedroom wondering why *she* felt guilty.

That he had some further complication to add to her already overburdened worry banks, there was no doubt. Just what it was she couldn't imagine. Well, she *could* ... but surely not 'that'? If so the 'young lady' with her 'memorable experience' was due for a surprise of her own!

She pulled on the shoes and stood to look into the mirror. What she saw was a completely outmoded, expensively dressed, idiot. She looked like a boy who had got hurriedly dressed in a bomb-distressed ballet chorus dressing room. The panama didn't go with the jacket. The jacket might have gone with the ski-pants – but nowhere she would have wanted to go. The shoes were the only familiar thing about herself.

What was she going to do? She looked a disaster and felt worse.

She was about to give up when she heard a brief tap on the bedroom door and, as she whirled round, ready to explode if he so much as smiled, saw him hesitate only briefly before breaking into an overly hearty greeting.

'George!' he beamed, 'I was wondering where you'd got to! Come, I've got us both a drink. You *do* drink don't you?'

Feeling that he must be either blind or more easily pleased than she thought, she followed him out of the room.

With a comradely arm about her shoulder he walked her across the expanse of the living area. 'I've been looking forward to having a talk with you, George.'

Leading her to a bar which seemed to have been born out of a bookcase – the first hint of crassness she had found in his furnishings – he handed her a tumbler of whisky.

'As you know,' he was saying, 'I've been seeing a great deal of your sister and quite frankly there are some things about her that puzzle me. I thought you might be able to help me with a pointer or two.' Jeffrey paused and smiled with patronising indulgence. 'Drink all right?'

She had gratefully taken a sizeable draught of the smooth malt but, still unsure of her voice, simply nodded in reply.

'Good!' he cried, leading her to sit on a couch opposite his own. Sitting himself down he beamed across at her. 'I mean, frankly, she's a bit of a tart, isn't she?'

She frowned and conveyed her dissension as best she could without yet daring to try out her voice.

He seemed to pick up on her dilemma and sorted it out. 'Now, George, I know your voice is about to break and you're embarrassed about it, but you can talk if you want to, you know.'

'She's not a tart!' she said positively.

'Well, you would say that wouldn't you? Being a loyal brother and all, and, of course, I respect that, but tell me, George, have you ever had a woman yourself?'

She reverted to a resentful shake of the head while waiting to see if this was going to lead to an explanation of the phone call.

'No, I suppose not. The Old School keeps to its regime of cold showers and avoiding "evil" thoughts, eh?' He paused and drew in a long breath as if contemplating the 'good old days', before going on. 'Matter of fact I was reading the other day that cold showers actually *stimulate* the libido. Did you know that?'

She shook her head.

'So you see, the Old School idea can lead to a lot of mischief in the showers.' Idly picking an imaginary thread from his jacket sleeve, he went on. 'Much of that going on still?'

Again she shook her head, aware that her 'twin brother' wasn't being very good at this. Despite the sanctioning of her unmasculine voice, she still couldn't speak because, having been reminded of where all this was supposed to be leading, she was scared to death. He *hadn't* been bluffing!

Seeing Jeffrey in the role of an 'old queen' intent on seducing a 'young boy' was unnerving to say the least. He was just a little too smooth and convincing for her taste. An added concern was the knowledge that there was a 'surprise' on its way.

Perversely, she also resented him thinking that any brother of hers, imaginary or not, would fall for such a line.

Jeffrey, who had been watching her/him for some silent moments, now gave the most sickly smile she could imagine before patting the couch beside him. 'You look so distant sitting over there. Why don't you come and sit by me?'

Feeling sickened and revolted – Jeffrey was that good at it – she warily moved to sit next to him as he had asked.

Jeffrey, laying a careless arm along the couch behind her, smiled again. 'Got a little treat on its way for you, George.'

A very real shudder of revulsion went through her body. 'Really?' she squeaked.

'Yes. Possibly something a young lad like you has never seen before.'

Quite suddenly she felt she wasn't there. It was as if her body had been invaded by another creature. Everything was suddenly unreal, even surreal. She really was starting to respond like a nervous schoolboy in the company of a disreputable uncle.

This was ridiculous. A waking nightmare. Could it be that she had been subtly hypnotised or even drugged?

When the arm, which had been 'carelessly' laid along the back of the couch, became a hug, she actually felt quite sick.

Abruptly, not quite sure where the impulse had come from, she found herself on her feet blurting out that she wanted to go.

Jeffrey was staring up at her, obviously taken aback. As they looked at each other in confusion the apartment door bell cut through the tension like a knife.

'Not now,' he said, getting to his feet. 'Surely,' he added, before turning away to answer the door.

She looked around for succour but none was apparent. She began to think she might be going mad when she strained to hear the subdued murmur of voices coming from the apartment's lobby.

Now, in total confusion, she felt as if she was suffocating.

Her brain had simply ceased functioning and the earlier 'disassociated' feeling grew even stronger.

The voices drew nearer and she turned to see Jeffrey returning accompanied by a tall slender girl wearing a full-length 'gowny' dress and, of all things, a feather boa over her shoulders.

'This is my young nephew, George,' he was saying to the girl. 'George, this is Lesley.'

Lesley came forward with a graciously extended hand. 'George' found 'himself' awkwardly shaking her hand and not knowing where to look.

Lesley, fortunately, seemed oblivious to anything about her but her own appearance. 'Darling,' she said, addressing Jeffrey. 'Put my music into a suitable slot, would you?'

Jeffrey, who seemed to be enjoying himself enormously, took a cassette from her and went off to place it in its 'suitable slot'.

Meanwhile Lesley was casting an assessing eye around the apartment, which gave Helen a chance for a good look at her.

The hair looked as if it was fighting for its life under layers of lacquer. The face had been made up by an undertaker and the word 'glitz' had been invented to describe the dress. All in all, Lesley was what her mother would have called 'extravagant' and she would have called, enamelled.

Jeffrey rejoined them to be received by an anxious enquiry from Lesley. 'My music, darling! Aren't you going to play it?'

Showing her a black box he was carrying, he smiled. 'Remote control,' he told her. 'Any time you're ready.'

Casting another despairing eye about the apartment Lesley spoke again. 'Yes, darling, but we'll have to do something about the lighting . . .' Lesley moved off around the apartment, turning off this lamp, turning that one on, until she came back murmuring, 'I suppose that'll have to do,' and struck a startling, dramatic pose; standing in profile to them with one hand raised in the air and the other knuckled to her forehead.

Turning to 'George', Jeffrey indicated that she should come to sit next to him on the couch, as Lesley hissed: 'My music, darling!'

Jeffrey hit the play button on the remote and, as the brassy show music filled the apartment, Lesley started making swooping, leg dragging movements about the space before the couches, only occasionally tripping on the hem of her gown in the deep rug piling.

Feeling that things were moving from the surreal to the preposterous Helen realised that Lesley was about to launch into a strip tease of the most excruciatingly embarrassing kind. She couldn't bring herself to look at Jeffrey – on the other hand, she could barely tear her eyes away from the ludicrous Lesley – but she did begin to wonder when he had decided to turn their 'affair', if their relationship could aspire to so grand a status, into farce.

Mouth involuntarily open in stupefaction she watched as Lesley slipped out of the gown to reveal black stockings on a garter belt framing surprisingly good legs, then used the feather boa to play peek-a-boo with her undersized breasts.

Having thought that things couldn't get worse she was appalled when Lesley started waltzing towards her, flicking the boa into her face. 'Have you been a *really* good boy? Lesley *loves* really good boys!'

Fortunately, Lesley waltzed off into a series of crotch-probing poses, enabling Helen to stop herself throwing up on the glass table before her.

When was this nightmare to end? She had never felt more

shamefully distressed in her life. Distress for the totally untalented Lesley who, somewhere, waited like a taxi to be summoned out to embarrass people.

The music was building to what had once been a show-stopping climax and she could pray that it signalled the end of this torture – a prospect which focused her mind on the horrendous potential the aftermath presented. Suicide would be the only rational response if Lesley were to be included.

Now their 'dancer' was dramatically sticking one long leg before the other as she advanced on 'George' with fixed gaze and malice aforethought. Then, throwing her arms and boa wide, she exposed her almost non-existent breasts as, looming menacingly closer, Lesley placed one leg on the glass table, threw her thighs wide to expose the diamante G-string, which 'George' realised, with horror, was about to come off!

It did! To reveal an even greater horror. There before her eyes was an unmistakably male penis! She felt unable to take her eyes from it as the music died away and total silence reigned.

'Want to feel it, darling?' asked the voice of 'Lesley'. 'It's a real one.'

Mesmerised, she heard Jeffrey speak. 'You have my permission . . .'

Slowly, she raised her eyes to the now grotesque face of 'Lesley' to see that he had whipped off the lacquered wig. As their eyes met Lesley spoke. 'I don't do penetration, darling, but if you want me to go down on you, that's cool!'

She heard a silly, squeaky voice protest, 'But I'm a girl!'

Lesley chuckled. 'That's all right, love. I don't discriminate.'

Feeling as if she had been transmuted into a waxworks tableau, she could find no thought, no words, other than a silent prayer that somehow the floor would open up and get her out of this.

Her prayer was answered by Jeffrey. With a sonorous clap of his hands he stood up and spoke the first sensible words she had heard all evening. 'Wonderful! Absolutely marvellous. Thank you Lesley, but, sorry, that's as far as we can take it tonight.'

Afraid to meet anyone's gaze Helen sensed Lesley immediately dropping out of character to fussily gather up her discarded props as Jeffrey shepherded her away.

Meanwhile 'George' sat feeling as if a dentist had sneaked up and injected her entire body with novacaine.

There was more murmuring at the door but, this time, thankfully, it was the sound of 'Lesley' departing. It was then she realised she was still wearing the hat. How long ago her preparation all seemed now! The hat lay in her hands like the reminder of another life.

When he came back into the room, thankfully alone, she found her voice. 'Why did you do that?' she asked him.

'It's what "us chaps" do.'

Silently, she looked at him. Were men an alien species? Had he imagined that what they had seen could, on any level, be construed as titillating, arousing or anything but humiliating to the onlookers?

'Sad, isn't it?' he asked, voicing her thoughts exactly.

When he came and reached down for her she went into his arms with a sob of relief. The nightmare was over and the world could resume its axis.

But not quite.

'Look,' he said, and she watched as he reached under the glass table and, pulling away a furry rug, revealed a mirror laid to reflect upward.

'What's that for?' she asked.

'For you,' he said. 'You told me you liked to watch yourself suffering.'

She felt herself jellifying. The protest her brain was making was choked off by the excitement in her throat.

His voice softly insistent, he said, 'Kneel on the table.' When she hesitated, he added, 'It won't break.'

Suddenly, the role intended for Lesley was clear. 'She' had been hired to witness her humiliation. As she tentatively did as he said, she reflected that, comparatively, it made what was to come an act of love.

'Stay quite still,' he murmured as she knelt on the table and looked through its transparent surface to her 'twin brother' looking back up at her.

She watched as Jeffrey reached round and loosened the rolled-up trouser tops and then eased the elasticised top over her hips. Fascinated, she felt distanced, like an audience watching a play, as he ran his hands over her rump. Then she flinched and gasped as she felt the lubricant jelly being worked into her.

Now she knew he really meant to go through with it she felt her body preparing itself – except it had gone into action in the wrong place!

'You're going to get a thorough screwing,' he told her, moving her raised buttocks towards the end of the table. 'You can scream and shout all you want. It won't make the slightest difference.' He was standing behind her now, as she stared down at the frightened face of her 'brother's' reflection as he waited with her.

Standing behind her, she felt him hard and probing. She gasped in anticipation of pain as he found her and tried to force entry.

With a tight grip on her hips he thrust again and she found

herself falling forward to rest her arms, to the elbows, on the glass top.

Then he withdrew, but the respite was fleeting, since he had withdrawn only to better prepare the ground. His jelly-laden fingers searched her out and acted as warning precursors for the giant that would follow in their path.

Again he addressed himself and this time the resisting sphincter muscle surrendered to him and she screamed as he surged into the breach.

The mirror relentlessly recorded every flicker of expression, each and every one of her protests against the strange sensation, but there was no escape now. He was lodged firmly and moving smoothly while she stared, in horror, at the maddened face in the mirror.

Now the rushing sensations were close to unbearable; layers of pain and pleasure so intermingled they seemed inseparable. Now she saw her reflection screaming and she cried out for the lash of him.

'Yes,' screamed the demented creature in the mirror. 'Yes!' and he responded, bucking and rearing into her with even greater vigour, ever greater cruelty. Now, having transmuted pain into pleasure, she rejoiced; she no longer cared about what he was doing to her. Happy only that he could harvest such pleasure from her body, she felt herself thrashing in the grip of an orgasmic wave.

Insensate to anything, overburdened with delight, she felt him throbbing and pumping, and filling her with his pleasure.

When his exhausted weight bore down on her she slid forward to lay on the glass, her head now turned sideways away from the indelicate, mirrored, vision and thanked any interested god that she had lived long enough to know this moment.

They lay for long minutes, he still inside her but now of more accommodating size, in silent communion until she got an uncontrollable fit of the giggles.

'What's so funny?' he asked, defensively acerbic.

'I was just thinking of poor Lesley,' she said. '"No penetration"! She doesn't know what "she's" missing!'

5

They woke like lovers.

Lying side by side in his huge bed beneath a single sheet, they held hands in silent communion, feeling no need to question or explain.

She was the one to break the potent silence. 'Yesterday, when I saw you on my door monitor you looked exactly like someone in an old newsreel.'

'Good news or bad news?' he asked in a slightly puzzled tone.

'At the time I didn't know, but now I do.'

'Really?'

'Yes. Because now I feel exactly the same.'

'As what?'

'As if I was in an old newsreel.'

Raising himself on one elbow he looked down into her smug, smiling face and was puzzled. 'Have I missed the point of this conversation – or what?'

She shook her head. 'I haven't come to the "point" yet.'

'Would you mind hurrying up? I have this uncontrollable urge to fuck you.'

She smiled, cat-like. 'You must have seen those old newsreels of the Allied troops liberating France.'

'Of course.'

'Well, right this minute, I feel like one of those French women, beside themselves with joy, clambering onto the tanks.'

Looking down, his expression was still puzzled.

'Liberated,' she told him. 'That's what you've done to me. Liberated me after months of oppression.'

His eyes flickered during a momentary stunned silence. 'I think that's about the best compliment I have ever received.'

'My hero!' she said, but couldn't contain the giggle.

His mouth nuzzling into her throat, he murmured, 'And how, exactly, did those newly liberated women reward their conquering heroes?'

Purring with pleasure at his caresses she could barely contain her mounting excitement. 'Well, first they would permit their hero to bring them chocolates and then, perhaps, allow a kiss. All most proper, of course. Then, another day, perhaps he would call with flowers and get two kisses. Some days later she might receive chocolates *and* flowers . . .' His lips on her breasts were creating tidal waves, making it difficult for her to maintain her little-girl tone so she broke off to indulge herself in moaning restlessness.

'And, after all this long drawn out courtship – what did he get?'

'Movietone never showed that,' she managed – the words barely escaping her throat.

'Shall we try an educated guess?' he asked as his lips moved to cover her urgent mouth.

Suddenly the bed was a battlefield. No more a place for bantering philosophers or, even, thought. Here only the animal responders could survive. Ecstatically, her body greeted his penetrating surge while her brain became fixed in a loop of joy.

This was right! This act between these two people at this time and place, she thought, was the true definition of consummation; the saturation and the wholesome, natural completion of self.

She welcomed his unstoppable climactic surge with genuine joy, screaming out with an intensity more appropriate to fear than pleasure. Suddenly they fell apart like broken dolls to lay appalled at the pleasure they had known at each other's loins.

She was the first to find words. '*Ah, mon Colonel! Où sont les autres?*'

He was still gasping for breath. 'For God's sake don't talk French to me. I can barely think in English!'

Filled with the joy of a confident temptress she rolled to press her breasts against his heaving chest. 'I wanted to know where the rest were?'

'Rest of what?' he gasped.

'Your Regiment! We liberated women do not stint to reward our liberators and we show no discrimination!'

'Or mercy!' he gasped.

Kissing her way down the centre seam of his chest and belly she came upon his fearful pride.

'*Pauvre petit!*' she murmured. '*Je crois trouver un héros tombé!*' With sinuous tongue she reached out to tease the 'fallen hero' now limply lying in repose, bringing a moan of delighted protest from him.

'I see it all now,' he said. 'The entire Machiavellian plot!' Reaching down he seized her head and turned her grinning face towards his own. 'You've insured me for a million pounds and now you're set on fucking me to death!'

Her laugh rang out in delight. 'The way I see it, is that it's got to be worth a damn good try!'

Dragging her up the length of his body he brought her nose to nose. ''Tis a far, far better thing I do now than I have ever done.'

She joined in to mangle his quote. 'That a man should give his life for a woman's pleasure?'

Closing his eyes against the intensity of his sigh he pushed her head to rest on his chest. 'This is a moment of such exquisite pleasure I feel there ought to be a way of preserving it forever in amber.'

Each pleasurably confident that their thoughts were identical, they lay in silent communion for some minutes before he spoke.

'Tell me something,' he said.

She smiled upward. 'Like yesterday?'

'No. Yesterday I asked you to say something you have never before dared say to a lover. This is different.'

She waited, confident that there was nothing she couldn't tell him.

'Tell me something about yourself that you've never told anyone. Not even your best friend.'

A twinge of pain, discomfort, shuddered through her. This man had plundered her body in the most absolute manner possible, and she had rejoiced in the surrender, but now it seemed he wanted to assault that most intimate part of her body – her mind.

She knew exactly what he wanted to know. Just as yesterday the five words that had hovered on the edge of her lips, unspoken for years, had struggled free, now her greatest secret was there, fully formed, and impatiently waiting its turn – but it was too painful to share, even with him.

When she was very young and still experimenting with her own sexuality she had discovered that the man who lived opposite her in Eastbourne had been spying into her bedroom with a telescope. Night after night she had tormented the man, sometimes giving him full view of what he sought and on others coming to the brink and then closing her blinds before he got what he wanted. She had been knowingly cruel in her exhibitionism and thought herself a monster while consoling herself with the thought that he was only getting what he deserved.

Night after night she had revelled in knowing his eyes were on her and, goaded into even more daring acts, she had felt like a latter-day Scheherazade and found fuel for her own fantasies. One night her mother, looking out from another room, had discovered the man spying from a tree to which her exhibitions had lured him, and called the police. The man had been dragged into court and lost his highly placed position with the local authority. He had, to his honour, never mentioned what must have been obvious to him – that she had known and conspired with him – while shame had prevented her saying a word about her own repeated complicity, and he had been hounded out of town, his reputation in ruins. This incident was known to no one but themselves and remained her most shameful secret. From time to time she would calculate how old the man must be by now, and by what standard he must judge her own behaviour. While that man lived, the only other guardian of her guilt, she knew she could never be truly free. Not even now, not even with this man who had brought her to the edge of paradise, could she share it. Instead she sought to divert him.

'I used to run an airline,' she said and then waited as he absorbed her meaning before reacting precisely as she had hoped he would.

Raising himself on one elbow he stared down at her. 'You what!?'

She laughed, delighted by his reaction. 'I did!' she insisted.

'An airline?' he asked.

She nodded, almost unable to contain her happiness that she had managed to surprise him.

'A real airline? I mean, one with aeroplanes that flew?'

She nodded again.

'Which one?' he demanded.

'Well, all right,' she confessed, 'it wasn't exactly an *airline*, but we did have planes and they did fly.'

'What was it then?'

'A club. There was this small airfield near where I used to live. The owners would sometimes rent their planes to other people and sometimes, if they were qualified, they would fly them as air taxis. I used to run the office.'

Sinking back onto the pillows he sighed with relief. 'For a moment I thought I was in bed with the Chairman of British Airways!'

Her laughter rang round the bedroom.

'I always wanted to learn to fly,' he said, and when she stayed silent, went on. 'Never had the time.'

Her silence had become palpable and, curious, he looked across to see that tears were flowing from her eyes.

'What's the matter?' he asked with immediate concern.

'That's where I met Kenneth.'

'Kenneth?' he asked and then immediately felt stricken as he remembered. 'Your husband?'

Her chin trembling now, she nodded.

'Christ!' he said feeling an idiot. 'I'm sorry. Look, I blundered into that! Millie had told me what happened, of course. The last thing I wanted was to upset you.'

Her shoulders were shaking now, and she turned away, murmuring into the pillows.

He reached for her but she, now openly weeping, shrugged him off.

'Look, there's nothing that's happened between us for you to be ashamed about.' He felt helpless seeing her pain and feeling he had nothing to offer. 'You're a young woman. No one could blame you. Please don't ...'

She spoke savagely into the pillow. 'You don't understand! I killed him!'

Her words jolted him for a moment until he understood they couldn't have literal meaning. Now he reached for her more positively and forced her anguished face to look at him. 'That's crazy!' he told her. 'How could you have killed him?'

She threw off his hand which sought to placate her, and fled to the bathroom. He would have followed and caught her but, as he moved, he found his foot tangled in the sheet and was held long enough for her to have shut and bolted the door.

'Open the door,' he pleaded. 'Please. I want us to talk.'

Her only reply was a muffled: 'Go away!'

Reluctantly, he forced himself to give her the time and space she so obviously needed.

Using a guest bathroom, he found himself making a mental inventory of his own bathroom for anything with which she might harm herself. With relief he concluded there was nothing. Not even aspirin, for which he had a lifelong aversion. The windows were fixed against the air-conditioning so it was impossible for her to hurl herself down the eight floors of the building. Even so he was concerned enough to come silently to the door and press his ear against it, listening for any sound inside.

His worst fear was that he would hear nothing so he felt almost pleased to hear the shower noisily gushing.

Dismissing his fears as melodramatic, he turned to dressing. She was, he assured himself, far too sensible a person to do anything like that.

Finally, remembering that this was a business day, he went out to the office section of the apartment, still cursing himself for having brought Kenneth into their bed.

'Idiot!' he yelled at himself, before picking up the telephone to tell Annabel that he was ready to start his working day.

She sat huddled in the corner of the shower cabinet and let the water pound down on her naked body. Not all the waters in all the world would be enough to wash away the self-disgust that gripped her. How could she have so piled treachery on betrayal? Even, back then, when Kenneth was dying, choking, drowning, she had lain, pleasuring herself on the deck, sensuously aware that the Diving Master was looking at the breasts she had bared to the sun.

When they had brought up Kenneth's body and she saw the agony of his dying in his face she had felt cursed by all the gods that ever were. Had she not panicked and left him she would have been, as she was meant to be, there to summon the help that would have saved him. She had been sickened then as she was sickened now.

Emerging from the bathroom, wrapped in an oversized robe – a reminder that she had come to this flat practically naked – she hesitated as she heard voices. His, and then the answering voice of a girl or woman. For a moment she shuddered at the memory of Lesley, and, then, as she came closer, she heard they were talking about the claim on the stolen Maserati.

The girl was tall. Her black hair was cut so dramatically close to her head it looked almost like a cap. She was strikingly attractive, perhaps a year or two older than herself, and when she looked up she revealed the most beautiful eyes Helen could ever remember.

'Ah,' Jeffrey cried, following Annabel's eyeline. 'This is Annabel,' my personal assistant.'

The two women smiled and then warily waited for some sign that the other intended to shake hands. Neither did.

'Let's all have some breakfast. Annabel, would you?'

Annabel picked up the telephone and spoke quietly in the background as he came to her. 'You all right now?' he asked, and when she nodded, went on, 'I feel a complete idiot. I'm sorry.'

Looking at him she managed a smile. 'It's hardly any of your fault.'

'It was my fault for blundering in like that. Especially then, at that moment.'

'What moment?' she asked.

He looked at her awkwardly. 'Well . . . just then I felt we were so close. You know,' he finished artlessly.

Looking at him she suddenly realised that this assertive, dominating man could also be vulnerable. 'It wasn't your fault,' she told him. 'It was a passing idiocy on my part.'

He was holding her now but not so close that they couldn't look into each other's eyes. 'I know that's not true. I know the memory of him is still an agony. I just want you to know that I will do anything to make it easier for you to bear.'

Laying her head against his chest she let the tears flow again, now a blending of gratitude and a feeling that his solicitude was welcomed but misplaced.

Annabel, coming to announce that breakfast was on its way up, was stilled by the intimacy embodied in their embrace. Silently, and a little in awe, she turned away, unable to disturb them.

Later that day as she lay in the solarium, listening to the distant voices of Jeffrey and Annabel as they worked, she found that she had regained some of her confidence. Having worked through the self-hatred of the early morning, she had concluded that if she was of no worth to herself she could, still, be of use to others. A category which was hastily reduced to an exclusive one. Jeffrey. He had shown concern. Consideration. Appreciation. She was capable of lighting his eyes with delight. If that were not a worthy function then she couldn't imagine what else might be.

Naked, she went to where he worked at his desk. Annabel was at a distance feeding paper into a fax machine, as Helen willed him to look up.

When he did, she saw with pride how his eyes flickered from her face to her breasts, to her naked pubis and back again.

'You don't demand enough of me,' she told him. 'If you want a whore then you have me.'

Jeffrey's mouth quivered, his lips tried to form words but none came.

Peripherally aware that Annabel was openly watching her, she turned and walked away across the deep-piled space to the bedroom.

It had been almost an hour since her declaration to Jeffrey. An hour she had spent staring into a mirror and asking, over and over again, the same question: 'Who are you?'

The real question she was asking of herself was 'Why did you do that?' Why had she made such a determined attempt to close down all her previous life and throw herself so totally into Jeffrey's hands? Chillingly, she realised it was not the first time she had made such a gesture.

When Kenneth had asked her to marry him she had been excited less by the culmination of a romantic dream but rather as a means of escape from her mother. For as long as she could remember, her mother had terrified her just as she had dominated her father.

'Extravagance!' was her mother's verdict on every birthday

present, every Christmas gift, her doting father had ever bought her. From an early age she had been aware that her mother thought of her as a rival and that never once, during all those years of her growing, had she ever managed to gain her approval. Kenneth's proposal had given her ammunition against her mother. An act of defiance to counter the many years of helplessness as she watched her beloved father sink further and further under the yoke of domination. How many times had she seen that smiling acceptance of his subservience and wanted to shake him, force life into him, because his acceptance of her mother's domination robbed her of any chance of successful rebellion. That was why she now sought out strong-willed men. Men behind whom she could find shelter from her mother's wrath.

Guiltily, she now saw that Kenneth had not been that man. He had simply been the means of escape and she doubted that she had ever truly loved him. Whether or not he would have developed the strength to provide the protection she so desperately craved, had never been put to the test. The accident had ended any such hopes and, instead, returned her to her mother's unrelenting pressure. The question now was could Jeffrey be that man? In going to him as she had, speaking as she had done, she now realised it had been an act not of submission to Jeffrey but another attempt to distance herself, to shut out forever, her mother.

When the door to the bedroom opened she saw Jeffrey coming into the room and, standing, she turned to face him.

'You are not my whore,' he told her. 'When you are free I will love you.'

'Free – of what?' she asked.

'Of your guilt.'

'You mean Kenneth?'

'There's a great deal more troubling you than simply Kenneth,' he said with finality.

His words struck so directly into her own thoughts that she felt almost elated that he could be so understanding. For confirmation she sought to challenge him. 'What makes you think you know so much about me?'

'I've been there,' he told her in the flat tones of confession. 'I know what it is to have guilt tearing into your guts. My father . . .' His words trailed away like water spilt in a thirsty desert. 'Let's just say: "I know".'

'So what do you propose doing about it?' she asked.

'I told you yesterday that the best way to beat a nightmare is not to run away but to turn and face it. I propose that we test that theory together.'

'How?'

'By means and times of my choosing. If you put yourself in my hands I think we could work it out. Are you willing to try?'

It was another demand for commitment. Once more he was asking for her submission. She had now, in this time and place, to make a decision which she knew would be irrevocable. As she stood there facing him across a room, which seemed suddenly a continent wide, her mind raced through the alternatives. If she refused this man she might be turning her back on her one salvation. If she submitted she had no idea of where it might lead. Remembering his earlier, milder, challenges and his talent for bringing her to previously unimagined heights of pleasure, she knew what her answer was going to be.

He was offering her a voyage on an uncharted sea but beyond the fear lay the possibility of undreamt of discovery.

Excitement gripping her in a rush, she slowly, deliberately, nodded.

'You have to say it,' he urged.

Looking him directly in the eye for the first time in many minutes, eyes flaring, she said: 'Yes. Do what you will.'

6

Standing before the mirror and staring at her gilded nipples, Helen was appalled by the commitment she had made. Five short words had condemned her to whatever dark fantasy might lie in the darkest recesses of Jeffrey's mind. Fear and excitement had always been close allies in her fantasy subconscious but she had declared herself to a man in open acknowledgement of what she was doing and left herself no escape clauses, no excuses she could make, and no means of dignified retreat.

Along with these fragile certainties came doubt. What had he thought of her? After hearing her declaration he had said nothing but had stared at her for what seemed an agonisingly long time. His lips had moved but the thought had withered before being spoken until, still wordless, he had turned away and out of the room.

The dull echo of her unanswered words, intended to be a challenging submission, now echoed in her mind like mere bravado, the garishly decorated breasts no more than a clown's make-up. Had he seen it as such? Had she assumed, too soon, that she had some hold on this man she, even now, barely knew? Was he now trying to grapple with the dilemma of what to do with a woman who had offered up a commitment he didn't want?

Her thoughts lashing her, she realised that what she dreaded most was total rejection. The thought terrified her. She knew that, should he do so, her confidence would be crippled and her soul seared for life. Once more she trembled on the edge of a precipice knowing there was only one person in the entire world who could save her.

When the door opened again she turned fearfully towards it, to see Jeffrey standing there smiling.

'We have a visitor,' he said, his voice light with confidence. 'Someone I know you will want to meet.'

The words had no real meaning – it was the melody with which he spoke them that warmed her. Had he said 'we' have a visitor? Had he said 'I know you will want'? Somewhere in her relieved mind the other words 'visitor' and 'meet' only signified that she had not been rejected and that there was something he wanted to share with her. At that moment she might have run to him, thrown her arms about him and sobbed with relief, but, instead, she simply smiled and murmured: 'Thank you.'

'For what?' he asked.

His puzzled face warmed her. The ice slid from her, melting before the beat of a renewed heart that reminded her she lived. Confidence surging back, she sought to challenge him. 'Shall I come naked?'

'Why not?' he asked.

Excitement triumphing over doubt she came, eyes fixed on his, slowly towards him, hoping perhaps that he would back down, deciding, she might, after all, cover herself. When she realised he was not going to back down before her challenge she felt a liberating thrill – as if passing through the bedroom door, licensed by Jeffrey to go naked to greet a stranger, was the threshold to a new dimension in her life. One thing was certain – her commitment could now be nothing but total.

The visitor was short in stature but huge in presence. A man, completely bald but vibrant with the simmer of a fulfilled life, he stood burned dark brown by endless summers whose aura of warmth he seemed to carry with him. Disdainful of the season, he was dressed for the sun in a light cotton short-sleeved shirt and white linen trousers, while on his feet he wore open espadrilles. His eyes, looking large in so small a face, widened as he saw her and she knew immediately who he was even before Jeffrey spoke the introduction.

'Qito, I'd like you to meet Helen Lloyd.'

'Magnificent!' cried Qito holding up both his hands as if to prevent her coming any further forward. 'How wonderful to meet a beautiful woman naked! Like a goddess! Such beauty *should* be brazen! The goddesses knew that but it is rare in mortal woman.'

Coming forward, Qito took her hand and, with a courtly bow, kissed it. Helen unconsciously squared her shoulders while his kiss travelled the length of her arm, creating ripples of pleasure. His touch seemed to infuse her with some part of this extraordinary man's energy and, when he looked up at her with his sparkling eyes, she felt disconcerted – as if she had shamelessly initiated some form of intimacy with him – while his open admiration filled her with a fierce pride.

It was then that her eyes fell on the glass-topped table on which she had been sodomised the night before. There lay scattered the sketches Jeffrey had made of her before bringing her here. How distant that time seemed now. It was the time before commitment. Was this to be Jeffrey's first 'test' of her?

Her thoughts were brought from reverie by words which resonated with future promise. 'I shall paint her!' Qito cried, then, coming even closer, his perfect teeth gleaming unnaturally white against his walnut skin, he smiled into her eyes.

'You are deserving of immortality.' She felt, uneasily, as if his piercing gaze could see deep into the wanton soul that now lived behind them. 'Come, child,' he said, and taking her by the hand led her to stand before him as he sat on the couch and brought her hips square to his eyes. 'Open yourself to me,' he murmured.

Helen knew exactly what he meant but hesitated. Glancing to Jeffrey she saw he had seated himself at some distance and now regarded her with an expression of aroused amusement before he gave an almost imperceptible nod. Even as her incredulous brain questioned its instructions, her hands reached down to her labia and, with a curious feeling of innocence, opened them.

'You see!' cried Qito. 'We look into the gateway of all life and the portal to Paradise!' Qito's fingers had joined hers to probe deeper into her. 'There are so many petals to this rose, and as each unfolds it reveals yet more mystery.' Addressing himself to Jeffrey, who discreetly stayed behind Helen, he cried: 'So why did Nature hide it away? Disguise it, entangle it with brambles through which every man must find his way back to his source? To hide such beauty while the male equivalent is flaunted, exposed, and displayed is ludicrous!' Qito's fingers left her warmed and now throbbing 'source'. 'Nature made a grotesque mistake.' Qito's scorn softened as he spoke directly to her. 'Come, child,' he said. 'Look!' Glancing down she saw that Qito had opened his trousers and was fully exposing himself. 'Compare this pathetic male answer to your woman's mystery.'

Drawn, either by his hand or her own volition – she was never able to say which – she found herself kneeling before the couch and taking his limp and wrinkled penis in her hands.

'It is a blunt instrument. No?' he was asking her. 'Without

the tender hand of a woman it has the significance of wet string. Tell me what you see,' he urged.

Her mind raced. She held in her hand the penis of a man who might be a world-acclaimed genius, but was also a man she had only just met while her lover stood silently aside and watched.

While she struggled for coherence she could only wonder why this act of intimacy with a stranger felt so natural and normal – as if she had previously greeted a hundred men this way.

Oppressively aware that Qito still waited for her answer she wondered what words she could use? *Were* there words for such a moment? At the same time she felt filled with a sense of discovery – as if this was the first penis she had ever seen or held – and, with Qito's eyes, she saw it as something strangely closed, hooded, vulnerable – timid even, and she felt moved to bow her head and tenderly kiss it as she might have to comfort a suffering child.

'A mother's response!' Qito's voice sounded full of delight as she reached forward just an inch further to take him softly and tenderly between her lips. When the penis flexed in her mouth she felt triumph flooding her body, soaking her with confidence. Filled with a sense of giving life, she now eagerly reached for him, suckled him, and was gratified by the fleshy swelling response. On her knees, naked before a stranger, she was consumed by a zeal to bring the helpless infant between her lips to threatening, punishing adulthood, yet curiously she also felt detached – as if what she was doing was not real but being done merely to prove Qito's point.

The act had no context unless it was that Jeffrey watched and, hopefully, approved – but did he? Beyond his initial nod she had heard no word of encouragement – no sign that he was even aware of what she was doing. She sucked on Qito but wanted the pleasure to be Jeffrey's. Her mouth fully enthused, she could not beg his judgement. With her eyes bent close into Qito's surprisingly firm belly she could not see him, and so her nostrils filled with the slightly pungent perfume of the man, she could only strain her ears for some sign that Jeffrey was near and knew that this was for him, not for Qito, and far less for herself.

When she felt the first sting of leather on her buttocks, excitement flooded through her entire body and she almost cried out with relief. Suddenly what she was doing made sense, was parenthesised and made a part of her relationship with Jeffrey. The leather teased fire from her loins, and, like a whipped horse, she redoubled her efforts, sinking the fully erected and engorged shaft deep into her throat.

Now she knew that Jeffrey was not only near but taking a part, punishment became reward. Hearing Qito begin giving out muted sounds of pleasure increased her excitement and she knew that victory was hers, even as Jeffrey raised her crouched haunches to make more prominent a target of her all too willing flesh.

As she felt the first awakening seed, low in the now fully hardened shaft, she impulsively broke off for a moment to call to Jeffrey for harder, faster strokes and, as they came, her spirit soared, exulted beyond anything she had ever before known and, predatory now, sank the flesh deeper into her mouth while her buttocks sang with the pleasure of Jeffrey's whipping. It was the first time she had known pleasure and absolving punishment to be served on the same dish – and it tasted sweet!

Qito came with the stinging heat of a volcanic eruption, and she was determined that not one drop of him should escape her voracious mouth. Feeling Qito softening in her mouth she wanted to cry out and voice her frustration. She wasn't finished, but so close she thought it would be a crime if she should be left distracted but unsatisfied. Then, even as she drew breath to protest she knew she should have trusted in Jeffrey.

His hands reached around her to lift her, bodily, still curled up in the kneeling position, from the carpet to the glass-topped scene of last night's immolation, and was thrilled to see that the mirror still lay there. Kneeling again, she looked down into the sweat-streaked face of a totally distracted, almost demented woman, who moaned in anticipation as she felt Jeffrey addressing himself.

'Fuck me!' that demented creature cried and then let the words become a long moan of pleasure as she climaxed the moment Jeffrey thrust himself deep inside her. 'Yes!' she screamed and, when Qito came to stand before her raised, kneeling figure, she grabbed for his hands and brought them to her lips. Jeffrey was so roused and hard that his thrusting, savage and punishing, was exactly what she wanted. 'Punish me!' she screamed into Qito's caressing hands. 'Punish me! Fuck me!' and then felt Jeffrey surging, erupting, embalming the pleasure forever in her mind.

Exhausted, Jeffrey withdrew and let her sink to lie, in a curled foetal position, on the glass table, where Qito looked down in glee. 'See,' he cried. 'Her whole body lies in the shape of a smile.'

Qito looked from the satiated but defensive posture to Jeffrey, where after a momentary exchange of locked glances they turned away, avoiding each other's eyes with the shy awareness that they had both been savagely aroused over the body of the same woman – an act that both united and separated men at one and the same time. It was to that same woman that Jeffrey leant to kiss her gently on the neck.

Helen, roused by the kiss, moaned and reached out a blind embracing arm and drew him into a kiss while turning over on the glass to offer up her whole body. Holding him close, so that she could look directly into his eyes, she smiled. 'Is your wanton forgiven?' she asked.

Jeffrey shook his head. 'She is cherished,' he murmured.

Confidence soaring, she looked for Qito and, bending her head backwards, found him stuffing his penis out of sight but still standing over her. Her arm now reached for his blessing and Qito – his eyes bright against the walnut colour of his tan – looked almost aflame as he leant forward and, awkwardly, upside down, confirmed on her the benediction she sought. 'Where did you find such a glorious creature?' he asked of Jeffrey.

Jeffrey, sitting tentatively on the glass-topped table, put an arm about her shoulders and drew her to him as he answered. 'Well, you know, Christmas and all, you get the most surprising gifts!'

Qito's laugh resounded. 'Every man should have such a gift!'

'Well, now, you've had her, too.'

'To have is not to possess!' Qito said.

Listening to the two men, Helen could hardly believe they were talking about her. Turning to Jeffrey for comfort she asked: 'Am I "possessed"?'

'Totally,' he assured her.

His words gave her comfort. 'Thank you,' she murmured.

Turning her face to him and begging a kiss, she marvelled that she had done something that a week before would have been unthinkable, and then heard it discussed as if it had been no more than a social courtesy.

Qito was turning away, his voice fading as he spoke. 'An old man has no place between lovers,' he declared. 'I am going to leave you . . .' He was coming back to them, shrugging a bulky fur-collared coat over his summery clothes. '. . . but I shall never forgive you if you do not bring this wild woman to my show tonight.'

'I've no intention of going *anywhere* without this woman!' Jeffrey retorted, and then, standing, hugged the diminutive teddy bear the top coat had made of Qito. Springing upward from the table Helen felt filled with enough love to spare a little for Qito. She had to dip her head to kiss his cheek as he pulled her into a strong, wiry, embrace.

'Together we shall make a masterpiece,' he told her. Then, waving a hand to Jeffrey, turned for the door. 'Until tonight,' he called.

It was only as she saw Annabel hurrying to see Qito out that Helen remembered her existence. Suddenly shocked with herself she turned to Jeffrey. 'Annabel was here?' she asked. 'Did she hear everything . . . ?' The look on Jeffrey's face told her that she had, and Helen stood, aghast – hand over her mouth – as she heard the door close and the soft sounds of Annabel's return.

'Would anyone like a drink?' Annabel asked with such insouciance that Helen almost burst out laughing.

'We'd love one,' answered Jeffrey.

The moment Annabel had gone, Helen turned to Jeffrey. 'Whatever must she think?' she asked in hollowed, self-horrified, tones.

'She probably thinks, as will everyone else, how lucky I am.'

She looked into his eyes and noticed for the first time that they were grey with exquisitely placed segments of black. They were beautiful eyes she decided, and she felt herself melting before them. 'Don't ever let it stop,' she whispered then, feeling her body starting to tremble, and hastily added, 'I rather like the idea of being possessed.'

'And *I* meant it – I want to possess you rather than just "have".'

'You already do. I just need you to keep reminding me.'

They stood apart, like duellists looking for an opening, with distinctively differing thoughts. Jeffrey felt blessed while she felt an irresistible, masochistic mist enshroud her.

'Do something to me,' she breathed. 'Now – this minute!'

Jeffrey's smile was lazy. 'Don't you think you ought to think about getting ready?'

'For what?'

'Didn't you hear Qito invite us to his showing this evening? It's a huge affair. A gala in fact. I want you to look devastating.'

'In *what*?' she seethed. 'You brought me here naked.'

'That would be devastating,' he agreed. 'But hardly suitable for presentation to the French President.'

'The President of France is going to be in London?' she demanded in a voice filled with sudden alarm.

'No,' said Jeffrey patiently. 'We are going to be in Paris.'

'Tonight?' she squealed.

'Well that's where Qito's gala preview is being held.'

Helen's mind was running wildly beyond coherence. 'But . . . Paris? Tonight?' Exasperated, she turned to Jeffrey. 'It's impossible!'

The infuriating smile still on his lips he spoke. 'No it isn't. Paris is a thirty-five minute plane ride – little more than a cab ride when you think about it.'

'But I'm not ready. I've nothing packed. Nothing *to* pack! Jeffrey – this is impossible!'

'Nothing's impossible,' he said, coming towards her and seeking an embrace. 'You have the gown I brought you.'

'That's still in my apartment.' Bustling with sudden urgency she turned back to Jeffrey. 'I'll have to go back to my place. What time are we expected?'

'A President of a Republic doesn't "expect" – he commands. We must be there by eight.'

'Oh Lord! How will I... how can I...?'

Jeffrey smiled. 'You will,' he told her. 'I'll have Turner drive you home and I'll pick you up from your place at six, but you'd better put something on in the meanwhile.'

Panicked, she started a fervent hunt for her long-discarded raincoat only to find that a smiling Annabel was already holding it out for her to slip into. 'I take it you've no time for the drink?' she asked.

'I've no time for *anything*!' Helen protested, then, as the coat settled about her shoulders, she was reminded that she had rarely been other than totally naked for the past twenty-four hours. The close proximity to Annabel also brought about another crushing memory. 'Did you...?' she asked, then, as Annabel smiled noncommittally, went on, 'I'm sorry if you were embarrassed.'

Shaking her head Annabel's smile not only continued but brightened. 'Envious, perhaps,' she said. 'But certainly not embarrassed.'

Flashing the girl a grateful smile, she turned as she heard Turner arrive. 'Jeffrey?' she called. 'I'm going.'

Jeffrey appeared from the depths of the apartment and, reaching out his arms, gave her a gentle kiss on one cheek and then, as he leant into the other, whispered under the eyes of the patiently waiting Turner, 'I'm tempted to fuck you again before you go.'

'No!' she laughed, her protest forcefully loud. 'I've got far too much to do before six!'

Smiling, Jeffrey handed her to the care of Turner before turning back to the attentive Annabel.

'Think you can handle her?' Annabel asked.

His answer was a spirited: 'It's got to be worth a try, don't you think?'

'I'll say!' she agreed.

7

Standing under the teeming shower Helen felt like a tired child on Christmas night trying to remember her new presents. So much had happened since she was last in her own apartment that she could barely believe it had been only two days. She knew she was not the same woman who had stepped out from this shower two days before. Not only was there Jeffrey and his exquisite talent for erotic surprise but the change that had been wrought in herself. She could now confidently cope with something like the sad Lesley; been made aware that her body was something in which she could take fierce pride; had, under the eyes of one lover, orally taken another, and then, under the eyes of the other, given herself fully to her true lover. With pride she considered she had carried all before her with cred-itable aplomb. The excitement was not knowing where else this path, on which she had taken only the first few faltering steps, might lead.

Drying herself and hurrying to offer her hair to the salvage of heated rollers, she realised that tonight she was going to an event she had not even heard of hours before and there, in the company of an enviable escort, would meet again the legend for whom even the President of France turned out, and whom she had sexually satisfied. It was then that the echo of his promise to have her pose for him returned. It was enough to still her hands as they curled up her hair. Was it possible that the face staring back out of the mirror was really worthy of, as Qito had claimed, immortality? Would, centuries from now, some man from an as yet undreamt-of generation, look on her body and feel lust for her? Had, she wondered, Mona Lisa harboured similar doubts before going to Da Vinci's studio when her immortal image was but an idea in the artist's mind?

One thing was certain, she thought, as she started on her base foundation, no woman had ever been so filled with certainty as she was at that moment.

When Jeffrey arrived she had yet to pack and still to dress and barely opened the door to him before fleeing back into the bedroom, aware of how little time there was before they had to leave.

'I'll only be a minute!' she called out to him as she sat before her mirror to apply an antique golden lip-gloss to her already made-up lips. Then she searched out a pair of silk stockings she'd bought the previous year and never, until now, found occasion to wear. Slipping into the fine silk gown she remembered how it had looked on her the first time she had worn it. How quickly it had responded to her body's warmth and clung so closely as to even outline her navel. Again she was reminded that to wear anything, even stockings, under the dress was impossible. The thought of going to this event near naked both bothered and thrilled her. Slipping into a pair of elegant evening mules she gave herself one last head-to-toe scrutiny before bracing herself for the presentation to Jeffrey.

'Well?' she asked him coyly. 'How do I look?'

'Unique!'

'"Unique"?'

Jeffrey nodded. 'There are very few women in this world who can look equally beautiful dressed or naked. You are among them.'

Pleased by the compliment she felt ready to be pedantically teasing. 'To be "among" a number is not to be "unique",' she said with as much false petulance as she could muster.

'Exquisite, then?' he offered. 'Is that better?'

Pretending deep consideration she loftily replied: '"Exquisitely beautiful" would be no more than acceptable ...'

Jeffrey laughed and, his eyes alight with pleasure, started towards her, meaning to embrace her, but she turned away. 'No. I've spent ages on my hair and make-up and I'm not having you ruin it!'

'I was just going to remind you that you're pledged to me,' he said. 'What if I want you naked? Now, this minute!'

'Absolutely no way!' she cried, and as he reached for her again, she remembered that the gown would be gone in seconds if he got his hands to the shoulder catches, and ran from him in a move which soon became a halting chase.

The chase was ended before it really got started when the telephone rang. She knew immediately, as if sensing it from the sternness of the ring, that it would be her, almost completely forgotten, mother.

Seeing Jeffrey stilled by the interruption she went to the telephone and lifted it.

Her mother's excited voice poured into her ears. 'Where on earth have you been? I've been calling and talking to that stupid machine of yours for days. Why haven't you called me back?'

'Mother, I've been busy ...' she looked back over her shoulder and shrugged an apology in Jeffrey's direction.

'Too busy to return the messages I left on your machine?'

'I'm sorry, Mother, I haven't had time to play them back and I'm in a tremendous rush just at the moment – can I call you later?'

'No!' cried her mother. 'We've been worried sick about you ...' With the stream of non-stop complaints ringing in her ears, Helen had dropped her guard against Jeffrey only to be forcefully reminded of that oversight when she felt his hands at the fastenings of the gown. The telephone in her hand prevented anything but the weakest attempt to still the downward slide of the clinging silk. Covering the mouthpiece she turned, genuinely angry, towards Jeffrey. 'No, Jeffrey ... we have to ... this is my mother ... I—'

Determined and unsmiling Jeffrey gently took away the one hand that stopped the gown from uncovering her entirely and she stared helplessly, and pleaded speechlessly, as the gown slid to the floor leaving her facing him, naked. 'Please ...' she begged, but Jeffrey was implacable.

She was turned and he thrust hard into her from behind. Her gasp at his penetration carried all the way to Eastbourne.

'Are you listening to a word I've said?' her mother was demanding. 'It's that man, isn't it? The one you brought down here? I suppose you've been with him all this time with never a thought that we might be worrying about you? I think I have a right to know ...'

Her mother's words were now only background as the convulsions Jeffrey was creating in her took command and extinguished all will to do anything but respond.

'Helen?' her mother's voice was calling down the line. 'What on earth is going on ...'

'Mother, please ...' she managed. 'Not now. There's someone here ...' she broke off, trying to silence her rising climax.

'*Who* is there? *Him?*' asked her mother and then, after a steely silence in which Helen could almost sense the keening ears, added in horrified tones, 'Oh, my God! You're doing "it" with him right this minute aren't you? What on earth ... ? How *dare* you?' Helen heard the phone being slammed down in her desperate ear.

'You bastard!' she seethed even as her body begged release.

Jeffrey pulled her hips tight to him as she, still holding the telephone in one paralysed hand, bent forward and gave him even greater access. 'You're my whore!' he breathed throatily as he bent over her to sink his teeth into her shoulder.

'Yes!' she yelled into his face. 'Fuck me! Fuck me, fuck me!' then gave vent to a scream as the onrush of orgasm vibrated inwards before bursting out to encompass her entire body. Within a second she felt him straighten and then, as his grip dug painfully into her flesh, surge into her.

'God, I must look a mess!' she said the moment she managed to disentangle herself from him. 'My hair! What am I going to do?' she wailed.

'You'll go as you are. The "just screwed" look is all the rage this year!'

Turning from the mirror where she was surveying the damage she was enraged. 'You pig!' she yelled at him. 'How could you do that to me?'

'Because you looked so beautiful,' he smiled. 'I had to put my mark on you.'

'My hair!' she wailed. 'My face! I spent hours getting ready and then you have to do that to me. I haven't packed anything yet, and . . .' her voice trailed into silence as she remembered with horror what her mother had said as she slammed down the phone. 'And my mother heard us!' she cried.

'You mean, until now, your mother imagined you were a virgin?' His tone was so close to sarcasm that she felt a sudden urge to hit him.

'You know perfectly well what I mean,' she said defiantly. 'Well, we'll just have to be late. I'm going to repair the damage.'

Jeffrey physically blocked her progress to the bedroom. 'There isn't time,' he said. 'You'll just have to do what you can in the car!'

Filled with a sudden need to show anger, she remembered she had once been told how grimly her face set when she needed to express rage. Fully aware that she now wore that expression she decided to let it out. 'Jeffrey, I'm warning you – I really mean this – get out of my way.'

Jeffrey stayed where he was. 'Shall I go?' he asked quietly.

The rush of blood that was carrying an affirmative response to her lips stopped dead in its tracks as with sudden, chilling clarity she saw the space where Jeffrey now stood would, if vacated, be nothing but a yawning void which, she knew, would haunt her for the rest of her life. All anger was suddenly frozen. Icicles, she would later swear, formed in her gut at that moment. 'No,' she murmured so quietly that he made her repeat the words more loudly.

'No, you bastard!' she yelled at him.

Seemingly much relieved, Jeffrey smiled. 'Lucky thing for you I changed my mind.'

'About what?'

'When I saw how gorgeous you looked I wanted to put my mark on you in another way.'

It took a moment to realise his meaning. 'You were thinking of spanking me – just before going out ...'

'We aren't "out", yet.'

'*Don't* think about it!' Her voice was pitched half way between plea and resolve.

'All right, but you should bear in mind that you will have to be punished later.'

Annoyed that the threat both warmed and thrilled her she agreed that there would be time in the car to repair her face and hair and, after throwing some things into an overnight bag, happily went down to the waiting Turner feeling that she had narrowly escaped disaster.

* * *

The limousine whisked them to a part of Heathrow she didn't know existed. This was the area, far from the commercial terminals, from which private planes departed. Jeffrey, she discovered, had rented an air taxi and so, with the minimum of formalities, they were in the air and en route to Le Bourget airport which, she was informed, was even closer to Paris than the sprawl of the Charles de Gaulle.

Waiting there was another chauffered limousine which took them directly to the reception hall. It had all been so effortless and quick that she understood what Jeffrey meant by Paris being only a cab ride away. All it took was money and a willingness to spend it.

Feeling pampered and flattered she took wicked pleasure in thinking of how horrified her mother would be by all this 'extravagance'!

They were barely inside the exhibition hall and had no time to pick out one face from another when an authoritative voice started calling out that the arrival of the President was imminent, and the person behind it fussily started lining up those who were to be presented.

Falling back among the lesser guests Helen and Jeffrey could now see Qito, who had deferred to the admonitory 'formal' dress only so far as donning a black T-shirt under a darkish jacket, and, towering over him, was the unmistakable figure of Carla Colardi. It was only then that Helen was reminded that Carla, still overwhelmingly beautiful, was Qito's wife of almost twenty years. Dressed in a glittering silver gown, cut aggressively low to display her famous bosom, the glitter theme continued with her jewellery which, all platinum and white gold, flashed in the lighting as if powered from Carla's own formidable personality – which seemed further emphasised by her 'big hair'. Two legends in the same household should have been fertile ground for the gossipmongers yet nothing had ever been found to besmirch their union.

Looking at Carla, Helen could not help relishing the thought that she had, if only momentarily, shared Qito with her. The *frisson* of excitement this engendered was rapidly followed by the daunting thought of what the formidable Carla's reaction might be if she ever found out.

It was then that Qito spotted her. 'Helen!' he called out with such excitement that she felt all eyes, tensed ready for the arrival of the President, turning to her. Qito was gesturing wildly for Helen to come to him. Aware of Carla's huge black lustrous eyes searching her out from top to toe, Helen turned to Jeffrey. 'What?' she asked.

'He wants you in the line up,' Jeffrey smiled. 'Go!'

Aware that everyone in the crowded room was now looking at her and wondering who the hell she might be, she felt Jeffrey's hand on the small of her back urging her forward. With a growing sense of unreality that this was really happening, Helen found the crowd opening up before her and the fussy organiser looming before her to demand her name. Having hastily added her name to the official list he ushered her forward to where she found Qito insisting that she stand to his right, between him and Carla.

'*Cara mio* . . .' Qito spoke across the highly embarrassed Helen to the highly interested Carla. 'This is the English girl I told you about. Isn't she incredible?'

Carla's look to Helen was, to say the least, smouldering but, whatever verbal response she might have made was lost in the sudden stirring of interest as the President's party arrived.

Standing next to Qito, Helen had the unsettling feeling that she was caught up in a fantasy made real. She watched with blurred vision and bated breath as the President's party paused in the doorway, as they were welcomed by the Gallery officials staging the exhibition. Then her vision was filled with the sight of the President making directly towards Qito. It was only then Helen realised she had absolutely no idea how one greeted a President and, since it seemed she would be the first female to be introduced, she would have little chance to learn by observation. Grimly, as the President all but embraced Qito, she thought it would have been simpler if the man had been royalty. Then it would only have been a matter of a quick curtsey. Desperately, her mind raced over the possibilities only to find her brain otherwise engaged when the thought of her recent violation at Jeffrey's hands chose that moment to leap into her head, creating a stirring in her groin and the resulting fervent juices to start trickling down her thighs.

Her heart thumping out a drum beat of impending disaster, she heard her name, as if at a great distance, being spoken and a Presidential hand being extended to her.

'My new inspiration,' Qito was saying by way of further introduction, and Helen, totally lost, settled for an ingratiatingly embarrassed smile.

'How charming ...' mused the President in a tone that managed to convey its uncertainty at why such a nonentity should be being introduced, and she felt enormous relief when the hand-shaking personage moved on to greet Carla with more obvious enthusiasm and genuine warmth.

It was then that her swimming vision brought Jeffrey's face, grinning at her from across the channel left in the crowd and, for a passing moment, she hated him for exposing her to such an occasion with barely an hour's notice. Carla's voice broke into her seething mind. 'Qito tells me you have inspired him.'

Looking into the familiar famous face, Helen felt even more lost. What is there to say to a wife when her husband has declared that he has been 'inspired'? Fortunately, Carla didn't wait for any cogent reply but instead murmured, 'So no doubt we will be meeting again,' before being caught up in a surging crowd of admirers which somehow managed to elbow Helen to one side. Jeffrey caught her arm. 'Hungry?' he asked.

'Aren't we going to look at Qito's work?' a bewildered Helen asked.

Jeffrey indicated the great crowds. 'We'd see nothing in this scrum. We can come back tomorrow if you want. Meantime, I don't know about you but I'm starving.'

Not sure if she was hungry, she was certainly ready to flee from the confusion of this sudden exposure to so many famous faces, so she readily agreed to his suggestion that they go and eat.

It wasn't until they were seated in the small but exclusive restaurant that she realised this was the first time they had formally eaten together.

Jeffrey's choice of conversational topic was, initially, surprising. 'When I was ten,' she heard him saying, 'my father caught me smoking one of his cigars. I thought he would be furious with me but instead he fooled me into thinking he was delighted. He sat me down and lectured me on the proper way to prepare and really appreciate a cigar. In fact he watched me smoke my way through that first one and then insisted I had another. I got about half way through it before I turned green and spent the rest of the evening in the bathroom. I have never smoked a cigar since.'

Smiling politely, and wondering why she was being exposed to such a mundane tale, she was startled when he came to the point. 'That's how I intend to deal with your masochism.'

Gripped with apprehension she managed, '"Deal" with it? Is it a sickness then?'

'Not *the* sickness – a symptom. To get at the root we have to cut away the undergrowth.'

Stilled with fear of what he might be about to propose she nevertheless found herself anxious to be told. 'To face my nightmares?' she asked.

'To find out whether or not the nightmares really exist.'

'I see,' she said, filling in time as her mind raced. 'And how do you propose to do that?'

'I don't,' he said. 'You have to do it yourself, but what I can do is show you the way. It will be up to you whether you go down that road or not.'

Again the challenge! Again, he was forcing her to commit herself. Once more she found herself excitedly willing to do just that.

'I'm in your hands,' she told him.

Jeffrey smiled and, reaching out, laid an admonishing finger on her lips. 'Now I sentence you to silence,' he murmured as she, with mounting excitement, reached her lips forward to nibble at his lingering finger. 'I've dismissed the limousine and rented a self-drive car instead,' he said, as her lit eyes fixed alertly on him, 'so I will be driving. You do remember our drive to Eastbourne, don't you? I asked you to do something that night and you refused. You will not refuse me tonight.' For answer she drew his fingers deep into her mouth and, uncaring what other diners or waiters might think, kept her eyes firmly fixed on his.

'It is quite a short drive so you will have to be particularly expert since you will be performing that small service totally naked.' As she stopped sucking on him and stared instead, he added, 'However, you may remain clothed until we are in the car. Shall we go?'

The formalities of paying the bill, him signing his charge slip and their finding the car, seemed to take forever. Her body was totally encased in the excitement of the moment and the trivial interests of others were merely obstacles in the way of opportunity.

Still trembling she was seated in the car as he turned the heater to full and waited for it to warm up.

When he drove away she, with a sense of assertiveness, reached to her shoulders for the catches that held the dress and let it slither down into her lap, leaving her breasts bare to the flash of passing lights and the eyes of pedestrians. It was then only a matter of shifting her weight, first this way then that, before she was completely free of the gown. Laying her head across his lap, her fingers sought out his already risen flesh.

The steering wheel rubbed hard against her head as she plunged him deep into her throat. There was only one thought in her mind – he must come before they ended the short drive. At that moment it became her only aim in life beyond which there was nothing. Feeling an exquisite moment of total self-abandonment she worked her lips and tongue feverishly around his stiffened cock, trying as she did so to remember everything she had ever learnt or read about this particular pleasure. She felt almost total despair as she realised that the car had stopped and she had yet to feel his first convulsion. Desperately, she ignored the possibility of passing strangers looking in on her and increased the tempo and intensity of her lips and mouth.

Eerily aware that Jeffrey had remained silent, she continued working on him while dreading that he might intercede and stop her and tell her she had failed. Sensing his first flesh-quickening throb she sucked deeper and harder, forcing herself to concentrate on what she now knew was inevitable. Feeling his hand resting lightly on the back of her head she waited eagerly for his gush but, even as it started, she heard him add yet another condition. 'Do not swallow it!' he gasped as he started to issue. 'I want you to take it and guard it in your mouth. You understand me?'

All she could do was nod as he filled her mouth. When he nudged her to indicate that she could now sit up, she found his imperative that she must not swallow his tribute almost impossible to obey. Having to fight against instinct she was aware that her puffed cheeks and strained throat must be making her look ridiculous. As he got out of the car she sat, still naked, and only vaguely aware that they were stopped in a wide, tree-lined avenue.

When Jeffrey opened the car's door a blast of the winter's night air flooded in to remind her that she was still naked. 'Come,' said Jeffrey.

Stepping out of the car she found herself keeping her eyes strictly to the front, not wanting to know if there was anyone there to see her. Instead she kept her eyes firmly fixed on his until he, smiling, turned away and led her still naked up the steps to a substantial villa. There he rang the bell and she had to wait interminably, the cold now piercing her body in places she was only vaguely aware existed, and wondered where it was she had been brought and what might lay behind the glossy shine of this green door.

8

Helen caught barely a glimpse of the girl who had opened the door before Jeffrey, taking her elbow, urged her into the long, high-ceilinged hallway. At the far end a woman appeared wearing the kind of long floral evening gown that overweight ladies use to disguise their widened hips. She was directing a broad smile at Jeffrey. 'I had almost given up hope,' she was saying, before directing her gaze to Helen.

'Helen, this is Madame Victoria. She runs the most famous House of Pain in Paris.'

Madame Victoria smiled. 'And all completely English. We English are renowned for our expertise in this field just as the French, in England, are sought out for their cooking. Each to its own, as it were.' Madame Victoria, whose eyes suggested she had seen everything, looked a little puzzled as Helen stayed silent. 'Doesn't she speak?' she asked Jeffrey sharply.

'Not at the moment. Her mouth is full.'

'Of what?'

'Of me.'

Victoria's mouth wrinkled into a smile. 'Excellent!' she cried and immediately took Helen's arm and walked her the length of the hallway and into a large room which seemed furnished entirely with a variety of couches. Here Helen registered two girls, one naked and one in an abbreviated rubbery-looking dress that constricted rather than fitted her, while a man sat crosslegged on the floor before the naked girl's feet. Conscious that all eyes were on her, she was led to stand in the open centre of the room. 'Kate!' Victoria waved to the naked girl, 'come here.'

Kate came forward looking directly into Helen's eyes as if expecting a challenge of some kind. 'You kneel,' Victoria said, and it took a moment for Helen to understand that the order had been directed at her. Thankfully the carpet was thick and quite comfortable against her knees. Helen felt her hair taken and grasped firmly, though not cruelly.

'Be very careful, now,' warned Madame Victoria. 'You are going to open your mouth but when you do so you must not swallow. Do you understand me?'

Desperate now that she could no longer see Jeffrey, Helen nodded, aware that she didn't know how she could avoid swallowing. The moment she had agreed she felt a slight tug on her hair and bent her head backwards until she looked directly up at the worked plaster ceiling. The movement had caused her eyes to close, shutting out the sight of Victoria, but leaving her aware that the woman was peering deep into her mouth and must surely see the liquid which she could feel thickly coating her tongue.

'Ah, yes,' murmured Victoria. 'Do you see it, Kate?'

Helen felt a pang of excruciating humiliation as she sensed movement in the room and knew the others were coming to peer into her mouth. Kneeling there, mouth open like a hungry chick in a nest, she wondered how Jeffrey could have known how excruciating this would be for her. She had always dreaded visiting the dentist. Not because, in these days of sophisticated painkillers, she would feel any discomfort beyond the initial needle, but because the man would be peering into her mouth in a manner she thought more intimate than that used in a gynaecological examination. Gynaecologists didn't loom over her mouth like a threatening lover!

'Kate will clean your mouth,' said Victoria in such quiet conversational tones that Helen didn't understand the significance until, opening her eyes, she saw the bright-eyed Kate leaning closer to her. Her mouth closed on hers and a seemingly huge tongue probed into her, leaving her desperately breathless, while scooping and seaching out every last drop of Jeffrey's deposit. Helen wanted to scream protest at being so intimately invaded by another girl. Her hands moved as to fend off Kate but were taken, even as they moved, and lightly but firmly clamped behind her back. Her vision filled with Kate, she was uncertain who had taken her hands until she heard, close to her ear, Jeffrey's voice. 'You are being tested.'

These simple words flushed away the protest of her rational mind. What was being done to her was now sanctioned – gifted to her – licensing her to dismiss any consideration but that Jeffrey wanted this to be done to her. An overwhelming sense of relief flooded through her. What she was doing was being done for Jeffrey, which gave it sense and meaning.

Eyes closed, she now gave her mouth to Kate's searching tongue, opening to it as if she opened to Jeffrey. It no longer mattered if four people – or four hundred – watched her as, giving way to a gentle pressure on her shoulders, she felt herself being laid back to stretch full-length onto the carpet.

Kate had shadowed her movements and now Helen felt the full length of another girl's naked body on her own for the first time in her life as the tongue pressed deep into her mouth. Consciously or otherwise she had opened her thighs and Kate lay between them – one pubic bone pressing hard against the other – and to her astonishment Helen's loins began to flow as if in answer to a lover. Confident that nobody but her could tell of this shaming response she became alarmed when Kate suddenly lifted herself and knelt to straddle Helen's belly but, instead of covering her, she felt an unseen hand searching out the damning evidence of her arousal. Distracted now she sought to wriggle free of the unknown fingers that probed her outer lips before entering her, but Kate's firm pressure restricted any such protest, which soon turned to writhing as she felt the hand replaced by the gentler pressure of a tongue. Doubly invaded she wanted to scream to them to stop before she betrayed herself totally, but then she heard the benediction of Jeffrey's voice: 'Relax. Go with it.'

Tearing herself free of Kate's relentless kiss she let go a long, repressed orgasmic scream as her entire body convulsed under tidal waves of release. Now, with Kate's head tucked in against the side of her own, her eyes were freed to roam wildly and search out Jeffrey.

In response to her silent appeal he came to lie beside her, his hands gently caressing her breasts. As she reached to embrace him he closed on her and gifted her a deeply searching kiss. The wave came again as the unknown tongue probed even more deeply and she was forced to break off from Jeffrey's kiss as yet another wave engulfed her.

Looking manically down to see who it was inducing such pleasure she saw the thinning hair of the other man, which unnerved her only momentarily until Jeffrey renewed his kiss.

'Screw me!' she gasped into his open mouth but was then shattered to hear Victoria's voice cut through her consciousness. 'Enough!'

Suddenly, all activity had ended. Kate had gone, the man with thinning hair had gone, and Jeffrey was standing at a distance, leaving her spread and totally exposed on the carpet, the centre of all eyes and feeling like a beached whale. Wildly she looked from one face to the other, trying to divine the meaning of this sudden abandonment. It was then she realised that everyone was waiting for Victoria to speak. 'Come with me,' she said, and it was Jeffrey who reached down to offer a hand to help Helen to her feet.

Looking at Jeffrey she saw him suddenly unwilling to look back at her, which filled her with foreboding. 'I'm waiting,' said Victoria from the door, and so Helen followed her flowing gown out of the room, along the hallway, and into another room in which stood a shower in what might have once been simply a bathroom, but was now swamped with closets and shelves.

'Take a shower and then I will dress you,' Madame Victoria told her, and then had her stand in the disconcertingly pliable plastic shower tray before turning on the water.

As the hand withdrew from the cascading water Helen experienced a crystal clear image of another time and another place.

Just short of her eighteenth birthday she had left home, for the first time in her life, to start a course of business studies. It was a confusing environment for someone so used to being completely cared for, especially as she sensed that none of the other girls were suffering the same maternal withdrawal symptoms as herself. It had been only after long and prolonged campaigning by her mother that she had been found a room in the scarce Halls of Residence accommodation without which her mother would have forbidden her to leave home at all.

On the second night in the room which she shared with

another girl they had been invaded by a group of girls from the more senior second year, who had told them they were about to be 'initiated'. She and her room-mate, Caroline, had been frog-marched out of the Halls of Residence and into the nearby gymnasium. There they had been forced to strip naked and had their hands tied behind their backs.

After a great deal of pummelling and squeezing of their breasts they had, now quite distressed, been taken to the showers where their hands were tied to the shower spigot pipes and the water repeatedly turned on, first cold then hot, until both girls were tearfully pleading for the torment to end.

It was the vision of the girl's hand that had turned off the water before leaving them there in the dark that had now returned so forcibly. Helen had hung there, helplessly listening to Caroline's sobs until they were found in the early hours of the morning by a Security Guard who, having released them, made a report which somehow got lost in the bureaucracy and never came to anything.

She and Caroline, although becoming firm friends, never talked about the incident, which Helen felt had shamed them both, until the celebration held to mark the successful end to their first-year. More than a little influenced by the amount of wine she had drunk Caroline had remarked how much she was looking forward to getting her hands on the new intake of first-year girls. Helen had been shocked. 'You wouldn't really do that to the new girls, would you?' she had asked.

'Damn right I would!' Caroline had laughed. 'And I will! Come on, be honest – that night – didn't it turn you on?'

Helen stared at the girl with whom she had shared a room for almost a year and who she never once suspected shared her own shameful secret. The incident, only in retrospect, had seemed exciting. In fantasy she had even extended the experience and made the middle-aged Security Guard into a handsome young buck who had taken advantage of her helplessness and ravaged her. It had never occurred to her that her emotions of that time could possibly be shared by another living being and, for the first time in her life, she began to think of her own fantasies as something other than a private sickness lodging in her head alone.

Jeffrey had brought a great deal of her secret thoughts into the glare of reality and tonight she had taken yet another step forward. The memory reinforced in her the resolve to rise to his challenge, no matter how daunting it might become.

Madame Victoria's voice brought her back to the present. 'You haven't dozed off in there, have you?'

She turned off the water, stepped out of the shower, and, taking one of many warmed towels, started drying herself as she watched the indomitable Victoria returning, holding in her hands an intricately worked basque in layers of appliquéd green and black leather. 'I'm going to put this on you,' she was told, before being peremptorily turned as Madame Victoria's expert hands wound the leather about her waist.

Submitting to what she considered to be the inevitable she stood passively as the corset was tightened about her torso to just under her breasts, which the leather left exposed, and then gasped as with firm hands Madame Victoria started drawing on the strings, causing the leather to groan as it compressed about her rib cage. She made gasping protests as the process continued until she was afraid she might faint.

'Please ...' she pleaded. 'It's too tight. I can't breathe!'

'Nonsense ...' replied Victoria and gave another breath-taking pull on the strings.

Helen's body felt gripped as if in a vice as she desperately gasped for air. 'I can't ...' she managed.

'Relax,' Madame Victoria told her. 'Enjoy the constriction, you'll find yourself forgetting about it. Here ...'

Desperately Helen looked round to see impossibly high-heeled boots being laid at her feet. 'Put these on,' she was told. Knowing that she couldn't possibly bend, Helen had to put one hand out to balance herself as she forced her feet into the tight-fitting boots. She was relieved to find them a little too large, so there was no crippling pain from her toes.

Still trying to orientate herself to the new high elevation to which the heels had raised her, she felt her hair being brushed back from her face before being wound into a tight pony-tail. 'Hold on to that,' she was told as Victoria turned aside, only to return with a fearsome-looking headdress, combined with a mask made in leathers to match the corset. After threading her pony-tailed hair through a hole in the back of the headdress, it was lowered and fitted snugly about her face to outline her eyes but expose her mouth and nostrils.

'Now you may look at yourself,' smiled Madame Victoria, turning her to face a mirror set into one wall.

There stood a fearsomely beautiful creature who might have stepped from a fantasy science fiction novel labelled as a bare-breasted Amazon queen. The heels gave her enormous height and, while the corset still felt oppressive and the boots constricting, she felt a surge of excitement as she registered that the creation in the mirror was a reflection of herself.

'There,' said Madame Victoria. 'Don't you think that image is worth a little discomfort?'

Continuing to stare at herself she thought she had never imagined how her breasts could be so engorged by contrast with her tiny waist, and how firm and rounded her thighs could be made. In the mirror she saw not herself but a woman, so distanced and of such imperious sexuality, that it excited her incredibly. 'Yes,' she breathed.

'You look wonderful,' cried Madame Victoria. 'Think what effect it will have on him!'

Suddenly her mind was filled with Jeffrey and the excitement of showing herself to him like this. Guiltily, she became aware that her hands had gone, seemingly of their accord, to cup and caress her own breasts. 'Can we go to him now?' she asked.

'Of course, my dear. But you will need this.'

Looking down, Helen saw that she was being offered the haft of a shiny lacquer-handled whip. Looking up, eyes wide with surprise, into Madame Victoria's clear, unblinking gaze, her question was transparent to the other woman's greater experience before she had asked it. 'You'll see,' smiled Madame Victoria and, still confused, Helen found herself being turned and urged out into the hallway.

She had expected to be returned to the sitting-room, so was surprised when she was turned instead in the opposite direction and led into a room where another shock awaited her. Strapped naked to a wooden frame which dominated the room was a man – his back facing her. At first she thought this might be Jeffrey but was soon able to see this man was both heavier and older. Led to face him, she saw Kate kneeling naked before him, looking expectantly for her instructions.

'How are you this evening?' asked Madame Victoria in casual conversational tones.

'Very well, thank you,' replied the man, who Helen now saw was somewhere in his florid-faced middle fifties.

'This lady is the Mistress Helen,' said Victoria. 'She is to assist me this evening.'

The man's eyes glowed as they lighted on the masked, tall, leather-encased figure. 'Thank you, Mistress Victoria,' he murmured.

'I intend we play a little game,' Victoria was saying. 'Kate here, will arouse you – make you naughty – while the Mistress Helen will punish you for the naughty, filthy little tyke we all know you to be. You understand me?' asked Victoria, reinforcing her words with a resounding slap about the helpless man's face.

'I do, Mistress,' gasped the man.

Turning to Kate, Victoria nodded. Still haunched, Kate sat up slightly and, reaching forward, took the man's flaccid penis between two fingers and delicately addressed it to her lips.

The man gasped. 'No, please Mistress,' he pleaded. 'Don't make me "naughty". I promised Mummy I'd be good today.'

'Silence!' roared Victoria. 'We already know what a liar you can be! Kate will prove it.' Victoria turned to Kate. 'Well?' she demanded.

For answer Kate withdrew her ravaging mouth and exposed the man as already half aroused. 'Time for firm measures,' said Victoria who, taking the whip from Helen's nerveless hands, took a measure before delivering three quick blows across his buttocks.

'Well?' demanded Victoria of Kate, but she got only a muffled reply since Kate's mouth was already back and hard at work.

Helen felt absent – as if none of this was really happening. She felt that if she stayed silent they might forget she was there and so neither involve her nor dismiss her. These thoughts forced her to acknowledge that she would hate to be sent from the room. She felt hypnotised by the man in bondage, and the livid patterns Victoria's whip had created. Having no doubt that this was what the man wanted – indeed had come to Victoria for – she found herself more than intrigued to find out just how such matters could be managed.

'How old is your daughter?' asked Madame Victoria of the man.

'Please . . .' the man sounded more pained by the question than the whip that had been laid across his quivering flesh.

Madame Victoria's hand made only the tiniest of flicks but the whip seared into the man's flesh again. 'I asked you a question.'

'Twelve!' gasped the man.

The whip snaked out again. 'Liar! How could she be twelve when you told me she was about to make you a grandfather. The truth now!'

'Twenty-four!'

Helen watched Madame Victoria nod. 'Twenty-four. That's more believable. Now let me see – that would make four groups of six strokes, would it not?'

'Yes, Mistress!'

'Good. You will keep the accounts and ensure no mistake is made. You understand me?'

'Yes, Mistress.'

When Victoria rapped out 'Mistress Helen!' she waited until the startled Helen looked at her. 'You will go to his front and report on his condition. You understand me?'

Nodding, feeling even less real, Helen moved to the front and saw how Kate's kneeling efforts had raised the man yet again to full erection. 'He is ready, Madame,' called Kate.

'I said that Mistress Helen would report to me!'

Fascinated, Helen moved forward and reached out a hand to touch the rigid flesh, made slick and shiny by Kate, and then looked up into his eyes. They looked desperate as he met her gaze and, for a moment, she felt sorry for him. But then as her hand, seemingly of itself, began to stroke and caress the man's penis, she saw a smile play about his lips and all sympathy vanished from her to be replaced by a sudden lurch in her loins.

Madame Victoria's voice cut into her reverie. 'Well?'

'He is ready, Madame,' Helen murmured, her eyes once more peering into the man's face.

'Very well, then,' said Victoria and Helen held his gaze and continued to caress him as Kate sat back to cede her place.

The sound of the whip cutting through the air and then biting deep into the man caused him to yell out as a convulsive wave swept through his body and into Helen's arm, shooting through her upper body before sinking like an electric surge to clench at her loins.

'One, Mistress,' cried the man.

Helen's eyes never left him nor did her hand stray from his softening penis. Again the whistle then the impact as the whip cut into him.

'Two, Mistress,' his voice now rising against the cumulative gathering of pain.

Helen turned to see that Kate was watching her closely. With a quick gesture Helen brought her forward to fall hungrily on the detumescent cock.

'Three, Mistress.'

The strokes became more rapid and the man's voice more forced as he kept what Victoria had called the 'accounts'. Helen watched the man's face, contorted when the blows landed, breathing deeply between each one, with a growing sense of excitement. She had never seen anyone else beaten before and found the experience uniquely powerful.

'Mistress Helen!' Victoria's voice brought her once again to understand that this was all really happening before her eyes. Looking up she saw Victoria looking directly at her with a curious smile on her face. 'Take it!' she said and, looking down to Victoria's extended hand, saw the whip being offered to her.

Feeling an emotion that might have been fear or excitement, or both, she took the ebony-handled whip in her hand and found her breathing shortening as her hand tightened around its sculpted haft.

'You will deliver the next six,' Victoria told her, and brought her to stand in precisely the right place.

Helen looked at the already heavily marked buttocks and felt, curiously, that she was the one about to be tested. 'I want to see each of them leave its mark,' Victoria warned her before moving out of her swing's reach.

Her entire body started to quiver as she measured out the first stroke on the vulnerable flesh before her. She swung back and then brought the stroke feebly across his buttocks.

The man didn't even flinch. 'We shall have to do better than that,' scoffed Victoria. 'Strike harder.'

Suddenly, seized with a desire to make this one count, Helen found her arm swinging back further and her wrist snaking in faster to deliver the next blow. The cry of the bound man shot through her, electrifying every nerve in her body.

'Thank you, Mistress,' gasped the man.

'Keep the count!' Victoria reminded him.

'Thirteen, Mistress!'

The words meant nothing to Helen's brain, which was seized by a paralysing madness. Almost completely detached from what the man might be feeling she was aware only of the tremendous sense of power that was charging her entire body. Now she struck out, barely waiting for the man's count, until his voice rose to almost total incoherence as the blows followed close on one another.

She had become totally unaware of the man or the pain. She knew only of herself and the alien excitement which had laid siege to her senses. Only when Victoria stepped forward to grab her already raised hand did she realise that she had been, literally, flogging the man until his 'count' had become a continuous wail.

'That's enough,' Victoria said sharply. 'Go to your Master.'

Helen felt her brain empty. 'Master?' she asked.

Victoria turned her to the door and all but pushed her through it. 'He's waiting for you in the sitting-room. Go to him. Leave this to us.'

Resentful at being so peremptorily dismissed she went, feeling she had failed the 'test', to find Jeffrey rising from one of the deep couches, his eyes wide at the sight of her in the leather costume. 'You look magnificent,' he told her. 'Tomorrow we must have something like this made for you.'

This sudden transition from the unbelievable events taking place just a wall away, to Jeffrey's presence, confused her.

'Here,' Jeffrey was saying, as he held out a drink to her. 'You look as if you need this.'

Taking the glass, Helen was only vaguely aware of the other girl, to whom she had not been introduced, sitting legs curled under herself on the couch opposite Jeffrey. Noting that the girl, who when last seen had been wearing a dress, now wore only a dressing gown gaping open to show most of her naked breasts, and wondering if, in her absence, anything had happened between the girl and Jeffrey, she heard herself asking: 'Did you fuck her?'

Jeffrey smiled. 'No. I was saving that for you.'

'Here,' her voice continued.

'No. I thought we'd go back to the hotel.'

'That wasn't a question,' she said with an assertiveness that surprised even her.

His face quivering with surprise, Jeffrey looked at her. 'Here?' he asked.

She nodded and turned to the girl. 'Is there another room – like that one?' Helen indicated the room she had just left.

The girl nodded cautiously. 'Show it to me,' she murmured.

Rising, the girl glanced at Jeffrey for confirmation that she should do as Helen asked, before leading the still-masked Helen into the hallway. She was led past the room from which she had so recently been sent and into another, slightly smaller but equally well equipped. As she looked around she was aware of the girl watching her.

'Help me out of this,' she said, indicating the basque.

The girl came forward immediately but made a mild protest. 'But you look so good in it. Didn't your man just admire it . . . ?'

Impatiently she started tugging at the front hooks herself but knew the strings at the back would need help. 'Do it!' she commanded, surprised at how like Victoria her tone sounded.

The girl's fingers moved nimbly over the restraining strings and soon Helen felt her abdominal muscles relax with relief as cooler air touched her heated skin.

Freed of the basque, but still masked, she went forward for a closer look at the chains that dangled from a ceiling frame. Extending one wrist she closed the leather band round it and motioned for the girl to come forward and secure it.

In seconds the girl's obviously well-practised fingers had closed the clasps, and she looked to Helen to have it confirmed that the other was to be treated in like manner.

When she was fully secured, feeling deliciously open and vulnerable, she sent the girl to summon Jeffrey. Balanced on the high-pointed heels of the boots, only the mask gave her any confidence that she would not disappoint him when he came to her.

On coming into the room Jeffrey was stunned by what he saw. Every sinew in her upper arms and shoulders seemed defined by the restraint in which she had been secured. Her stomach had all but disappeared into her rib cage while her breasts appeared firmer with their nipples, aroused and engorged, pointing almost ceilingwards.

'The whips,' she gasped to him. 'Use them ...'

When Jeffrey nodded as if to dismiss the girl from the room, Helen called out again. 'No! I want her to stay!'

Jeffrey, smiling quietly, came to stand directly in front of her. 'Since the girl is to stay I suggest we make use of her. Shall I have her whip you?'

Feeling something akin to anger at his delay she spat her words out through gritted teeth. 'I don't care who whips me just as long as it hurts!'

'What a greedy little slave you've become,' said Jeffrey quietly, reaching out to tease both nipples with his fingers. 'Every time you tell me you love me she will strike five times,' he added.

Taking a deep breath Helen braced herself before uttering the fatal words.

When, some thirty minutes later, she saw, through hooded eyes, Victoria come into the room, she felt immense pride as that jaded lady winced at the sight of Helen's lividly marked buttocks and thighs.

The man that was with Victoria looked unfamiliar to her until she realised that his strangeness was due to the fact that he was now dressed. The man's eyes bulged at seeing her whip marks but he came forward, and reached both hands to encompass her head before kissing her lightly on both cheeks. 'Thank you, Mistress Helen,' he murmured.

Victoria looked significantly to Jeffrey before turning to usher the man out of the room, leaving her once more alone with Jeffrey and the girl. Defiantly, she held Jeffrey's eyes as he looked back at her. 'Now you can have me,' she told him.

9

Helen woke thick headed and feeling as if she might be coming down with something, only to find an enthused Jeffrey at her side.

'Helen!' he was excitedly calling before she was even fully awake. 'Marvellous news. They've found my car!'

Her head still heavy with sleep, Helen tried to concentrate. 'Your car?'

'Yes. At, of all places, the German/Polish border! Annabel called me from London. Apparently the border police got suspicious because the thieves – who can't be very bright – had put false French plates on a right hand drive car! They checked it out and found it was listed as stolen.'

'What on earth were they doing trying to take it into Poland?'

'Apparently there's a big market in Russia for that kind of car at the right price. Isn't it marvellous? I thought I'd go and collect it and drive it back. You could come with me if you want but I don't think the German/Polish border is the most appealing of places. What do you say?'

Helen felt confusion closing in rapidly. 'I'm sorry, Jeffrey, I'm not awake yet. As a matter of fact I feel exhausted still.' She paused, trying to absorb this sudden change of plan – an effort made worse by Jeffrey's obvious excitement at the prospect of getting his car returned. 'What do you suggest I do?'

'I'll only be gone a couple of days at the most. Why not just stay here?'

'Alone?' she asked.

'No. Annabel's coming over. I need the registration documents, the insurance – all that kerfuffle – to prove the damn thing's mine. She can stay with you – you two could go round the shops together.'

'I'd rather wait until you get back.'

Jeffrey nodded and then looked as if there was something else on his mind. Watching him she was filled with a sudden dread.

'Is something wrong?' she asked tentatively.

The question seemed to surprise him and he looked, for a moment, as if he'd been caught out thinking something shameful.

'No!' His denial was too effusive to be convincing. 'It's just that – well, there is something I wanted to discuss later but my having to go off like this ...' He let his voice trail off. 'No,' he said, as if his mind was made up. 'This isn't the time to get into that.'

'What?' she asked sharply.

His eyes, avoiding hers, focused randomly about the room for a moment before, taking a deep breath, he turned back to look directly at her. 'I'm a fraud,' he finally sighed.

Stricken with the thought that she was about to hear something she'd rather not, she spoke with quiet insistence. 'What sort of fraud?'

'You came to me with your guilt-stricken vulnerability, looking for strength and the means to forget – obliterate, if you like – the agony you've been put through. The trouble is I'm not as strong as you might imagine.' He hesitated as she watched him. Filled with a sudden feeling that everything was about to go wrong she, nevertheless, felt obliged to give him the space he so obviously needed. 'This may sound crazy but, you see, I've never felt entitled to anything I have,' Jeffrey said flatly. 'Not even you.'

His last words startled her. They had come so suddenly and sounded like the crack of doom to her apprehensive ears. 'What do you mean?' she asked. 'You have me. I'm here. My God, Jeffrey, we might not have known each other long but the things we've shared ... don't start doubting us.'

'I don't doubt *you*!' he protested. 'You're a fantastic girl. You're beautiful, sexual, intelligent and ... maybe that's the trouble. I've begun to think I'm exploiting your vulnerability.'

'That's total nonsense! I haven't done anything I didn't want to do – and there's things we've done I want to do again. Please don't feel guilty about me. I meant it when I told you you'd liberated me. Jeffrey, I need your strength – don't start doubting yourself now.'

His smile was wry as he looked away, staring blankly and without interest, at anywhere but her. 'My strength?' he asked with heavy sarcasm. 'Don't you realise that my only strength is in your submission?'

It took her a moment to absorb this surprising concept but when she did she found herself encouraged. 'Fine!' she said. 'That's fine with me. I'm totally yours.'

His smile remained glacial but at least, she thought, he's looking at me again. 'My father once told me that the only time you ever know what you possess is when you give it away, sell it, dispose of it. Only in losing it could you be sure you ever had it.'

The ice rushed back into her soul, making her next words brittle. 'Are you saying you want to be rid of me?'

'That's not what I'm saying at all. My greatest fear is that, having found you, I might lose you. I couldn't bear that.'

'So that makes us even,' she told him. 'I don't want to lose you either.'

As he looked steadily at her she read agony in his eyes. The source of this worried her. He had been in a confessional mood but had said nothing to explain this sudden despair. At the same time there was, gnawing at the back of her mind, the certainty that he hadn't told her everything. She couldn't imagine ever again being as intimate and open with anyone other than Jeffrey, and she found the thought of being without him terrifying. More terrifying than knowing the worst. 'What is it you're *not* telling me?' she asked.

'You might hate me,' he finally said.

'I doubt it,' she answered, her voice edgy with preparedness.

'I started some enquiries ...' he said hesitantly.

'Enquiries? About me?'

He shook his head as if dismissing that suggestion as ridiculous. 'About Kenneth.' Seeing her go into a shocked and puzzled silence, he rushed on. 'Millie told me about the accident and everything before I even met you. It didn't sound right to me then but it was none of my business so ...' he shrugged before going on. 'But after we'd met – when I realised how affected you were by what you thought had happened – I started some enquiries.'

Helen stayed silent. Her first reaction was much as if she had found him rifling her diary, reading her letters or checking her bank account, but then she remembered that she had felt precisely the same during the police enquiries and the inquest and when the facts – as the world saw them – had become public property. There was no reason Jeffrey shouldn't know as much as total strangers but his phrase 'by what you *thought* had happened' rang discordantly in her ears. 'And what did you find out?' she asked.

'Nothing. Not yet, anyway. I mean it's only been a few days – the real investigation hasn't even begun yet.'

'And what do you expect to discover?'

Jeffrey looked painfully awkward. 'I honestly don't know. I've done some scuba diving myself but I'm not expert, so I checked with a friend of mine who is. He confirmed my first reaction.'

'Which is?'

'That it is extremely unlikely that in a properly supervised dive, a member of the team could go missing for over an hour and not be missed. You told me Kenneth was an experienced diver and yet he got entangled with some wreck's hawsers and just stayed there waiting to die? That doesn't ring true. There had to be something they didn't tell you.'

'What?'

'That's what I hope we'll find out.' He looked at her with eyes pleading their sincerity. 'Whatever it is, or might be, it can't be worse than your imaginings – or the guilt you're carrying around.'

Feeling increasingly that the situation was becoming weird she attempted to inject a note of realism. 'Jeffrey, there was an investigation, then an inquest. If there was anything to find out it would have come out.'

'Inquest verdicts are not always what they seem,' he murmured.

'Are you saying that the verdict on Kenneth was fixed?'

'Of course not. All I'm saying is that, sometimes, a verdict isn't what's true but what's best.'

'For who, or what?'

'Who knows? It could be politics – it could be a negative effect on tourism . . . It could be – right now – almost anything. All I'm saying is that what you were told doesn't sound right – an experienced diver could have done a dozen things to alert people to what was going on. The last thing he'd do is just hang there and wait for his air to run out.'

Helen felt totally numb. She almost wished she could feel

anger but recognised that Jeffrey thought he had acted in her best interests. What concerned her was that he had thrust himself so deeply into her business without consulting her. Suddenly the wonderful lover sitting opposite her was not the man she had imagined him to be. 'Jeffrey,' she murmured out of her confusion, 'I think I'd like some time alone to think.'

'This is what I was afraid of,' he muttered. 'Please don't go cold on me now. I did this because I was worried about you.'

'Apparently not worried enough to discuss it with me first.'

'I thought you'd try and stop me.'

'Maybe I would have,' she said. 'It's something I've been trying to put behind me. Something I don't want to think about any more than I have to.'

'That's where you're wrong,' cried Jeffrey. 'What you've been really trying to do is run away. Do you imagine that by ignoring what happened you'll be able to forget it? You never will. All you'll succeed in doing is putting up barriers – barriers which, sooner or later, will come tumbling down and crush you. I knew that. I knew that's why you came to me. I didn't flatter myself that it was my magnetic personality that drew you. You wanted just to stop *thinking* – and not only about Kenneth, but everything. In me you imagined you'd found someone strong enough to distract you. You won't ever be able to put this thing to rest and I can't do it for you, unless you turn around and face it – for better or worse.'

'Like nightmares?' she asked with a wry smile.

'*Exactly* like nightmares.'

While recognising that there was truth in Jeffrey's words, she also recognised a greater truth – she now needed nothing so much as time and space to sift through the many confusing thoughts that were saturating her mind. She was experiencing her first doubts about Jeffrey but wasn't quite sure where they were coming from. Finally, she spoke quietly. 'Maybe it's not the best time to be talking like this. I'm too tired. I'm afraid I might be going down with flu, and I would like to get some more sleep if I can.'

Nodding, Jeffrey rose from the bed. 'Sorry, I was so excited at the news I didn't stop to think. Is there anything you want? For the flu, I mean?'

Helen, amused at his sudden concern, shook her head. Jeffrey nodded. 'OK. Get some sleep and maybe later you'll feel well enough to have dinner with us.'

'Us?'

'Annabel. I told you, she's on her way over. Should be here any minute.'

Jeffrey left her with many sudden doubts. Cursing the dead feeling in her head, she remembered her chilling naked walk to Madame Victoria's and, mentally, upgraded her symptoms from flu to pneumonia.

Helen's next memory was of being gently woken by the sound of Jeffrey's concerned voice. 'Helen, I'm leaving now. There's an early plane to Berlin – the sooner I get started the sooner I'll be back.'

Still asleep, a befuddled Helen tried to rouse herself to understand what he was saying. 'Tonight?' she asked.

'It isn't tonight. It's morning. You've slept round the clock.'

Startled, Helen stared at Jeffrey. 'Morning? How long have I been asleep?'

'On and off – something like eighteen hours, but you obviously needed it. I'll be gone at least two days, I suppose. It's a chance for you to get rested.'

With a vague feeling that everything was coming unravelled, Helen tried to put her arms around Jeffrey, feeling it was important to hold on to him at that moment. Gently Jeffrey unwound her embrace. 'I have to go or I'll miss the flight and that'll make the trip that much longer.' Leaning in, he gave her what, in her present mood, seemed no more than a patronising kiss and left her gazing after him as he hurried off to the door. 'I'll call you this evening and let you know how things are going.'

Muddled and cursing herself for being barely awake at the moment of his leaving, she lay back on the bed engulfed in a growing sense of unease. The bedside clock told her it was barely 7 am – 6 am London time she told herself for no logical reason she could think of.

Turning on her side she ruminated that she had a great deal to consider, but the problems grew more indistinct the more she thought about them. Gratefully she felt sleep once more overtaking her and decided to slide into its comforting embrace and worry about her indeterminate troubles later.

At first she thought she was dreaming of being attacked and became panicked when she realised it was real and that she was awake. A man was holding her in his arms and laying fervent kisses on her forehead and cheeks. Anger pumping adrenalin, she started fighting the man off furiously until she, amazed, saw that her 'attacker' was Qito!

'You are a very strong woman,' he was saying, ruefully nursing a bruised cheek before a broad, sparkling smile broke out of his deeply tanned face. 'You looked so beautiful lying there – I couldn't resist you!'

Dragging the covers defensively about her she stared at Qito. 'What are you doing here?' she demanded.

'We came to invite you and Jeffrey! Carla and I are leaving at noon for Basse Terre. We wanted you both to come with us. I want to paint you.'

'Jeffrey's not here,' she told him, aware that he must already know that. 'How did you get in?'

'Annabel kindly let us in. She and Carla are having breakfast right now. Will you come?'

'To breakfast?'

'To Basse Terre.'

'I don't even know where that is.'

'It's the capital of Guadeloupe – a *département* of France – a domestic flight from Paris.'

Helen felt herself being buried under an avalanche of confusion. Jeffrey had wanted to take her to Germany. Now Qito was proposing she go, immediately, to a place she had never heard of. If she had been tied between two horses and about to be torn to pieces she couldn't have felt more perplexed. She just wished her head, seemingly filled with concrete, would clear.

'You'll have to talk to Jeffrey about that, and he's not here.'

'I don't need Jeffrey. It's you I want to paint.'

'Well, I'm sorry, I can't go anywhere – I . . .' Helen broke off and then, feeling distinctly uncomfortable, made a more direct appeal. 'Look, I can't think like this. Let me get up and then we can talk.'

Spreading his hands expansively, Qito rose from the bed. 'Of course, but we haven't much time. We have to be at the airport in an hour. Don't take too long!' he cried breezily before going out.

Left alone, Helen lay in the bed and considered that her world, already disordered, was now in chaos. The one thing she knew for certain was that she wasn't going anywhere before she spoke to Jeffrey, but that thought only served to remind her that she, presently, had no way of contacting him.

Emerging into the suite's sitting-room she was surprised to see Annabel rising from the breakfast table still wearing a dressing-gown. This item brought a rush of even more confusing thoughts about just where Annabel and, more especially, Jeffrey had spent the night. Carla was agitatedly mobile, inspecting the hotel suite as if she might be considering buying it.

'They've re-decorated since I was last in this hotel,' Carla was saying as she looked disapprovingly at a silk lamp shade. 'Pity they didn't take the opportunity to *improve* it.' Then, finally acknowledging Helen's presence, she swooped towards her. 'It seems we are fated to meet constantly,' she cooed as she grabbed a startled Helen and delivered a swift kiss on each cheek. 'Qito is positively enraptured by you, darling!' Carla's words managed to convey that she did not entirely go along with that assessment.

Annabel came to Helen's startled assistance. 'How are you feeling?' Annabel asked. 'Jeffrey said he thought you might be coming down with flu or something. In any case, you look as if you could use a hot drink. Come.'

With a growing feeling that she had, during her sleep, become something of an outsider – even an intruder – it took an effort of will to remind herself that she was here with Jeffrey and it was they, if anyone, that were intruding on her. Burying herself in the fine porcelain teacup, Helen felt some of her vital life signs slowly returning.

Carla, meanwhile, was continuing her peripatetic inspection of the premises. 'If you are having influenza stay away from me. I catch everything!'

Qito joined in. 'The best thing for the grippe is warm sea air! Guadeloupe is just the place for that. Take my advice – pack a bag and jump on the plane with us.'

'Qito,' Carla's voice contained a threatening note of caution. 'Give the girl a chance. There's always another time.'

Qito's response was explosive. 'Another time! You don't know what you're talking about. You never understand! I have my muse – ' Helen was startled to find that role assigned to her. 'I have the place – the island we found last year – and I have the inspiration. You imagine I can switch such things on and off like a tap?' Turning to Annabel he demanded, 'Where is Jeffrey? I must speak to him immediately.'

Annabel shrugged. 'Not possible, I'm afraid. He's probably somewhere in the air between here and Berlin. After that he has to find his way to the Polish border but I'm sure we'll hear from him tonight.'

'Ridiculous!' cried Qito. 'We will be on our way to Guadeloupe by then. There's only one solution. Helen comes with us and you tell Jeffrey to join us later in Guadeloupe.'

'Wait a moment!' cried an exasperated Helen. 'Don't I count for anything in this conversation? In the first place, I'm not going anywhere – certainly not to some place I've never heard of – without, at least, speaking to Jeffrey and, in the second place, I don't even want to.'

Qito stared at her in horror. 'You don't know what you're saying!' he cried. 'Don't you understand? I *need* you!'

Suddenly angry, Helen found herself on her feet and shouting at Qito. 'What an arrogant little man you are!' she cried. 'You *need* so the whole world has to fall into line? Well *I* don't!'

Having left herself with no other place to go, Helen fled the breakfast room, taking with her the image of Qito's astonished face and leaving behind a solid stunned silence broken only by Carla's cry of approval and solitary applause.

In her bedroom Helen was still seething. Everything this wakening was off kilter. Immediately realising that her anger was due to an uncomfortable feeling that she had been 'dumped' in Paris in favour of Jeffrey's almost frenetic enthusiasm to recover his precious car. There was also the unsettling discovery that Jeffrey had spent the night in the suite where the only alternative to Helen's bed had been Annabel's. Added to which, this ludicrous assumption that she would be thrilled to go off to some unknown destination with a virtual stranger, made her feel as if she had stumbled into a Parisian version of the Mad Hatter's Tea Party.

Agitated wasn't the word for it!

When Qito came cautiously after her she felt ready to vent herself more fully but his soulful eyes dissuaded her until he'd spoken. '*Cara* ...' he murmured, coming forward and reaching out for an embrace which she, with conscious petulance, avoided. 'I didn't mean to upset you,' he was saying in his softest tones. 'Truly, Jeffrey is one of my oldest and truest friends. Had he been here, I know he would have agreed at once – maybe not to come with us immediately – but, maybe, to follow on in a day or two. I meant no insult by my suggestion.'

Despite herself Helen found his obvious sincerity beguiling, but she still had no coherent answer to make.

'I have a suggestion,' Qito was saying. 'I will leave first class tickets at the airport desk for both you and Jeffrey. That way you can join us as my guests whenever you wish. Is that fair?' he asked before adding in the face of her continuing confusion, 'Am I forgiven?'

Finding his tone conciliatory, and the pressure of the need to make a decision lifting, she managed a smile. 'I'm sorry. I just feel a little irritable this morning. I don't know what's wrong with me. Maybe I am coming down with something but I shouldn't have spoken to you as I did. I'm sorry.'

Qito's face positively beamed with relief. 'Then everyone forgives everyone else!' This time as he came forward she allowed him to take her into a light embrace. 'When you've spoken to Jeffrey, and you feel better, come. It's a beautiful place. The sun shines, the water is warm and, there, they don't know what a grey day is. It would do you good!' Holding her at arm's length he beamed. 'And I need you to inspire me!'

The cosy warmth that had been established between them was peremptorily interrupted by the cutting edge of Carla's voice. 'Qito!' she said sharply. 'We have to go if we are to catch that flight.'

Stepping back with an alacrity that suggested guilt, Qito turned to his wife. 'Of course. *Subito!*' he said.

Helen found herself quite pleased – even flattered – to be the subject of a withering look from Carla before the lady turned abruptly from the bedroom.

'So, I may hope to see you in Guadeloupe!' Qito was insisting.

Smiling, Helen told him she would have to speak to Jeffrey and see what he said. This answer seemed to satisfy Qito as he turned, chastened, to join the impatiently waiting Carla.

'Don't forget,' Qito cautioned her on leaving. 'Tickets will be waiting!'

With the barest of polite goodbyes Carla all but dragged Qito from the suite, leaving Helen to face Annabel whose dressing-gown reminded her again of unresolved doubts, best left, she decided, until another time.

'Aren't you excited?' Annabel asked.

'About what?'

'That Qito, of all people, wants you to pose for him. He would immortalise you!'

At any other time Helen might have found Annabel's enthusiasm faintly comic but, in her present mood, she could find nothing even remotely funny. 'Maybe,' she said as she made her way into her room and, settling on the bed, felt in need of a damn good cry.

That evening, feeling that Annabel had dragged her across half of Paris, Helen returned to the hotel anxious not to miss Jeffrey's promised telephone call. She was frustrated to find a message from him that he was sorry to have missed her and would call again later.

Beginning to find Annabel's presence oppressive, she bluntly asked her how long she meant to stay. Annabel shrugged. 'Jeffrey did ask me to look after you while he was gone.'

'I don't need looking after,' she said, not bothering to disguise her acid tone.

Annabel seemed quite at ease and Helen got the distinct impression the girl was enjoying the discomfort of her presence. 'It's a little late to go back to London tonight.' Annabel smiled. 'Perhaps in the morning – that is, if Jeffrey doesn't want me to stay on.'

Aware that she had been subtly reminded that Jeffrey had the last word in the arrangements, Helen felt a surge of bitterness. 'Well, at least,' she said with deliberate sarcasm, 'you'll have the bed to yourself tonight, won't you?'

Annabel opened her mouth as if to say something but settled for an inscrutable smile which infuriated Helen even more. Turning on her heel, Helen went to her own room and closed the door with noisy emphasis.

When, later, Annabel called through the door to ask if she should order a room-service dinner, Helen told her she wasn't hungry and settled in for a grumpy night, not caring that she was behaving badly.

Jeffrey's promised call didn't materialise and so it was an even more unsettled Helen that faced Annabel the following morning.

In answer to Helen's somewhat forlorn enquiry, Annabel told her that the only call had come from the airline to confirm that they were holding tickets in the names of Helen Lloyd and Jeffrey Hacking.

Not wanting to leave the hotel in case she again missed Jeffrey's call, Helen waited impatiently throughout the morning until, close to two in the afternoon, she finally heard Jeffrey's voice.

'Hi! I'm sorry about this. There's more red tape than you can imagine. I've had to hire a local lawyer to try and fight my way through it but he hardly speaks English and my German is atrocious. I'm afraid this could take longer than I thought. There's talk that they will have to hold the car as evidence until the smugglers come up for trial.'

'But that could take weeks!' Helen protested. 'Surely you don't intend staying there that long?'

Her heart sank as she heard Jeffrey's sigh. 'Well, no, but I think I should stay at least another couple of days and see what can be done to speed things up.' As if trying to cheer her up, he added, 'By the way, I've seen the car and it's totally undamaged. That's something, don't you think?'

Helen didn't think it was much and let that into her tone as she answered. 'I feel pretty silly sitting in Paris on my own. The best thing I can do is go back to London – but I'm not sure how to settle the bill.'

'Don't worry about that. Let me talk to Annabel ...'

Handing over the telephone Helen felt even more out of place than before Jeffrey's call.

She heard the efficient Annabel assuring Jeffrey that she would take care of everything, and then, without offering Helen the chance for a last word with Jeffrey, hung up.

'Nothing's easy,' smiled Annabel. 'I even told him not to expect too much before he left. He's crazy about that car.'

'To the exclusion of all else it seems,' murmured Helen.

'What a shame you didn't accept Qito's invitation,' Annabel said brightly.

Reminded that she hadn't even thought to mention the invitation to Jeffrey she asked, 'You don't imagine I had any serious intention of going, did you?'

Annabel looked bemused. 'How many chances at immortality are you going to get?' she asked. 'I know what I'd do,' Annabel added.

Looking up, Helen saw a strangely thoughtful looking Annabel handing her a drink. As she gratefully reached for it she had little idea that her, already shaky confidence was about to be totally shattered.

'You do know he's married, don't you?' asked Annabel.

Helen smiled. 'Qito? Of course. Carla was right here.'

'I meant Jeffrey,' said Annabel.

10

To be confused was one thing. To be confused about why she was confused was demeaning. She had run away. That fact was clear in her mind even as she had blundered out of the hotel and taken a cab to the airport. They had the ticket and, since nothing could be too much trouble for anyone connected with Qito, she found herself caught up in a highly efficient process which demanded nothing of her but her presence. She had given no thought to where she was going but only to what she was leaving behind.

She felt emotionally violated. She had opened herself completely to Jeffrey, more so than any other living being and he had betrayed her. She remembered him saying that there were things he had yet to tell her, but thought the basic fact of his being married left unsaid was unforgivable, and it was this that was the source of her confusion. The issue of marriage had never been mentioned and, indeed, given the short time they had known each other, it would have been ludicrous. However, given that, in little more than a week, they had explored each other's sexuality with such complete abandon, she did consider that it entitled her to believe that a bond of trust had been formed, which Annabel's news had totally shattered.

Now, riding in this plane to an unknown future, she could not wipe away the image of Jeffrey as she had seen him in arousal, and the knowledge that behind that face, during all those excursions, had been this other man who had kept a secret.

It was this that confused her. She had been made foolish in his eyes, which was demeaning enough, but there was also the knowledge that, somewhere in this world, was a woman with a greater claim to him than her.

Stupid! Stupid! Stupid! These two syllables repeated endlessly in her mind, blocking out any attempt to rationalise what she was really doing by flying in this aircraft to an unknown and, until yesterday, unheard-of destination.

When the meals had been cleared away and the duty-free trolley wheeled down the aisle she realised the flight was going on for what seemed an inordinate length of time for a domestic flight. It was only then that it occurred to her to check her ticket. The 24-hour clock system always confused her but she was still able to work out that the scheduled flying time was four hours and, she thought, that must include some time-zone reduction – maybe an hour or so – so, having been already in flight for two or more hours they must, surely, be almost there. Could it be that it was possible to fly for three hours and still be in France? It was then she realised she hadn't the least idea where Guadeloupe was. She had imagined it might be some off-shore possession in the Mediterranean like Corsica, but even with her limited knowledge of geography she didn't imagine Corsica to be more than two hours flying time from Paris, yet her video display showed them gaining height.

She cornered a passing attendant and asked her for an explanation.

'But, madame, the explanation is in the time zones. The flight only appears to be four hours because those are local times. To that you must add the five-hour time difference.'

'*Add* the time difference?' a bewildered Helen asked. 'But surely if we are flying east the time difference is deducted?'

'But we are flying west, madame,' the girl explained in patient tones.

'West? You mean across the Atlantic? But I thought this was a domestic flight.'

'It is. Guadeloupe is a *département* of France, but it is in the Caribbean. Our flying time will be a little over eight hours.'

The smiling girl moved off, little realising that her words had left a corpse in the shell of Helen's body. She who had, but moments ago, felt herself betrayed was now herself a betrayer. She was flying into the ocean that had killed Kenneth. Before her eyes lay his pain-wracked death mask, which now stared at her to ask what she thought she was doing.

Why was it she had never once in her life ever asked the obvious questions? Sometime, in the few quiet moments she had known with Jeffrey, there had been room to ask why a man of his age and affluence had not married. Surely, before so precipitously fleeing that man, she might have taken a moment to ask where Guadeloupe was? Had she known it lay in the same ocean that had taken Kenneth she would never have come. She felt totally lost in a nightmare of her own making and, but for the almost sepulchral dignity and quiet of her fellow passengers, she might have broken out into a primal scream. Instead, she sat in her seat numbed with the thought that she had already died.

She felt trapped. Once more committed to an insanity because she had failed to ask the right question. Catching the arm of the passing attendant she asked for more champagne. If there was no physical way out of this sealed cigar in the sky she would seek escape from herself and the self-loathing that was suddenly welling inside her, and champagne seemed as good an anaesthetic as any other.

Two or three glasses of their excellent champagne later, the movie she had chosen to watch seemed to be getting duller and more out of focus. It was a welcome relief when the flight attendant came back to lean in on her confidentially.

'Madame, the Captain asked if you would like to visit the flight deck?'

Thinking that one of the best ideas she had heard in a long time, Helen got to her feet and was surprised to find the plane's floor seeming so unstable. The attendant even took her arm as she led her forward and through a door into the capacious cockpit.

This was a totally different world to the passenger sections. Here was a confusing array of different coloured lights, dials and switches, most of which seemed to be displayed on monitors. It looked like a video-game player's heaven.

From out of the left-hand seat a shirt-sleeved man in his middle forties was smiling at her as if from a toothpaste ad.

'Welcome to our workbench,' he called in a warmly accented voice. A younger man rose and came to lead her even further into the alchemist's kitchen of confusing technology. With the champagne singing in her blood, Helen was gently edged towards the right-hand seat.

'Would you like to sit there?' the younger man asked.

He helped her into the extremely comfortable control seat and she was thrilled by the thought of sitting before the controls of a powerful machine, but terrified of touching anything in case she caused a sudden disaster. The younger man was meanwhile fitting a headset over her hair and arranging it about her ears. Suddenly the Captain's voice was a whisper in her ear.

'Have you ever been taken up front in a plane before?' he asked. The question struck her as extremely funny and she went off into peals of laughter. 'What's funny?' he asked as she fought to control her giggles.

'No,' she said. 'But I'm willing to try anything once.'

It took a moment for the Captain to translate his own double entendre but when he did his voice became a great deal warmer.

'Well, in that case, we must see what we can do for such a lovely lady.'

Helen looked across at the man's face, lit as it was by the green glow of the electronic instrument panel, and decided he was extremely attractive. 'My name is Lucas,' he told her. 'My First Officer is Hubert.'

Helen turned awkwardly in the seat to shake the hand of the younger man. Hubert was even more attractive, she decided.

'Are you going to Guadeloupe on vacation?' asked the Captain's voice close in her headset.

The question, confused as she was about her own motivations, stilled her for a moment. Rather than launch into a long explanation she decided it would be simpler to agree.

'Alone?' was the next question.

'As you see,' she told him.

Aware that a meaningful glance had passed between the Captain and the First Officer, Helen felt a surge of returning confidence. The questions, and the revelation that the Captain already knew she was travelling alone, made it clear to her that she had been 'targeted'. Obviously the Captain had sent his cabin staff to scout for an attractive woman travelling alone, and she had been selected. Helen found she didn't mind one bit!

'We have a two-day stop over in Guadeloupe,' the Captain was saying. 'Maybe I would be lucky enough to have dinner with you one evening?'

While looking across at his chiselled profile, Helen realised that ten days ago she would have fled, embarrassed, from such an open pass but Jeffrey had taught her differently. That, and the generous amount of champagne she had drunk, seemed suddenly to have fired up her blood and she found nothing wrong in answering the Captain boldly. 'It might be that you could get *very* lucky,' she told him. His answer came as a confident chuckle into her ear.

It was then, keenly aware of a glow in her loins, that she noticed something missing from the area immediately in front of her. There seemed to be no control stick. 'Excuse me,' she asked. 'But shouldn't there be something here to steer the plane by? What do you call it . . . a joy stick?'

'Not any more,' the Captain told her and, pressing himself back into the leather of his seat, indicated a tiny lever by his left hand. 'These days we have only this.'

'It seems very small,' Helen murmured, then hurriedly added, 'I mean to control such a huge machine.'

'Size is not everything,' smiled the Captain. 'Mind you,' he added in his warm French voice which was, by now, insinuating through her like warm treacle, 'we still carry joy sticks in case of emergency.'

'You do?' asked Helen innocently.

'Of course,' he smiled and, turning round, called to his First Officer. 'Hubert will be happy to show you his . . .' The Captain broke off and Helen, turning to see what had caused his hesitation, saw that they had been joined by one of the flight attendants – a somewhat subdued-looking, pretty young woman.

The Captain greeted her. 'Ah! Of course – our *nouvelle*.'

Helen, realising that the Captain had spoken in English for her benefit, turned to study the newcomer with some interest.

The girl had fine blonde hair and fine china-blue eyes which flashed uncertainly from one to the other of the three but finally centred on the Captain, whose voice continued to whisper into Helen's headset.

‘Michelle is newly graduated from our training school. This is her first operational flight. We have a tradition of initiating our new girls in a particularly interesting little ritual. Would you be interested in witnessing it?’

Her interest even more aroused, Helen turned fully in the seat to study the stewardess even more closely. She saw the young woman’s lips parted in an uncertain smile with the lower lip visibly trembling. Helen clearly read aroused sexual excitement, barely repressed, in Michelle’s expression. She not only saw it but began to feel it herself.

‘I’d love to,’ she breathed.

The Captain nodded as if this confirmed his own judgement. Looking across at his maturely handsome face, Helen felt a stab of insight. This man, in charge of a highly sophisticated aeroplane, was all that stood between her – along with approximately two or three hundred others – and plunging to her death. It was his skill that kept her safe and, quite suddenly, she thought of him as no longer a man but, given his power of life or death, some kind of latter-day deity. That thought combined with his obvious good looks – not to mention the uniform – caused her body to heat up as an air of highly charged eroticism blanketed the flight deck.

Meanwhile, the Captain was addressing the apprehensive Michelle. ‘Are your passengers settled down?’

‘Yes, Captain,’ murmured the girl.

‘And so you have some time to devote to us?’

The girl flashed a side-long glance at the attentive Helen before nodding.

The Captain’s voice came once more into Helen’s headset. ‘There is a strict dress code for the new recruits,’ he said, his voice light and amused. ‘It is my duty to now check that Michelle has conformed to that code.’

‘What “code”?’ asked an avidly interested Helen.

'You will see,' said the Captain, before turning to address Michelle directly. 'Are you properly dressed?' he asked.

She nodded, her hands already anticipating his next order as she reached for the buttons of her blouse.

'You understand it is necessary for me to confirm your report?'

Michelle, anxiously nodding, whispered, 'Yes.'

'Very well. Continue.'

Helen's eyes grew rounded with excitement as she saw the woman's trembling fingers complete the opening of her blouse to reveal her pleasantly rounded, pink-tipped breasts.

The Captain continued his commentary. 'New girls are not permitted underwear on their inaugural flights,' he told Helen.

Helen found herself, enormously aroused, unable to take her eyes from the woman now unzipping her uniform skirt and handing it to the First Officer, who was hovering behind her ready to take it. Michelle then turned to face the Captain wearing only a pair of high-heeled shoes, hold-ups and an apprehensive expression.

'At this point ...' the Captain said through the headset, 'it is necessary to check if the initiate is truly enjoying herself. Would you care to assess her condition?'

Barely believing she was doing this, Helen agreed enthusiastically and, with no doubt of what was being asked of her, removed the headset and stood to look directly into the face of the startled flight attendant.

Feeling that the past few days had primed her for this unconventional moment, Helen spoke words which, even to her ears, sounded alien. 'Hands on your head.' The girl nervously obeyed but visibly shuddered at Helen's next order. 'Spread your legs.'

Michelle almost stumbled and fell as she shuffled her uncertain feet apart and the First Officer had to extend a steadying hand.

[illegible]d with a surging sense of power, Helen held her gaze as she reached down and, with her fingers, felt the woman's spread inner thighs which were seemingly melting with excitement. Helen's voice came out burdened with an unfamiliar huskiness as she reported Michelle's condition. 'She's ready for anything.'

'So what do you suggest we do with her?' he asked.

Helen looked to him. 'You need me to tell you that?'

The Captain shook his head. 'But what about me?' he asked. 'Do you not wish to check on my "readiness"?'

Helen hesitated a moment as her impulse to go immediately to the man was tempered by an even greater impulse to survive. 'Who's going to fly the plane?' she asked.

'Madame!' protested the Captain. 'Computers have been flying the plane since we left the Charles de Gaulle air-traffic control. You have nothing to fear but my penis.'

Fearlessly, Helen went forward and, kneeling at his side, felt a surge of unutterable daring as she reached for his trouser zip. He was standing tall and aroused as she searched him out and leant forward to tease him before plunging him deep into her throat.

As she hungrily sucked, she fantasised about the context. The Captain had her life in his hands since he controlled the sophisticated machine that contained them all, and it thrilled her to imagine that her safety depended on this man's pleasure. It was, therefore, with some affront that she felt Michelle's breasts brush past her bobbing head and realised that the attendant was being bent over her own kneeling figure to plunge her tongue into the Captain's mouth. She was even more distracted to feel Michelle's knees pressing against her and, breaking off for a moment, she turned to see that the First Officer was vigorously taking Michelle from behind.

A slight pressure on her head brought her attention back to

her 'duties' and she took the Captain once more into her mouth as Michelle started screaming in orgasmic ecstasy. Then, pressing forward, Michelle all but thrust Helen to one side in her anxiety to reach and straddle the Captain in his seat, where, having torn his cock from Helen's grasp, thrust it deep into her own spread thighs.

Helen had little time for resentment when she, at the First Officer's urging, turned to be confronted with an enormous, risen penis standing out from his uniform trousers. The distant roar of the engines sang in her ears. This was a moment out of time and she felt like a woman truly privileged to be breaking every one of polite society's conventions. Thinking only of the hurt Jeffrey had delivered to her, and revelling in this opportunity for instant revenge, she took the risen flesh deep into her throat where her taste buds were immediately assailed by the taste of strawberries. It was the first flavoured condom she had ever tasted and, for some reason, it struck her as hilariously funny.

11

Helen stepped from the plane feeling more an alien than a visitor. Even the pristine blue sky and the all-embracing heat seemed to mock her – and ask her what she imagined she was doing. Having left Paris in precipitate haste, feeling feverish and confused, she now found herself filled with the doubts and bewilderment of a refugee and the suspicion that she might have made a momentous mistake. Since the flight from Paris to Guadeloupe was classified as domestic, there were few formalities on arrival other than to reclaim the baggage.

It was in the baggage hall that Carla, accompanied by a stick-like young man, found her. 'There you are!' she cried, closing to embrace Helen as she might have her oldest and dearest friend.

Surprised as much by the warmth of the greeting as anything else, Helen relaxed, aware that everyone in the baggage hall was excited to find a famous face – Carla's – in their midst.

'Qito is beside himself with excitement,' Carla told her as she supervised the young man retrieving her one, sad-looking, bag. 'Did I introduce Jimmy?' she asked as they started from the baggage claim hall. 'Jimmy travels with me everywhere. He claims to be my hairdresser but actually he simply cannot live without me.' Only Carla's self-deprecating shout of laughter took the edge off her remark. 'We are only two minutes from the harbour,' she added.

'Harbour?' asked Helen.

Carla nodded. 'We are guests on my friend's yacht.'

Coming out of the airport was, for Helen, fresh from the wintry north, like stepping into an oven. On the short walk to the waiting car, Helen was struck by the fetid balmy air, perfumed by the scent of uncountable flowers striking at her nostrils like a cheap perfume. There was a spiciness to it that caught at the back of her throat like the very essence of excitement.

It seemed impossible to believe that this place, drenched in sunshine and filled with the colour of flowers, could be on the same planet as the wintry grey streets of Paris or London.

'I'm surprised Jeffrey hasn't come with you,' murmured Carla as they sped through the alien streets of this other world.

Distracted from gazing in awe at the colours of the overwhelming green of the flora and the equally colourful dress of the people, Helen turned to her. 'He doesn't know I've come yet,' she said adding, in the face of Carla's incredulous stare, 'he was still in Germany when I made up my mind.'

This seemed to give Carla pause for some thought until, her brow clearing, she smiled. 'Qito will be flattered,' she said.

As the car started drawing into what appeared to be a mixed mooring for expensive boats and workaday fishing boats, she was reminded of the yacht. 'Whose yacht is it?' she asked.

'It belongs to a man called Martinez. He has loved me for twenty-two years and will do anything for me – or, of course, Qito.'

Beginning to wonder just how many devoted admirers, like Jimmy, Carla might have, she heard herself blurting out: 'He's your lover?'

The scorn seared through Carla's reply. 'No! He loves me but that doesn't mean we are lovers. Impossible!' Carla's tone suggested she thought the question was ridiculous.

A chastened Helen was further distracted when the car drew

to a halt at the gangway of a boat which seemed to her to have the proportions of a minor warship.

A white-uniformed crewman leapt forward to open the doors of the car and Helen stepped out to better see the sleek lines of the beautiful craft. Two other crewmen, both oriental, appeared as if by magic to seize on her one piece of luggage while she and Carla, with the weedy hairdresser, Jimmy, coming a poor third, walked up the gangway to where a smiling man in his mid-fifties was waiting to greet them.

'Martinez!' cried Carla on greeting the man. 'This is the English girl that Qito is so madly in love with!'

Martinez wore a moustache and his fiftyish, handsome face was sparkling with two rows of teeth which seemed to be crowding out of his tanned face. Murmuring in Spanish he bent low over Helen's hand before straightening to add, in a pleasantly accented English, 'Qito will be beside himself that you've come.'

Never having seen a yacht like this before, far less ever been on one, Helen found it hard to believe that anything like this could be private property. On board, the boat seemed even bigger than it had from the outside. Martinez waved forward a petite, slim Chinese girl who wore a very tight-fitting cheongsam and what appeared to be a permanent smile.

'Tsai, would you show our guest to the Golden Stateroom.'

'Of course,' said the brightly smiling girl.

Helen was led from the aft deck through a huge sunlit deck cabin that was furnished with an extravagance of white leather couches set about beautifully carved oriental tables. Beyond that was a carpeted hallway leading to a short flight of winding stairs which gave, in turn, into a lower hallway which was bounded on one side by wide windows and on the other by several doors, each of which seemed to have a panel of different colour. The door which was opened for her revealed a room walled with gold panelling and soft velvets, while the gold-bordered white carpet was so silkily smooth she felt guilty to even tread on it.

'This will be yours,' Tsai told her and started a conducted tour of the facilities during which, she noted, that her baggage had not only arrived but been unpacked and her clothes hung in closets. She marvelled at the speed with which this must have been done.

Gazing in at the glittering gold bathroom, the dressing room and the king-sized bed, Helen could only reflect that her own apartment would comfortably fit in here and leave room to spare.

'It's incredible,' she murmured when, at the end of the tour, Tsai stood smilingly awaiting her verdict. 'I never imagined there could be cabins like this on a yacht.'

Looking around, Helen felt uneasy with her lack of experience with anything as grandiose as this before and, since there was no one to ask but Tsai, turned to her. 'What do I do?'

Tsai seemed puzzled by the question. 'Do? You do as you wish.' Helen nodded and let the girl go, before turning to survey her meagre wardrobe. This totally unexpected journey to a warm climate left her with very little choice. She was still pondering on the best compromise when her legs felt suddenly weary and in need of rest. Not wishing to further crease her dress, she slipped out of it and lay down on the top of the bed intending to close her eyes for a few moments. Helen drifted into a dream in which she imagined she was flying in an aircraft so big it had a dance floor on which naked couples were either upright and dancing, or horizontal and copulating.

Ghostly hands seized her and lifted her to be impaled on a huge pink phallus that dominated the interior of the aeroplane. Jeffrey was there, encouraging the two uniformed pilots to bear down with all their weight on her legs while her mother sat on a high stool knitting and shaking her head in disapproval.

She was startled awake as she consciously felt a hand laid gently on her forehead. Opening her eyes, she saw Tsai standing over her. 'Madame is not well?' the girl asked.

Helen, in truth, was not sure how she was and, for a moment, even felt unsure of *where* she was. It was only when she heard the slap of water against the yacht's sides that she remembered. Seeing Tsai was still patiently waiting for an answer she shook her head. 'No, thank you. I'm fine.'

Swinging her legs to the side of the bed she realised that she had lain down naked. Someone had, while she slept, covered her with a white linen sheet.

'Madame Carla sent me to enquire if you would wish to join the company for dinner tonight,' Tsai said. 'If so, it will be in one hour.'

'Is it night already?' asked Helen, looking to the long narrow windows that lined the seaward wall of her stateroom.

'It is seven o'clock in the evening,' Tsai said. 'Come, let me help you. It is difficult if you are not used to the sea.'

Beginning to suspect that life had become unnecessarily complicated, Helen allowed herself to be led into the bathroom which, she saw, was now dominated by a massage table which had been put there since she last saw the room.

'I make you feel better,' Tsai said with enthusiastic confidence. 'Just lie on the table and I massage you. You'll feel better.'

Feeling that she could cope only with the least line of resistance, Helen obediently stretched herself face down on the towel-covered bench, and, feeling that her body was a mass of knotted tensions, was grateful to feel Tsai's hands soothing away the aches with oils. 'That's marvellous, thank you,' she sighed, giving herself over entirely to the girl's expertise.

Helen lay moaning with pleasure at the girl's ministrations until she realised with a start that she could easily be lulled back to sleep if she allowed her to continue. 'I think that's enough,' she said, turning to sit up on the couch and looking into the Chinese girl's worried face. 'It's not that I don't appreciate it. It's simply that you're relaxing me so much I might doze off again.'

The worried frown on the girl's face cleared to be replaced by a sunny understanding smile. 'Ah, no!' the girl cried, 'I know it. Do not worry.' The girl reached forward to push firmly on Helen's shoulders until she lay on her back. 'I fix that,' Tsai told her and produced a bunch of twigs. 'This stimulates the blood,' she said.

Worried that the girl might be about to beat her with the twigs, in Finnish sauna style, Helen moved to protest but then groaned with pleasure as she felt the twigs drawn firmly along the length of her legs to leave in their wake a tingling, scratchy feeling that aroused her flesh to the most delicious sensations. 'That's nice . . .' she murmured, lying back and closing her eyes to better concentrate the sensation as the twigs progressed across her belly and then made a tingling Devil's dance on her breasts. Embarrassed to feel her nipples rousing and hardening she moved her hands to protect them from further stimulation, only to find Tsai's own hands intercepting them and pressing them back – this time above her head. 'You wish?' asked the girl. Not understanding what she was being asked, Helen opened her startled eyes as she felt Tsai's fingers seeking out her clitoris and her lips hovering only centimetres above her nipples.

'No!' she cried, sitting up and aware that the middleclass girl from Eastbourne was reverberating with shock at the oriental girl's suggestion.

The beautiful girl from Taiwan was now standing back with

the expression of a whipped puppy. 'I am most deeply sorry,' the girl was saying. 'Others like me to do that for them. Please forgive me.'

Helen still felt ruffled as she wrapped herself in a towel but, seeing the hang-dog expression on the girl's face, felt Eastbourne rapidly draining from her. 'I'm sorry,' she said. 'I would enjoy it too, I'm sure but, for the moment, I'm so tired it might exhaust me.'

Looking up, Tsai's face looked much brighter. 'Now I give you shower and after you feel much better.'

'I can do that for myself,' smiled Helen and tried to shake off the girl by ducking into the shower stall and turning on the water. She was still trying to keep it out of her hair when she was startled to see a now naked Tsai joining her.

'Look, this isn't necessary ...' she started to protest.

Tsai's face furrowed as if worried that her expertise was being challenged. 'I do this all the time,' she assured Helen, 'please.'

Deciding that further protest would only lead to greater misunderstandings, Helen relaxed and let the girl's, admittedly expert, hands go to work. Tsai's promise to make her feel better was more than fulfilled until the point where Helen found herself again becoming embarrassingly aroused. 'That's enough for now,' she told her as she brusquely moved to snatch up a towel before Tsai could offer it to her.

'You are angry with me?' Tsai asked.

'Of course not,' smiled Helen. 'Tell me, have you any idea how the ladies dress for dinner?'

'Very formally,' said Tsai Lo, her expression still anxious. 'All the ladies look most beautiful for dinner.'

This was bad news for Helen. She had packed only the gown Jeffrey had given her and both Carla and Qito had already seen that. She was still trying to decide what might best serve in its place when she noticed a long pale-pink dress with intricate gold thread embroidery hanging from the closet door. 'Where did this come from?' she asked.

'It's Madame Carla's suggestion that you might like to wear this for dinner.'

'How did Madame Carla know I hadn't brought anything suitable?'

Tsai stared at the carpet as she murmured, 'She asked me after I unpacked for you. Are you angry with me, madame?'

Somewhere deep inside, Helen did indeed feel that she was being treated as something akin to a charity case but, after a moment's reflection, saw that the gesture did solve a difficult problem. 'It's beautiful,' she said finally and was amused to hear Tsai's held breath audibly exhausted.

'I shall help you with your hair and make-up,' she enthused. 'I have training in such things.'

Giving herself once more over to Tsai she found the multi-talented girl able to work minor miracles with both her hair and make-up with amazing facility. After dressing in Carla's gown, she surveyed herself in the mirror and only then noticed the distinctly oriental lift that Tsai had given to her eyes. It was different but not at all unflattering. Giving herself a final check over she announced herself ready and, as Tsai bowed her out of the stateroom, Helen thought she could, so easily, accustom herself to this life.

Tsai led her to the door of the aft deck saloon where the company were assembled for aperitifs. Carla, seeing her, hurried forward. 'My dear, how lovely you look!' Linking arms, Carla brought her the considerable distance across the salon to where the others were gathered. Martinez rose politely as she would have expected, but Qito's reaction was startling to say the least. Hurrying forward he brushed aside the bowing Martinez to pull Helen into an embarrassingly close embrace accompanied by multiple kisses on both cheeks.

'I thought you'd never get here!' he was enthusing. 'I know exactly where I will paint you. I have the island all picked out and ready for us. Together we shall make it immortal!'

Overwhelmed by this unexpected deluge of affection Helen looked up to see Carla's steely eyes fixed on her – a look which silently spoke warning volumes.

'Well,' said Carla with an undisguised sarcasm. 'Now that our revered guest of honour has joined us, I suggest we go in to dinner.'

Qito and Carla took the heads of the long, gold-laden, dinner table while Helen was seated to Qito's right. Martinez, who, as Host, might have been expected to head the table, was seated to Carla's right, while Jimmy was placed on her left. Qito seemed determined to dominate Helen's entire attention to the exclusion of all others. He enthused, almost without pause, over 'his' island where, she learnt to her consternation, he intended to isolate both himself and her for several days. 'I am filled with fire,' he told her, eyes shining. 'I have never before been so certain that I shall create a masterpiece.'

Carla's voice was the only one to which Qito attended. 'Qito, *caro*, please let our guest have some peace.'

'Peace?' cried an indignant Qito. 'For what does she want peace? She is to be the instrument of immortality!'

Carla's voice was carefully even-tempered but cutting in tone. 'Qito ... If you want to fuck the girl, go ahead but don't bore us with hyperbole.'

The stunned silence that greeted this remark only increased Helen's embarrassment, which became intense when Qito threw down his napkin and leapt to his feet to let go a stream of Italian that Helen was grateful not to understand.

Carla too was on her feet answering in equally angry tones and the two were soon standing almost toe to toe exchanging what were obviously gutter insults. Helen dared a glance towards the others at the table. Jimmy the hairdresser sat with eyes closed and visibly shook as if the insults being hurled at Carla were digging out pieces of his heart. Martinez had risen to his feet and gone to stand at Carla's shoulder as if willing to intervene if the shouting match came to blows. Helen, who felt the cause of all this, just wished there was some way to slide invisibly out of her seat and to the calm of her own cabin.

The raised voices had attracted a worried gathering of the stewards who were standing, staring in from the service door.

It ended with Qito raising a hand as if to strike Carla but, as she challengingly stuck out her head as if defying him, he turned to stalk from the dining room with Carla in hot pursuit and still shouting.

In the nervous silence that followed the warring pair's exit, Martinez turned to the remainder of his guests. 'Shall we take coffee and brandy in the library?' he asked.

Grateful to be distracted, Helen and Jimmy dutifully trooped after Martinez to an upper saloon whose walls were lined with books – all trapped behind panelled wire and glass doors to prevent them being dislodged during rough weather.

There, already in place, was a large-screen, high definition, TV whose presence Martinez explained as the silent stewards distributed after-dinner brandies. 'I have my favourite movie of all time to show you,' he told the guests. '*Messalina*, which, of course, stars our honoured guest Carla.'

The opening music and titles were played out over a scene of Carla wearing little more than a superior expression and a sprinkling of diamante, as she was carried through the streets of ancient Rome. Helen was just marvelling at how fantastically beautifully Carla photographed when the original herself came storming into the darkened library and, pausing only to pick out Helen in the reflected light from the screen, marched to her, grabbed her hand and dragged her to her feet. 'You!' she all but screamed in Helen's face. 'Come with me!'

Dragged off balance by Carla's determined tow, Helen feared for the hem of the gown she was wearing as her uncertain feet sought to keep up with her body. Feeling that an angry protest was in order she tugged her hand free of Carla's. 'What do you think you're doing?' Helen demanded.

It was when Carla turned back to face her, here in the fuller light of the passageway, that Helen was shocked to see Carla's eyes brimming with tears. Suddenly all the aggressiveness was gone from her stance. 'I love him!' she cried, and Helen found herself moving forward to take her in her arms. They stood, frozen in mutual surprise for some minutes before Carla made an effort to control herself. 'Come,' she said.

In Carla's stateroom, even grander than the one assigned to Helen, Carla appeared to have regained her self-control.

Without asking she poured them both whiskies from a side table and lifted her glass in salute before sitting down to stare directly at Helen. 'How could you understand?' Carla asked a bewildered Helen. 'Look at you! Comfortable bourgeois upbringing. Nice school, where they taught nice manners and how to be polite. My school was different,' Carla said sourly.

Not having the least idea of how to respond, Helen sat silent.

'I had no childhood,' Carla was saying, so quietly it seemed she might be speaking only to herself. 'At nine I found out that begging bread was not enough. Men were the answer. Dear God – the men! When I was twelve I met this skinny little guy who said he was a painter. He took me to his studio where I found out he was eating even less than me. So now, genius that I was, I had two mouths to feed instead of just my own.' Carla looked up at Helen with eyes that could coruscate a soul, let alone a camera. 'But now I had a purpose other than just surviving. You see? I became a much better whore, and we ate well. I fed my genius when he would have starved. I kept him alive to be the Qito who now has the world kneeling before him.' Carla fell silent and stared into her glass for a long moment. 'Never once has he ever touched me.' Those terrifying eyes flared upwards to fix on Helen. 'Not once!' she added.

By some means other than her own volition Helen found she had moved from her chair to sit next to Carla on the couch. Reaching out a hand that was meant to be comforting, she said, 'Carla, I'm sorry. Look, if it will make things any better, I'll leave.'

Carla's street-loud laugh filled the room. 'Stupid girl,' she cried. 'We're in the middle of the Caribbean – at sea! Where do you suppose you can go?' adding scornfully, 'Don't you understand anything?'

Startled at the sudden mood shift, Helen took back her hand and stared at Carla. 'What do you want me to do?' she asked.

Carla indicated a bedside panel of buttons. 'Press that second button down,' she said, a curious smile now playing about her mouth.

Helen did as she was asked before turning back to Carla.

Carla's voice when she spoke was deeper and more controlled. 'It's time for a lesson your polite school never taught. You want Qito? Then you'll damn well pay your dues!'

Helen protested. 'But I don't want Qito. Not in that sense. He wants to paint me – nothing more!'

Carla's smile was like that of a contented serpent who knew the kill was certain. 'Get naked,' she said.

The blood thundering in her ears, Helen stared stunned for one moment as she decided whether to stay or run.

Reminding herself that it was, after all, Carla's gown and that she was at sea with nowhere to run and, since even the owner deferred to Carla, there was no one on board to whom she could run. With those huge, famously beautiful eyes scrutinising her she felt something undefinable.

Fear certainly, but also a mixture of pride and resentment which amounted, so her liquid loins proclaimed, to excitement. Coyly turning away from the blaze of Carla's gaze, Helen reached for the fastenings and, as gracefully as she could manage, stepped naked from the gown. Taking a deep breath, she turned to face Carla.

Carla rose from the couch and came forward to stand immediately in front of her. 'You have a beautiful body, but let's make it more so. Put your hands on your head ... and brace your arms back ... You see what that does for your breasts?'

Helen found her voice lost in her throat and could only nod.

'Now open your legs a little,' she said as she reached out a gentle hand to cup the side of Helen's face. This touch caused Helen to flinch as if struck, and when the hand travelled down her face to her neck and the firm flesh of her shoulders, she shuddered and, involuntarily, turned towards the hand as if to beg that it move to her breasts. 'Look at me,' said Carla. 'Look only into my eyes.'

Bringing her own eyes to meet those dazzling, devastating ones, Helen felt lost.

'Do you know what I am doing to you?' Carla asked and, reading the answer in Helen's desperate eyes, she smiled. 'And is that what you want me to do to you?'

Finding a hoarse voice and nodding, Helen said: 'Yes.'

Carla lifted her head and, reminding Helen to keep her eyes open and on hers, moved her hand with agonising slowness to caress her breasts, first with her fingertips and then with nerve tingling trails of her long nails, brushing against Helen's urgently roused nipples. 'Ah!' sighed Carla. 'You like that, do you? Do you like pain?'

Her throat once more numbed, Helen could only nod.

'A flicker of pain to spice the moment or the crescendo of feeling that comes with the whip?'

Helen shook her head. 'Not the whip,' she managed.

Carla nodded as if that answer was pleasing to her. 'But my caress? You find that pleasant?' Helen's nod was answered with a sudden nip of Carla's nails on her aroused flesh. 'Answer me properly.'

'Yes.'

'Look nowhere but into my eyes,' Carla said as her hands sought out the swell of Helen's belly and the fingers of one hand traced the contours of her pubis while the other gently played with her half-opened lips.

Despite everything, Helen raised up onto tip-toe to thrust herself towards Carla's hand. Carla's smile showed she understood the plea in Helen's eyes, which now stung with the effort of holding Carla's gaze. 'Do I judge that I may do with you as I will?' asked Carla.

'Yes. Please!' Helen all but screamed as Carla's roving fingers plunged deeply, causing her body to crease almost double, an action which brought her mouth into contact with Carla's throat where her lips, as if of their own volition, kissed greedily. A tug at her hair brought Helen's head suddenly back to stare into Carla's now wild eyes. 'I will tell you when you may kiss me,' she seethed through angry lips as the hand left Helen's belly to streak across her cheek. 'Now apologise.'

'I'm sorry,' Helen murmured.

Carla, still holding Helen's hair in a tight grip, nodded. 'Good.' There was a pause while Carla seemed to be considering what she might do next. Helen was startled to hear her address a third party.

'Tsai, my lovely, come here.'

Into Helen's peripheral gaze came the beautiful girl who

had come into the stateroom so silently that this was the first Helen knew of her presence.

Tsai Lo, wearing a green silken cheongsam, came to stand at Carla's shoulder. Her flawless face reflected no emotion as her clear eyes looked into Helen's. 'Earlier,' Carla was saying to Helen, 'you had the temerity to refuse Tsai's caresses. You will apologise to her. Get onto your knees.'

Feeling that her entire body had been eviscerated and replaced with ice, Helen knelt.

'Look at us,' Carla ordered.

Raising her eyes, Helen was immediately struck with the resemblance between the two beautiful women – born ten thousand miles apart – but as similar as sisters with their black hair, almond-shaped eyes and flawless skins. The only real difference between them was the structure of their facial bones and that the slim and dainty Tsai looked like a two-thirds scale model of the exquisite Carla. Helen was now forced to watch as Carla's hands caressed the shoulders of the impassive oriental girl until one hand sought out the fastenings of the cheongsam and, flicking them open, let the material fall away to reveal her perfectly formed small breasts. It was Tsai who stepped from the cheongsam and cast it aside before resuming her docile stance in Carla's half embrace. 'You may kiss Tsai's feet and tell her you are sorry for your impudence,' Carla ordered.

Kneeling further forward Helen felt that she had somehow been caught up in an oriental ritual. Tsai's feet were shod with green silk sandal-like shoes of such exquisite beauty that it added to the electric thrill of humiliation she felt. Kissing first one then the other of the tiny feet that seemed sculpted from ivory, she murmured her plea to be forgiven to Tsai.

'Good,' said Carla in a more positive tone. 'Now you will move yourself to lie on the bed.'

Rising to her feet, unable to look at either woman, Helen obediently padded to the bed where her uncertainty about how she was to lie was ended by Carla. 'On your back,' she told her.

As Helen lay back she had a rush of understanding of how well she had been prepared by Jeffrey for this moment. It was as if he were there in this cabin continuing her sensual education. The memory of Madame Victoria's brought her a sudden rush of confidence. 'May I be tied?' she asked as Carla came to loom over her.

Carla nodded and presented two thick ribbons of padded silk. 'I was about to do just that,' she answered. Making a loop at one end of the silk ribbon, Carla snapped it closed about Helen's wrist before turning it several times about the bedhead as if tethering a horse. Moving round the bed she stretched Helen's other wrist to the fullest before securing that. Helen lay there revelling in her now total helplessness.

Her excitedly lit eyes came once more to Carla to see that she held yet another band of silk in her hand. 'Yes,' she purred in agreement as the silk was tied about her eyes to make a blindfold.

There followed a period of almost total silence in which the only sounds were of rustling material which, Helen's heightened senses judged, must mean that Tsai was undressing Carla. When she heard whispers passing between them, the waiting Helen, her loins now totally liquid, felt a stab of jealousy as she imagined caresses passing between them while her own body was crying out for their touch.

'Please!' she called out of her voided sight and, as if in answer, she felt a slight sway of the bed as someone's weight was lowered to it. The next sensation was that of fingernails being drawn the full length of her leg to score inside her thighs, making earthquakes under her skin. The hand that came to press down on her pubic bone was answered with Helen's own upthrust and thrash of her legs as she sought to wrap them about her tormentor. The girl, now identifiable as Tsai, lay her weight to still those searching legs, and Helen felt Tsai's soft breasts pressing against the answering muscle of her inner thighs. Slim fingers sought to open her vulvic lips and peel back the inner layers before the searing contact of a firm tongue sought Helen out, causing her to cry out her pleasure in a fully vented scream. Her legs, now freed, went out to wrap themselves about the slim Chinese girl as Tsai's tongue went deep inside to expertly ravage her.

A gentle finger, laid to her lips, stilled her cries and she quietly reached to take the finger into her mouth, sucking on it and the two others that followed, with a rising need to have everything.

Next she felt Carla's generous naked body stretching out alongside the length of her own and the suckled fingers were withdrawn to be replaced by soft lips closing on hers. There was a clash of tongues as her own sought to duel with Carla's. Devastated by the twin attack on her senses she felt her body convulsing as the sheer pleasure of total surrender overwhelmed her.

Tsai's lips had, meanwhile, found her aroused clitoris where they alternately sucked and then nipped the tender bud. The sensation redoubled as Carla's teeth closed on her soaring, marble-hard nipples.

Then the sheer joy of Carla's, now liquidly aroused voice murmuring into her ear. 'Shall I ravage you?'

Without waiting to question the feasibility of the suggestion, Helen heard her own voice calling out in affirmation. She waited, breathless, as she felt Tsai's slight weight leaving her to be replaced with the more substantial Carla. Keening to feel everything that might be done to her she felt a nudge at her soaked entrance and then the surprise of a solid phallus. Her pleasure echoed at the top of her voice; it mattered nothing that this might be counterfeit. It mattered only that Carla's arms were round her, Carla's mouth on hers and that the upward thrusts of her own body were met with the generous press of Carla's breasts.

Her legs wrapped about the other woman's body, bliss searing deep inside her. The thought that she was giving pleasure to this wondrous creature only served to heighten the pleasure that was being returned.

Orgasmic waves rolled thunderously throughout her delighted body and she would have cried out but for the deep penetrating tongue that ravaged her throat.

It was only when Carla broke off to voice her own mounting climax that Helen could join in the relieved chorus. Pounding into her with welcomed savagery, Carla finally fell exhausted, her heated body sliding to one side and dragging the counterfeit cock from Helen as she did so.

Now Helen regretted her tied hands since she wanted nothing more desperately than to reach out and embrace Carla as she lay beside her with her head heavily on one of Helen's arms. 'Thank you,' Helen murmured into the stillness that ensued then, almost immediately, was once more convulsed as she felt Tsai's hands, now oiled with the scents of jasmine and rose petals, soothing her sweated skin.

From the pleasured sounds coming from Carla, Helen judged that Tsai must be anointing them both simultaneously and, delighted, she opened her mouth and reached with her tongue to test the air and savour the taste of the oils that now filled the room.

The massaging ended, Tsai stretched herself out on the bed and Helen heard the sounds of tiny kisses being exchanged between the two women before Tsai's body moved across

Helen's to lie on the other side of her as Carla's fingers came again to tease her painful nipples.

Carla leant in so that her words breathed across Helen's open mouth. 'You imagine that Qito could do anything like that for you?'

Startled to be reminded of their differing status, Helen could only shake her head. Carla laid a finger on her lips.

'I promise you he cannot,' she declared with a throatiness that was excitingly threatening. 'So, our little beauty is to spend five days alone on an island with my husband, is she?' Carla broke off for a tiny chuckle. 'And what do you suppose is going to happen to that "little beauty" when she is delivered back to me?'

'I'll probably be screwed senseless,' Helen groaned.

Carla chuckled ominously. 'You imagine an anxious wife would *reward* you?' she asked, indicating that she would answer the question herself with a tut-tutting sound. 'Oh, no! That is not the way of the Italian wife. You will scream for me again – but not with pleasure.'

Helen's racing excitement at these words was quenched in a deluge of kisses. Opening herself wide to Carla, she gasped as she was re-entered.

'Yes!' called Helen as the dildo once more battered at pleasure's gate. It mattered little when she realised that it was now Tsai that was entering her. The slim girl's weight pressed down on her, her smaller, but firmer breasts clashing with her own as she rose to meet her thrusting pressure, even as her body protested that there was now soreness and discomfort amounting to pain in this new assault, since in her ear was the balm of Carla's threatening voice.

'I shall enjoy myself with you,' Carla was saying. 'Every gram of pleasure you have ever known will be paid for with a kilo of pain.' Carla's voice was becoming strained and excited as her hands thrust between the slight body of Tsai and Helen's to dig her nails viciously into Helen's nipples. 'Will you scream for me?' Carla was asking.

'Yes! Yes! Yes!' cried Helen as pain gave way to a totally consuming pleasure. Tsai, who had not uttered a sound, much less a word, during her assault, now withdrew leaving Helen spread and gasping with no inclination to close herself.

Swaying gently on the couch from her own gratification, Helen heard some whispering and then the opening and closing of a door.

Carla took the blindfold from her and Helen looked up into her huge eyes, now bright with tenderness. 'I dismissed Tsai to spare your blushes,' the fabled beauty told her.

Hearing the door open once more Helen looked in astonishment as she saw Martinez come into the room, totally naked except for black leather straps which crisscrossed his body. Rising from the bed Carla went to greet the newcomer who stood trembling – whether with fear or excitement, or a mixture of both, Helen could not judge. 'Do you love me?' Carla asked of the man.

'You are my mistress and entitled to do with me as you wish,' he answered in careful English.

Beaming with delight Carla brought Martinez to stand over the wide-eyed Helen. 'And what do you think of my friend?'

'She is beautiful, mistress,' said Martinez.

Nodding, as if acknowledging this to be the correct answer, Carla moved away, admonishing Martinez to stay as he was, only to return a few moments later carrying a short-handled, many-tailed whip.

Helen's eyes blinked rapidly from Martinez to the whip in Carla's hands and wondered who it was intended for. The answer was not long in coming.

Carla's hand snaked out to bring the whip lightly across

Martinez's buttocks. 'You have my permission to become erect,' she told him.

Helen could only watch in amazement as the sanctioned member started immediately to stir and grow. More light taps of the whip followed as the tumescence rose under Helen's eyes until it stood, frighteningly big, straight out from his firm belly.

Her loins beginning to drool in expectation, Helen was disappointed to hear that Martinez's erection was not for her.

'You have my permission to bring yourself off on her body,' Carla drawled.

Immediately Martinez's shaking hands went to his hardened cock and started stroking it as the slaps from Carla's whip became both harder and faster. As if anxious to keep pace, Martinez's hands flew up and down on his burgeoning penis.

'It's going to be wasted!' Helen cried out.

Carla stared at Helen, as, smiling, she moved to the other side of the bed. 'Did you say something?' she asked.

Helen, looking at Carla and knowing she was about to feel the sting of the whip, felt her body convulsing. 'Let him take me!' she spat.

For answer the leather strips were brought down on Helen's thighs, the ends seeking out and stinging her labia. Defiantly, Helen raised her body to meet the blows but, before Carla could take advantage, Martinez cried out, and, shouting, begged permission from Carla to come.

Carla's attention turned to him as she, in furious tones, ordered Martinez to kneel up on the bed.

As he did so the whip snaked out and rapped him sharply about the chest as, with a great cry, he spouted a copious stream of sperm which landed, hot and wet, on Helen's heaving belly and breasts.

Feeling cheated, Helen gasped out a protest which Carla ignored as she spoke to Martinez. 'You have my permission to clean her with your tongue,' she told him.

The tongue touched off a totally unexpected wave deep inside Helen and she, under Carla's approving eye, twisted and turned her body to bring Martinez's cleansing tongue to her, but it wasn't until Carla gave her express permission that Martinez dared to do as Helen wanted.

Being far less expert than either Tsai or Carla he managed, nevertheless, after much effort, to bring her to a quiet but perfectly satisfactory orgasm.

12

It was the strong tang of freshly brewed coffee, irritating her nostrils, which woke Helen to a new day. Opening her eyes she saw Tsai moving about the stateroom in her usual wraith-like manner. For a moment she lay as if still asleep while she worked on the problem of precisely how to greet the girl after the previous night's intimacies. It was quite a surprise to herself to realise that this was her only problem. She felt no shame and certainly no regrets about what had happened. As she allowed herself to stir she felt only a strange release, feeling as if she had been admitted to a sorority of freedom in which guilt and regret had no place. Deciding that the simplest approach was the best, she sat up in the bed and sang out a 'Good morning'.

Tsai turned towards her smiling. 'Good morning, madame,' she said, hurrying to pick up a breakfast tray, appetisingly laden with a mixture of croissant-like rolls and fruit. 'I was uncertain whether madame would prefer to bathe or to shower.'

'Shower,' decided Helen, sitting up feeling wickedly indulged to be fussed over so thoroughly. Gratefully starting with the tiny glass of orange juice she went quickly to drink greedily of the delicious coffee while watching Tsai move about the room as if determined to find something to tidy. It was then that it dawned on Helen that the almost imperceptible vibration caused by the boat's engines had ceased.

'Are we moored somewhere?' she asked.

Tsai turned to her, face beaming. 'Yes, madame. At an island which, I am told, is called Far Lee Island.'

Helen threw back the covers and hurried to one of the long narrow windows to draw up the slatted blind that covered it. She could see nothing but the endless ocean. 'Where is it?' she asked.

'On the port side, madame. We are looking to starboard from here.'

'Well, what sort of place is it?'

'Deserted, madame. No one lives there. Mr Qito has chosen this place for you and he to work on.'

'And there's nobody else on it?'

'No, madame.'

Helen turned away with a great deal to ponder. When Carla had said she would be alone with Qito she had taken that as a figure of speech. Had it really meant they were to be little more than castaways? Finding her appetite for breakfast gone Helen went directly to the bathroom where she turned on the shower full blast.

Tsai was waiting for her with warmed towels as she stepped from the shower, seemingly willing to dry her back and legs as Helen caressed her front. Her breasts seemed rudely aroused by this double assault, and Helen's mind took her to the massage bench which still stood erected in the bathroom.

Without a further word she lay face down on it. With equally tacit silence Tsai Lo's hands started to stroke oils into her skin.

Lying there, Helen contemplated what the next five days might bring. She felt that she had most certainly paid the admission price but wondered precisely how the performance might play. She vaguely remembered seeing a film about a girl stranded on an island with a man she came to hate and the memory of it brought her little comfort. These thoughts, combined with Tsai's expert hands, led her to dreamily remember the last occasion she had lain on this bench. Times had since changed!

Languorously, she turned her awakened body onto its back and looked up into Tsai's beautiful face. She awaited the girl's reaction with a feeling of voluptuous abandonment. Tsai allowed herself only the tiniest smile of satisfaction at this overt gesture as her hands began spreading their fiery message across Helen's stomach and breasts. Tsai said nothing until her hands were gently massaging Helen's throat. 'Madame would like?' she asked.

'Madame would like very much,' said Helen and, closing her eyes, passively gave herself over to the now openly arousing caress.

Using only her soft hands Tsai gently stroked Helen's most sensitive flesh, her oiled fingers stimulating and stinging her openness to a convulsing climax.

Opening her eyes she saw that Tsai, duty done, had turned away and was once more the purposeful maid, picking up the dampened bath towels and turning back with them in her arms. 'Has madame decided what she wishes to wear today?' asked the girl, as if nothing untoward had occurred between them.

Picking up on the workaday mood, Helen shook her head. 'What is the usual dress for morning?' she asked.

Tsai smiled. 'Perhaps a simple sarong, madame?'

'Sounds perfect, except I haven't got one.'

'Oh no!' cried Tsai. 'We have plenty!'

Curious, Helen followed Tsai out into the stateroom where she watched as drawer after drawer was opened to reveal neatly folded ranks of the soft silken garments. Called upon to choose, Helen arbitrarily pointed out one decorated with oversized red flowers, which seemed to please Tsai who insisted on showing her how to wind it under her arms to tuck in above the left breast. Tsai insisted this was the way it was worn in the Polynesian islands. From the breakfast tray Tsai took a fresh flower which was almost the twin of those on the material, and hesitated over which side of the head Helen would prefer to wear it.

'What difference does it make?' Helen asked.

'Is very important,' cautioned Tsai Lo. 'For the unmarried woman it is worn on the right, but a married woman wears it on the left side.'

'What do you mean by "unmarried"?'

Tsai glanced coyly away. 'Virgin,' she whispered.

Helen laughed. 'Let's not push our luck,' she said, taking the flower and carefully pushing it into her hair above her left ear.

Coming up onto the main deck gave Helen the first sight of the island on which Qito apparently intended they should spend some days alone. The yacht was moored in a pristine bay, some hundred yards offshore.

At first sight it seemed as if a careless deity had dropped a handful of greenery in the middle of the ocean. From behind the edge of the white sand beach, dotted with clumps of elegant palms, rose the steep sides of a volcanic hill covered in a verdant carpet of shrubs and trees.

Looking at it Helen thought that it, at least, was not the desert island of legend. On the contrary, it looked quite cool and inviting.

An approaching steward interrupted her reverie and offered her breakfast, which she refused. Since there seemed to be no other guests about, Helen took the opportunity to have her first real look at this amazingly huge boat. From the dining salon there was a view forward over an immaculately clean deck of polished mahogany to the elegantly shaped bows.

Stepping out of the salon Helen was overwhelmed by the scents being wafted seawards from the island. Looking to the source of Nature's perfume she caught a flash of reflected light and, guarding her eyes against the gleaming sea, saw that one of the yacht's motored tenders was dragged up on the beach and manned by two of the white-uniformed crew.

'Good morning, madame,' said a quietly accented voice beside her. Turning, she saw an officer in a white duck shirt and shorts. He was shorter than herself and looked vaguely Latin. 'I am the Captain,' the man was saying. 'Captain Miguel de Soledad. Most of the guests have gone ashore. May I show you the ship?'

Accepting, Helen was led up a flight of steep chrome-railed stairs to a quarter-deck which spread the full width of the ship and seemed filled with a confusing array of instruments and television monitors.

'The boat is equipped with most of the very latest navigating and guidance systems.' Fearing that her technological blindness would afflict her she tried to look intelligent as it was explained to her that satellite positioning made it possible for the crew to know the yacht's position to within a metre or two, anywhere in the world. Of more interest was the array of communications equipment, by which they could send or receive fax or telephone communications. It occurred to Helen that she might try calling her mother to tell her where she was, but then decided against it as her mother would surely consider it 'extravagant'.

Although she had no knowledge of such things, it was still impressive to learn that the yacht had a displacement of 750 tons, was nearly four hundred feet in length, and carried a crew of twenty-nine.

'It must cost of fortune to run a boat like this,' she said.

'More money in a year than most people would expect to see in a lifetime,' the Captain smiled.

One of the crew came into the wheelhouse to report something to the Captain in what sounded like Portuguese.

The Captain turned to her. 'The others have started back from the island,' he told her.

Looking down from the wing of the bridge Helen saw that the launch was fast coming back towards the boat. On board she could see Martinez and Jimmy but no sign of Carla or Qito. Leaving the bridge she moved down the steps to the main deck, ready to greet them as they came aboard.

Martinez was the first to come on board. From the warmth of his smile and his bear hug of a greeting, Helen judged that he must have enjoyed the previous night's events. 'It's going to be fantastic!' he told her. 'Qito is like a crazy man waiting for you.'

'He's already ashore?'

'Ashore and raring to get to work. The tender will take you to him.'

'Now? But I haven't prepared anything ... I've no idea what I'll need.'

Martinez smiled expansively. 'Nothing,' he said. 'You'll want for nothing. It's like a paradise on there.'

'But what about food and ...? I presume we *are* going to eat?'

'My crew have been working since daylight,' said Martinez. 'What you have on there is a mini Hilton,' adding, with an encouraging shoo-ing motion, 'Go. The tender is waiting just for you.'

Still confused by the pace of events, Helen suddenly saw Carla on an upper deck looking at her with an expression that threatened thunder.

'Go!' said Martinez urging her forward to the gangway with a gentle nudge.

One more glance in Carla's direction made the possibility

of getting away onto the island more appealing. Still feeling that this was completely unreal she stepped onto the gangway and into the assisting hands of the two crewmen.

The launch started away from the yacht the moment she was on board and, looking back, Helen suddenly realised a sense of just how isolated she was going to be.

Turning away from the impressive lines of the yacht and looking to the island, she couldn't shake off the feeling that she was being transported as some form of ritual sacrifice. Rapidly she tried to remember what she knew of Qito. That first meeting with Jeffrey . . . the reception in Paris and then his visit to the hotel. Their encounters on the yacht added very little, and she might, for all she knew, be about to be delivered to an ogre to do with as he wished. One thought, above all others, seethed in her disordered mind – that whatever he might do to her, Qito, secure within his international prestige, would not be held to account. Throughout her sexually aware life she had always sought to pass the responsibility for her actions to others, secure in the knowledge that the man would behave to a set of principles. Now she was being offered, almost literally naked, to the mercies of a man who would not likely be held accountable, in a place from which she had no escape.

She tried desperately, as the launch nudged up into the soft sand of the beach, to take refuge in her masochism and be thrilled by her jeopardy, but somehow the call went unanswered and, as she stepped from the boat onto the beach, she felt only a cold dread of what might be to come mingled with the feel of warm water and soft sand.

Seeing no sign of Qito, and so having no idea of what she might be expected to do next, she hesitated. One of the crewmen called out to her. 'Lady?' Turning back to the man she saw him pointing into the palms which fringed the beach area. 'You go there,' the man added as she still hesitated.

Seeing little alternative, Helen started blindly up the gently shelving beach to the line of sighing palms. As she began to peer into the shadowed gloom under the trees she heard the murmuring of the launch's motor and, turning, saw that it was already backing away from the beach.

Fighting off an impulse to run after it, she heard a sound in the shrubs to her front and, turning, saw a smiling Qito, his compact but powerful body completely naked, coming towards her. 'It's perfect!' he cried. 'At least we won't have those cretins –' he waved a hand at the yacht '– disturbing us. Come.'

When Qito turned, Helen followed him across some grass which bit coarsely at her bare feet. Within a few yards the colourful undergrowth opened up to a sandy-based clearing in which stood a very substantial-looking tent around which were piled crates and boxes. A little way off from the tent stood a propane-fuelled cooking range that would have looked well in her kitchen. At least they weren't going to starve to death.

Qito had momentarily disappeared into the tent, only to emerge carrying a large plastic bottle. 'Get that off,' he said, indicating the sarong she had wound about herself that morning.

Defensively she asked, 'What for?'

'So I can spread this on you,' he told her, indicating the plastic bottle. 'Sun shield. You're going to need it on your white skin. It's factor thirty so you should come to no harm.'

Somewhat reassured, she reached for the bottle. 'I can do it for myself,' she told him warily.

'Nonsense!' cried Qito, 'besides, I want to feel the contours of your body. If I'm to paint you I must feel the plasticity of you.'

Not at all sure that his statement had any validity, Helen felt curiously shy as she unwound the sarong and, not for the first time, stood naked before him. Qito came forward and, humming an unfamiliar tune through closed teeth, set about coating her body with the sunscreen. As he worked, he talked. 'After we get you protected we can walk up to the spring. Fantastic! You'll love it as I do. God is a wonderful set decorator.'

Helen stood submissively as Qito, the infuriatingly repetitive tune endlessly repeated, liberally coated her body, actually going on his knees before her to stroke the oil into her legs. 'You'll have to do this every morning and, again, after you swim,' he told her.

Filled with a sudden sense of the absurdity of the situation, Helen felt brave enough to quip, 'Aren't you going to do it for me, then?'

'No time,' said Qito as he stood up and looked critically at her to seek out any spots he might have missed. 'You trimmed your pubic hair and shaved your armpits,' he told her, as if noticing for the first time.

'I usually do,' she told him.

'Ridiculous habit,' muttered Qito. 'Hair is grown for a purpose and you're supposed to be my wild creature of the forest.' With a deep sigh he turned away to return the sunscreen to the tent.

'Now,' he said, 'I'll take you up to the spring and afterwards I'll make us some lunch. After lunch I like to sleep a little and then this afternoon we'll start work. That suit you?'

Helen shrugged. 'I could cook if you like,' she offered.

Qito let out an exasperated gasp. 'Women can't cook!' he told her and then turned away, obviously expecting her to follow.

Helen picked up the discarded sarong and was about to wind it about herself when Qito, already some yards off, called back, 'You don't need that. There's nobody here but us. Come on.'

Unwilling to so immediately assume the status of naked savage, but neither wishing to dispute with Qito – already out of sight in the trackless bush – she compromised, and, bunching the strip of material in her hand, started after him.

Qito may have been thirty years older than her but his legs seemed to carry him up the hillside with the ability of a mountain goat. Helen found her heart and lungs protesting as she ground up after him, so it was with some relief that she saw him halt at the top of a rise.

Puffing up to stand beside him, Helen looked down into a rocky depression. From half way up a sheer rock face came a shimmering but sparse column of water which, sparkling in the sunlight, looked like so many diamonds. The sun's heat seemed focused on the water and, before it struck the smooth, saucer-like depression in the rock beneath, it almost completely petered out so that what fell was no more than a mist which drifted airily away on the breeze. It was magical. A fairy-tale place where legends could be played out.

'Isn't it wondrous?' asked Qito.

'Fabulous,' breathed Helen.

'Imagine how long that water must have been falling. It must have taken millions of years for that drizzle to have worn away the rocks. It's inspiring,' he told her. 'Civilisations, worlds even, have been created and lost while that steady drip waited for our eyes to find it.'

Looking to Qito's absorbed profile, his eyes fired with delight, she felt a surge of privilege. This *was* a truly magical place – the kind she might have wanted to share with a lover, and for one passing moment she all but promoted Qito into that role.

'Is this where you mean to paint me?' she asked.

'Down there!' cried Qito. 'Exactly where the water strikes the ground. I mean that you should look as if the water had carved you out of the rocks.'

His enthused tone fired her so that she could see what the finished picture might be. Suddenly everything – the flight to Guadeloupe, the yacht and being stranded on the island with Qito – made sense. The chain of events which had brought her here, ragged and unplanned, now seemed like an intricately stitched tapestry. In that moment there was no other world and, it was almost possible to imagine, no other people. In such a place, she decided, anything was possible.

It was Qito who broke the mood. 'Let's go and eat,' he said, and started back down the path they had so recently created through the coarse undergrowth. Helen hesitated and gave one more lingering look into the magical dell. No matter what was to come, she decided, it was going to be worth it.

While Qito monopolised the cooking range Helen wandered through the thin screen of shrubbery to the gently lapping water's edge. Tiny fish were being driven up onto the beach with every eddy. Looking further out into the translucent waters of the lagoon she saw the flash of other bodies as they teemed, seemingly fighting for sea room, in their crowded world. Impulsively she waded knee deep into the water and laughed out loud when she saw how her legs appeared to bend in the mirrored clarity. Fish eagerly approached her intrusive legs and she yelped with delight as they fearlessly nudged against her in the hope she might present them with a meal.

Lifting her eyes to look beyond the white water breaking on the reef, she saw an endless placidity and imagined this to be a friendly place that had opened its arms in welcome and granted her peace.

A half-heard yell from Qito brought her wading back from the busy ocean to find him already greedily scooping up forkfuls of a creamy pasta and drinking deep into a glass of blood-red wine. She felt an intense sadness for the workers who, she imagined, sweated in the dark noisy factories to produce durable goods which had been brought to a paradise they would never see.

Qito indicated her plate set down on a table. The sauce was delicious – tangy enough to soften her conscience at enjoying the rich creamy indulgence. Qito, who seemed to wolf his food, was almost finished. She had barely had time to savour hers, and compliment him on it, before he was on his feet, stretching, belching delicately, and turning to go into the tent. 'I'll sleep for an hour then we'll make a start,' he told her.

Grateful not to have been invited to join his siesta Helen, after eating, walked down to the water's edge to sluice the plates and watch the fish excitedly nudge at the dregs of the meal. She idly wondered how they might react to this new taste sensation before having a pang of conscience about how it might also damage their digestive systems.

'The hell with it!' she called to them. 'A short happy life is better than a long miserable one! That's my motto.' Consoling herself with the thought that these creatures had never known a wet, grey city landscape she paused for a moment and looked towards the shrubs that screened the campsite. She was overwhelmed with a sudden stabbing need for a lover to magically appear beside her and throw her to the sand. With a guilty start she realised that this lover had no face. At that moment she would have allowed herself to be taken by anyone – including Qito who, anyway, would give her no choice.

For some reason this thought inflamed her. Going to the folding table, so immaculate with its clipped-on, pristine white linen cover, she poured more of the heavy red wine and drank it down in one huge gulp. With her head buzzing with alcohol she turned away and found a sensuously curved palm tree. She lay there, her back against the sharply ridged trunk, while letting the fingers of one hand seek out her sex.

Opening her thighs slightly, so not to disturb her evenly balanced body, she sought out her hardened and aroused bud. Moistened and ready, her fingers gently stroked the apex of her pleasure, dispatching waves of toe-curling energy to the furthest ends of her body.

Giving way totally, she felt the warm tropical air blanketing her as she rocked herself harder and faster into an unconscious riot of emotion, leading to her heavily breathed, choked words. 'Hurt me!' she gasped. 'Hurt me, take me! Hurt me!' she told the palm as she ground her naked back into the tearing ridges of the tree bark.

At the moment of orgasm there was only one thought in her head. 'Jeffrey!' she called into the still warm air, and then collapsed as all the energy flooded out of her.

Levering herself from the tree, aware that she had all but rubbed her back raw, she lay on the mattress-like texture of the sand and felt totally miserable.

'Why did you have to be married?' she asked the gritty sand.

13

Standing beneath the drifting mist of water Helen had time and space to think. Posing, she decided, was a mindless task, but the thoughts that crowded in to fill the unengaged space in her head were unsettling.

She marvelled at the pandemonium of events which had brought her to be standing naked on an uninhabited island in the company of a man whose name had, less than a week ago, been but a legend.

With only the occasional screech of an outraged bird to break the all-pervading silence, her mind was free to retrace the steps that had brought her here.

Carla. Astonishing that she had shared intimacy with yet another legend and done so without remorse or shame. The yacht, although a magnificent experience in itself, had become no more than, as her mother would have said, an 'extravagant' means of transportation peopled by beings from another world in which she remained an alien.

In boarding the jet which had brought her from Paris she had been taking flight in more senses than one. She had been fleeing from Jeffrey. A man with whom, in the intimacy of a bed, she had exposed her body, and, even more intimately, her inner fears, more totally than to any other living being. That he had harboured significant secrets while presuming to delve even deeper into her own life, had shattered her. It wasn't the fact of his being married that bothered her so much. After all, she had no such expectations of him, but that he, in the face of her confessions, should not have found time to mention it, appalled her, and told her that he was not the man she had thought him to be.

The incident with the flight crew had been sheer vengeance. As that thought entered her head she wondered why she didn't think of the intimacy with Carla in the same light, before realising that there was a very great difference. What she had done with the pilots had been of her choice, while Carla, while not coercive, had *imposed* intimacy on her.

The same was true of Jeffrey. He had come into her life like a whirlwind and, gathering her up like a latter-day Dorothy, had taken her down the yellow brick road which had led, not to Oz, but to disappointment. She had wanted Jeffrey to be the all-knowing Wizard able to grant her every wish, but instead she found him to be the Tin Man who had no heart. Of even less comfort to her was the suspicion that she had cast herself in the role of the Scarecrow – all outward appearance and no substance – a victim but now resolved to be a victim no more.

'The light's going. Let's call it a day.' Qito's voice echoed dully about the glade and was heard by Helen with enormous relief. Her arms, which she had been holding above her head, throbbed with relief when she lowered them and, for a moment, she was back in Jeffrey's penthouse recovering from his bondage of her in the conservatory.

Hoping for a glimpse at his progress Helen was disappointed to see him hastily lower a canvas flap to cover the painting. Anticipating her protest he told her she could only see it when it was complete.

Her offer to help him carry the canvas back to the camp was dismissed. 'No need,' he told her. 'There's no one else on the island.'

'It might rain.'

'Not likely and, in any case, the cover is waterproof. Moving a wet oil is likely to do more damage than leaving it where it is.' Helen saw that Qito looked drawn and tired as he turned and started leading the way through the flowering shrubs to the beach.

'Shall I help with the evening meal?' she asked.

'No. I can't stand people watching me work – whether it's painting or cooking. You go have a swim or something. I'll call you when it's ready.'

Standing on the beach watching the sun redden and start its seemingly headlong plunge over the horizon, Helen felt a sense of acute isolation as she realised the immensity of the ocean at her feet and her own insignificant occupancy of this tiny speck of earth. Had it not been for Qito she would, at that moment, have thought herself totally forgotten by the teeming outside world. She sought refuge from her thoughts by wading hip-deep into the warm tropical water and then, plunging head first, sought to swim herself into a state of exhaustion.

Tiring quickly from her initial exertions, she turned on her back and gazed upward into the even greater immensity of a sky which was already starting to light up its stars. Lazily she swam and floated until, feeling more relaxed, she was overjoyed to hear Qito's voice calling her to come to the table.

Qito had lit and strung four oil lamps from a rope suspended between the trees, while on the table lay dishes of food which stingingly reminded her she was famished.

Qito had magicked a dish of an exotic fish under a thick piquant sauce accompanied by pasta and a salad which, as she ate, filled her with a reassuring sense of well-being. 'This is delicious,' she told him. 'Where did you learn to cook like this?'

'Only when you've known real hunger,' he told her, 'do you learn to appreciate food.'

Looking at the famed face in the light of the lamps Helen remembered Carla talking about finding someone even hungrier than she had been and, with a pang of envy, she saw that the bond that had been forged between the two of them was close to unbreakable. Idly, she played with the idea of scouring the attics of London to find herself a similar cause deserving of devotion but then decided, with her luck, she would devote twenty or thirty years to a no-hoper and, in any case, thirty years was a long time to wait for posterity to catch up.

Helen ate silently for some moments, aware that Qito, having wolfed down his food, was now enjoying his third or fourth glass of wine and was watching her closely. She hoped his mind wasn't speculating on anything sexual and she was startled when he seemed to have tuned into the thought.

'Is it too boring?' he asked her.

'Posing?' she asked. 'Not boring, but I had no idea how tiring it could be.'

'I meant being here with me,' he insisted. 'With a lover this place could be paradise for a young woman. Unfortunately, when I work, I am impotent with everything but my paints, so I cannot fill that role for you even had you wanted me to.'

Uncomfortable with the thought that he might be reading her mind, she sought to divert him. 'Carla did warn me.'

Qito nodded. 'Carla is extremely possessive of me, but she earned that right.'

'Aren't you jealous of her?'

This question was greeted with a scornful laugh. 'Any man who marries a beautiful woman and imagines she cannot be tempted by other admirers is a fool. Jealousy is a total waste of energies which can be better employed in seeking redemption.'

Helen found the word 'redemption' laying heavily on the

table. Big philosophical concepts had always made her uneasy since she suspected she would never understand them. 'Are you a religious man?' she asked.

Shaking his head, Qito reached out to refill her glass. 'I believe in the soul. That is my perception of what life is – a striving to find a soul. When we have that, we have redemption. Not in the eyes of some prescient, all-seeing deity, but for ourselves. A simple self-justification for having lived.'

'You've found it then,' smiled Helen. 'In your art, I mean.'

'In the eyes of others, perhaps. I have yet to find it in myself. Redemption calls for discipline; gratification is much more accessible so we take the easier path and, in the struggle, lose purity, without which, all is lost.'

'Your philosophy sounds almost monastic.'

Roaring with laughter, Qito rose from the table. 'The monks wouldn't have me!' he cried and, reaching for a bottle of brandy, poured himself a generous draught. 'Which of them was it prayed: "God grant me chastity – but not yet!"? That is my downfall, you see?'

Helen shrugged off the question as Qito came round the table, cupped his hands about her face and lifted her bodily to her feet. 'You are a very beautiful woman,' he told her, 'but I am a tired old man and must now go to my rest. We shall meet again at dawn.' Planting a chaste kiss to each of her cheeks, he wished her goodnight and disappeared into the tent.

Helen watched the tent flap drop back into place behind him and couldn't escape a feeling of rejection. Perversely, she felt he might at least have tried something with her if only to give her the virtue of rejecting him. Now, instead, she found herself, revitalised by food, facing a long empty evening.

A stir of the palm fronds reminded her that a night breeze had sprung up, so, finding a blanket, she wrapped it around herself and was drawn towards the brilliantly moonlit beach.

There, watching the liquid silver ocean rippling under the full moon, she thought of herself as standing on the edge of eternity. Qito had said life was a quest for the soul and here, she decided, was as good a place to look for it as any other.

She spread the blanket, lay down on the still, warm sands and looked into the immense sky above her. The combination of wine and sun and Qito's philosophising – not to mention his working 'impotence' – had induced in her a warm glow of relaxation which, for Helen, always brought about a sensual awareness. Qito had been right in one thing. This was a place to be shared with a lover but where was he to come from? With one hand trailing over her groin and another cupping her breasts, she was reminded of Qito's words: 'Gratification is much more accessible,' and that, her questing fingers reminded her, was certainly true but she lacked the fantasy to stimulate herself. Carla? The pilots? Both conjured up a background of sophisticated technology which was far from her mood.

Closing her eyes, she sought out her old favourite. The regiment of sex-starved men, but even they were out of ear-shot, and she was left with nothing but the physical stimulation of herself.

It was then that some sixth sense, or, perhaps, some tiny sound, caused her to open her eyes. There, rearing above her, the whites of his eyes bright in the moonlight, stood a man. Curiously Helen felt no fear and was, only afterwards, to understand why. In the moment of opening her eyes and registering the man's presence she had imagined him a manifestation of her own longings.

After a moment of stilled surprise Helen found herself smiling a welcome. The man said nothing. His body, bare to the rope that supported his baggy sailcloth trousers, was athletically dark and polished, with the moonlight bright enough to shadow the deep contours of a powerful chest. Feeling that to speak would break the magical moment, she instead spread her thighs and arms in invitation. The man's expression barely flickered and she saw that more was demanded of her.

She laid a hand on the man's groin and, feeling him already hardening, reached for the knotted rope that supported his trousers. The man brushed aside her feebly questing fingers to quickly dispose of the knot himself. The baggy trousers slid from his taut, muscular stomach and Helen, now more fervent, took him fully into her fist, thrilled to find that her fingers could barely meet about the thickness of the still-growing penis. She drew him down to kneel beside her in the sand. Unwilling to lose her daring initiative she guided the intimidating size of him down over her belly to where her readied sheath awaited his sword.

It was then, inevitably, that she ceded all control. Now the man, his body tangy with salt, lay above her, staring directly into her widened expectant eyes, seeming to ask if she had enough courage to take him. Gathering both her wrists in one huge, roughly textured hand, he effortlessly pulled them rigidly above her head, pinning her helplessly under his body, which now bore down on her with threatening weight and slab-like solidity. Searching the man's eyes, she could see no sign of curiosity about who she might be and, more worryingly, no sign of mercy. Helen wanted to speak – to give consent, reassure him that her reaction was that he paid her homage rather than rape, but his intense, set expression muted her, and made her know that what was about to happen would be devoid of tenderness and that pain and pleasure would be mixed in equal parts.

When he moved to gently probe at the outermost sides of her pubis she could not suppress the gasp of welcome that escaped her tight lips. Urgently she rose to meet him, swallow him, but he paused, teasing her to the point of torture. Shuddering with expectation, she tried tearing her hands from his indomitable grasp to wind them round him and use her nails to goad him into her, but still he waited, his face expressionless. As her body begged, he ended the agony of expectation. And so it was with relief and apprehension that she felt him pressing gently forward, opening her up to penetrate, with deliberate slowness, deep into the centre of her soul, until she writhed, her body pleading, even as her fear mounted that she could never accommodate him. Just when she was certain she would be split in two he began to withdraw – so slowly and with such deliberation that she feared he meant to drive her to distraction.

Shamelessly, fearing that he meant to abandon her, she pressed herself against him, her legs around his broad hips, until she was all but lifted from the blanket. It was then, when she was at her most vulnerable, that he plunged with surprising accuracy deep into her to rub against the tender flesh inside her. He brought forth a gasp which ripped through the silence of the night as, having shown her the worst, he once more withdrew with tantalising slowness to hover at the gate.

There his solid cock rested, teasing and threatening before, when she least expected it, it again plunged deep into her, ravaging her senses to be immediately followed by another, even more hearty thrust, causing her to voice yet another scream of triumphant pleasure.

His movements became a mix of slow withdrawals and inward thrusts. There was no tender smile, no brush of his lips to reassure a vulnerable Helen. Instead, he held himself away from her upwardly arching body, creating a space of intense heat between them, making her skin as liquid as the fire he stoked in her loins. Not one word had passed between them as he plunged himself, huge and vibrating, inside her. The sheer strength of this assault excited her as she strained to intensify her own pain by squeezing her stretched, outer lips, vainly attempting to trap his huge, pulsating cock.

The only sounds between them had been her alternating cries and sighs, lending an almost ritual air to her exquisite torment. When she felt the helpless embrace of her own orgasm rushing through her, it seemed almost impertinent. He, this man, this stranger, this totally unknown lover, gave no sign that he felt anything other than a delight in assailing the willing flesh laid open to his mercy.

Consciously aware that this was animal savagery, she cried out in the certainty that this was right. To couple without preliminary, without even a word, was totally in tune with the primaeval setting and her own mood. Waves of orgasm swept through her, as she abandoned every doubt and restraint imposed by hundreds and thousands of years of social pretensions. Qito had spoken of redemption and now, naked and savage, she felt she was close to knowing it – red in tooth and claw!

His expression didn't alter one iota as he continued orchestrating one unstoppable wave after another – his heavy sac banging into her until, without warning, he pulled completely out of her. His grip still firm on her wrists, he raised himself until she could feel the dead weight of him between her breasts. With his free hand he took both her breasts to squeeze them tight about his huge erection so that she felt his throbbing climax long before the first gouts of his heated offering spurted forth to lay a sticky trail across her throat and lips. With this came the first sign of humanity in the man as his body relaxed and his weight came down, threatening to crush her as her freed hands forced themselves between their sweat-streaked bodies, to seek out the precious fluid that lay there.

Smearing her breasts and belly, as if anxious to coat herself in the memory of him, she reached up and tried, with the other arm, to draw him down to her, shamelessly seeking some moderating tenderness in which she could express her thanks in the only language her fevered mind could recall.

The man seemed puzzled by this gesture and, despite her protest, levered himself out of her attempted embrace to stand over her. Muted by the immensity of him, she continued to work the rapidly cooling semen in a vain attempt to soothe her aching breasts. Unable to summon the will to move, she lay, her eyes filled with the still half-erected hugeness of him, and passively watched him reach for his discarded trousers. With eyes that never left her, he put them on, tied the rope and, still expressionless, turned away.

Only then did she find the strength to move. Scrambling to her feet she saw that he was walking down the beach to where – she saw for the first time – a small dinghy-like boat, a bright lamp hung over its stern, was drawn up onto the beach.

She stood silently watching as he pushed the boat into the water and athletically leapt aboard. The rasp of rope on the pulley signalled the raising of the one triangular sail which, filling immediately, with the light night breeze, brought silent life to the boat as it arced its way seawards, leaving a phosphorescent trail in its wake.

As the boat gathered pace, Helen felt filled with something akin to awe. This stranger had appeared, full-fledged as if from a fantasy, and now was, it seemed to her inflamed imagination, returning to the mythical Valhalla from which he had sprung.

Breathless, she watched the bobbing bright light which marked his boat's passage and began, even then, to wonder if it had really happened. The tingling ache in her sex reassured her that it had, but it was still difficult to believe that anything that fierce and animalistic could be so satisfying. Drawn to the water's edge, she scooped up water to wash herself down in its warm saltiness while her eyes remained fixed on the lighted boat until it was lost in the vastness of the ocean beyond the reef.

When she did turn away she was filled, not with sadness at something lost, but a certainty that she had lived a day which would be fixed forever in her memory. Had she perhaps, she wondered, found the first strand of what Qito had called her quest for a soul?

While certain that such a momentous experience must have more significance than mere gratification, the stranger had left no room for her to take refuge in any delusion of romance.

He had come out of the night and delivered precisely what she had craved. More than enough, and certainly nothing less. If he had been a messenger from the prescient deity that Qito denied, he had left in her a soaring confidence which filled her with joy.

As she came into the tent and saw that Qito slept on undisturbed by the activities, the sounds of which must surely have carried to the campsite, she felt even greater pleasure in knowing that the experience was hers alone with no need to explain or account to anyone.

Hugging the memory of the night close to her breasts, as she might have done with a favourite teddy bear, she summoned up the image that had lodged most firmly in her mind – the moment when, satiated, he had stood over her, his still half-hardened cock standing proudly out from his muscular stomach. Her groin went into spasm as she regretted that he had not allowed her the pleasure of re-arousal – nor the wanton abandoning of self that taking him into her mouth would have given.

Had the stranger even understood how completely he had been welcomed? Demanding only her submission, he had not even allowed her the pleasure of acquiescence, but, once more safe, she acknowledged that he had been right.

They had coupled as two animals meeting in the night. No words had been used and, what words were needed, she wondered, to communicate the most basic of needs?

In the dark stillness of her desert island tent, with only Qito's nasal snorts for company, she felt herself in communion with thousands of past generations of women. Tonight she had known what it was to be truly, consentingly, *taken*. Not romanced, not seduced, with no pretence at anything other than an urgent response to a mutual need.

She knew with certainty that nothing was ever going to be the same again.

Content that she now knew something granted to few women, she slipped into the sleep of the innocent.

14

Waking the next morning Helen was pleased to find she was alone. It gave her the space to appreciate the sensation of peace and a freedom from guilt that warmed her entire body. To be able, as she was, to rise naked from the light covering of her camp-cot and step out of the tent into an unthreatened peace and bathe in warm sunshine, was, to her, the definition of what it is to be alive.

Finding coffee, still warm in a pot, she poured herself a cup and stepped through the margin of brush that separated the campsite from the beach to feel the comforting ooze of warm sand pressing between her toes. Looking out over the sparkling lagoon towards the white water of the reef, she imagined that anyone looking at her would see a body carved, as Qito had once remarked, in the shape of a smile. To be happy was one thing but to *know* it – to feel it settled about her shoulders like a comforting blanket – was sheer bliss.

Suddenly, it was important to her to establish the reality of last night's 'fantasy' encounter. Walking around a slight bend in the immaculate shoreline she came upon an area of disturbed sand. Was this the place? She wasn't sure. The tide had lapped away at where the boat might have been moored while the sun beat down, bleaching out signs of where she might have lain and received the man. Deciding it would take the skill of a forensic scientist to find traces of the night's debauch, she smiled happily in the knowledge that it didn't matter. Nothing mattered. This morning, as no other she could ever remember, she felt in love with a world which had, it seemed, suddenly chosen to focus all the blessings it could offer on herself.

Wading into the bounteous sea she washed herself down with the warm water, and felt her stimulated body sing with happiness. A distant voice, calling her name, carried to her. Looking round she could see nothing but the extravagant greenery of the island's vegetation soaring steeply up the hill towards the glade in which Qito had posed her.

Making her way up the scarcely discernible path, her body being rapidly sun-dried, she came upon Qito sketching a detail of the rock formations with such concentration that he hadn't noticed Helen's arrival.

She stood a moment and watched him at work, filled with a throbbing awareness of being in the company of genius. Bathed in the glowing awareness of privilege, she moved forward to let him know of her presence.

'There you are,' he said, straightening from his crouch. 'I was beginning to wonder if you were ever going to wake.'

'Sorry if I'm late.'

Qito shook his head. 'The light won't be right until the afternoon anyway. Have you noticed how the rocks soften in the evening light?'

Shaking her head she happily felt she would never again be able to rid her expression of the smile which seemed to start somewhere deep in her body.

'You look different this morning,' Qito murmured.

Nodding happily and, prompted by her overwhelming feeling of invulnerability, she went towards him and gently wrapped her arms about his diminutive body. 'I feel different,' she told him. 'This is a magical place. It makes me happy.' Aware that Qito was standing very still and making not the slightest attempt to return her loose embrace, she drew back her head and looked down into his widened brown eyes. 'Today anything is possible,' she told him. 'Today I love you.'

Qito's eyes softened before suddenly flaring with decision. Reaching for her hands, now resting lightly on his shoulders, he drew them aside. 'My God,' he said. 'I must have those eyes.' Turning her so that she was half faced into the sunlight filtering through the overhang of foliage, he took up his sketch pad. 'Your eyes are incredible this morning. If Carla saw them she would know.'

'Know what?'

'That you were in love.'

'With you?'

'Since I'm the only other being here she might be justified in thinking so, don't you think?'

Helen felt her inward smile turn to a satisfied grin. How little this intense man knew! Content that her fantasy was lodged safely and secretly, she found she could look back at him innocent and unblinking as he stared into her eyes, the silence broken only by the scratch of his pencil on the coarsely textured pad.

Throughout that morning Qito seemed quietly intent on capturing every tiny detail of her face and its unvarying expression of happiness, until hunger drove him to thoughts of lunch.

Dismissed from witnessing the mysteries of his preparations, she went again to swim in the lagoon, exquisitely conscious that the same water in which she bathed was, somewhere, lapping at the keel of the fisherman's boat which would, that night, bring him to her.

Called back to the campsite she found chilled melon, Parma ham, an odoriferous but delicious cheese and bread so flakily crisp that it forced its way between her teeth to edge sharply against her gums.

'Do we have a refrigerator on the island?' she asked.

Qito nodded enthusiastically. 'And a freezer.'

'That's incredible. How is it powered?'

Qito waved a hand vaguely in the direction of a panel of glass. 'Solar panels,' he said. 'Just because we have left civilisation it doesn't mean we have to reject it.'

As she ate, Helen found herself filled with unworthy suspicions about the source of Qito's gastronomic feats and decided that she would have to investigate the contents of their amazing freezer.

Immediately after eating, Qito took himself off for his hour's siesta while Helen decided to force all thoughts of skin melanoma, and Qito's insistence that she coat herself in sun blocker, from her mind while she lay on the sand and worked on getting some colour into her skin.

It was Qito's angry voice that roused her from an intense but immediately forgotten dream. 'Are you crazy?' he was shouting at her while dragging her to her feet and back to the shaded campsite. 'Look at you! You're on fire! You'll be lucky not to have sun-stroke. My God, you could get ill and we wouldn't be able to work. You Anglos go crazy in the sun!'

'I'll be all right,' she murmured, feeling her earlier felicitous mood rapidly diminishing.

Later that afternoon, posing in the sylvan glade, she needed all her will-power to disguise from Qito just how light-headed and dizzy she felt. Daunted by the belief that Qito knew just how much she was suffering, but determined not to acknowledge it, it was with great relief that she heard him finally call 'enough'.

Back at the campsite, Qito insisted she lay in the cool of

the tent where he carefully smoothed more cream to her outraged skin. Feeling quite sick, Helen was happy to agree to his suggestion that she rest while he prepared the evening meal.

She had gone to bed with no intention of sleeping for any length of time but when she woke she found the evening had slipped into the deep silence of night. Qito was asleep and it was with the excitement of a daring teenager eluding the vigilance of a parent that she started towards the beach. She had been staring out to sea, eagerly watching for the dancing light on the stern of the fisherman's boat for some minutes before she found the night breeze, striking chill on her breasts, intolerable and turned back to sneak out a blanket.

The moment she came out of the tent she saw, through the shrubs, the gleam of a light out at sea and rushed, breathless, to watch with rising excitement as the boat found the break in the reef and turned towards the shore.

Unable to contain her patience, discarding the blanket, she waded into the still-warm water for some yards before plunging headlong into it and swimming out to meet the oncoming boat. There was a moment when she feared her headlong dash would end in disaster as he, not seeing her in the dark water, might have run her down. Seeing her only at the last moment he turned the boat so that she was swept along its side. With one immensely strong arm he reached down to lift her bodily from the water and cast her, breathless and spread, across the wooden slats at the bottom of the boat – which were still slimy from the entrails of past catches.

There was no pretence possible between them. Both knew why she had come so eagerly to greet him, but he had other things to do. Turning aside from her brazen, open invitation, he knocked away a piece of wood which brought the single sail crashing down the mast.

Flinging out a sea anchor he turned to her as if she were but one more chore to be taken care of before work could begin. Pulling away the rope that held up his trousers he came to stand magnificently naked and fully aroused over her liquid body.

Scrambling up, she would have paid homage to his risen flesh with her mouth but this man had no patience for such subtleties and, instead, caught her up, turned her around and penetrated her from behind – all in one swift movement which knocked the breath from her body.

Ravaging her, she felt his hands tight about her shoulders as if to prevent her escape, he brought her gasping to a rapid climax and, while she hoped for more, he pulled out of her and let her feel the shower of him pulsing onto her arching back. With a murmur of protest she tried to turn to take some part of him into her mouth but, instead, found herself lifted into his arms and carried over the side of the boat. Fearing that he simply meant to dump her, she rejoiced when he stepped into the now-shallow water and waded ashore while she felt a featherweight in his arms.

Dumping her unceremoniously on the sand he came down heavily on her, her legs pressed wide and high, and she was astonished to feel his already fully rearoused flesh probing deep into her.

Anxious to hear him speak, she tried to provoke him with urgent murmurings, but received only grunts as his hugeness delved deeper and more painfully into her. Reaching a climax, she wound her legs about him, gripping him tightly, determined that, this time, he would deliver himself into her and not on her belly, but this man had some deeply imprinted objection to coming inside her and, with great force, wrenched himself from her and levered himself upward. Not to be cheated, letting out a cry of frustration, Helen grabbed at his already erupting penis and sunk its convulsive size deep into her mouth. He made a move as if to protest but his orgasm had weakened him, so she had little difficulty in easing him onto his back where she triumphantly sucked on him until the last convulsive spurt. Straddling him, she looked down into his closed face and felt that she had conquered. The beast, now moaning with pleasure, lay vanquished between her thighs as she felt a soaring sense of fulfilment.

'Say something!' she told him harshly.

The man's eyes opened and she was shocked to see in them a flicker of shame.

Suddenly, it occurred to her that it was possible that no woman had ever taken him in her mouth before. Their few encounters had been animal – wild, even. Could it be that he thought of women as simple victims who could only be taken by brute force?

As the man continued to stare silently up at her, as if at some strange alien species, she was overwhelmed with the feeling that she had made him vulnerable – frightened of her, even – and moved to reassure him. Moving her body down over his she laid her head on the firm muscles of his tensed stomach and reached for his now sad-looking penis. Taking it gently between two fingers, she reached out with her tongue and touched its most sensitive point.

His reaction was instantaneous. Two huge hands reached about her ribs and lifted her bodily, as if she were no more substantial than a china doll, then turned her so that she was held at arm's length above his body with only her legs drooping to contact the ground. The breath driven from her, she felt totally vulnerable as fear rushed in to replace her earlier feeling of superiority.

His lips parted to reveal a shining row of perfect teeth and she felt herself being lowered onto his waiting cock. There she felt his flesh re-erected and waiting for her. Gasping at his entry, still dangling helpless above his head, she was effortlessly raised and lowered as he teased her by plunging her deep down onto him and then lifting her so that only the point of him nudged at her flowing sex.

He was reasserting himself, reminding her that he was master here and that her attempts to take the initiative were not to be held of any account. The ache of her ribs, where he held her, lessened in direct ratio to the reawakened fire between her legs. Gasping, breathless, she felt deliciously helpless and used. As her body burned, her mind reeled with the thought that she was, literally, no more than a toy in his hands to be used and tossed aside like any other masturbatory aid.

In the fear and humiliation she found an intense and worrying excitement. The power of the man that could so easily dispose of her as he wished, brought her quickly to climax and, as she gasped out her appreciation, she heard him murmuring the first word she had ever heard him speak. '*Puta!*' he growled.

Two things then happened so synchronously that they appeared for a moment to be cause *and* effect.

The man rammed her rigid body down onto his throbbing flesh, surging fully and cruelly deep into her, while a blinding white light shone into her face.

Concentrating on the one, and, for the moment, ignoring the other, she yelled out in climactic orgasm which became protest, as the man under her unceremoniously dropped her and scrambled to his feet.

Lying abandoned and helpless in the soft, warm sand she heard Qito's voice murmuring something that sounded like an Italian apology. Abstractedly she realised that her cries must have drawn Qito to the scene but she, still light-headed, found she didn't care.

The torch was switched off and allowed her to see Qito turning away down the beach. The man had disappeared by the time she looked for him and, resenting the abrupt end to their encounter, she got to her feet and hurried towards where the boat had been beached.

Frustrated to see the bright lamp at the boat's stern already some metres from the beach, her first impulse was to call out and reassure him that there was nothing to fear, but the hand she had raised to wave him to come back, went instead to smother the cry that had come to her lips as she stood and watched helplessly as the beacon that signalled her pleasure sailed away.

Coming back to the campsite she found Qito, his back resolutely turned to her, making coffee. Feeling curiously assertive she spoke to challenge his silence. 'Did we wake you?' she asked.

Qito turned and looked at her. 'Do you know what "*puta*" means?' he asked her and, when she shook her head, went on. 'It means whore,' he said, before walking round her and into the tent.

Had there been a solid door on the tent frame Helen felt certain he would have slammed it. Instead, she savoured the word and its meaning in her head to combine it with the almost certain feeling that Qito had been jealous. Self-embracing her tingling body she was even tempted to offer herself to Qito as he lay on his tent cot, but instead she turned away to the beach where, registering that the light of the dinghy was now far out to sea, she waded into the water and washed herself.

The following morning she woke to find Qito fussily working the camping oven and producing hot crispy croissants while keeping his back turned, firmly, towards her.

Amused at his petulance she sang out a 'Good morning' with all the genuine happiness that she felt.

Putting the coffee pot heavily in front of her he stood over her with just enough silence to let his annoyance show. 'Who is he?' he demanded.

'None of your business,' she told him, happily ladling butter and delicious apricot jam on her already overrich pastry.

'It is my business when you are too tired to stand still!'

'Yesterday wasn't anything to do with that. I'd had too much sun, that's all. Besides, I'm not your employee. I do as I want.'

For a moment she thought Qito was going to explode with anger but, to her relief, the fight went out of him as he sank down to sit at the table and look steadily at her. 'Jeffrey is my friend,' he said flatly.

'It has nothing to do with him either.' She let Qito wait while she sank her teeth greedily into the flaky croissant. 'He's married.'

Qito looked genuinely surprised. 'Married?' he asked. 'Jeffrey? No. It's not possible!' Qito paused a moment as if searching his memory to see if he could be mistaken before going on. 'I have known Jeffrey since he appeared on my doorstep fifteen years ago. A tall, skinny student who could talk sensibly about my work. We have been friends ever since. I have never known him to be married.' Qito paused a moment. 'Who told you of this marriage?'

'His assistant.'

Enlightenment, along with a knowing smile that bordered on the amused, crossed Qito's face. 'You mean that pretty girl – what's her name . . . ?'

About to supply Annabel's name, Helen was crushed with the sudden realisation of just how precipitately she had accepted Annabel's word. It was obvious that Qito didn't believe Jeffrey capable of such a deception and, in the colder perspective of time and distance, she found it hard to believe herself.

What if it were not true – or a misunderstanding? The thought that her every revenge might have had no basis appalled her.

Looking into Qito's waiting sceptical eyes, she found the only response was defensive. 'Why would Annabel have lied about something like that?'

Raising his hands as if to ward off an intruder, Qito smiled. 'You are asking me, a *man*, to divine the motives of a *woman*? Impossible! All I can say is that, until you have spoken to Jeffrey, I would caution you to withhold judgement.' As he was speaking, Qito gathered up his sketch pad and bundle of pencils. 'I'm off to do some work on my own,' he told her. 'We'll work on the canvas this afternoon.'

Alone with her thoughts, Helen considered what she might do if Annabel had been lying or misleading her. Would Jeffrey ever forgive her for her 'revenge'? The likelihood of keeping it from him after last night's discovery by Qito seemed distant. The more she thought, the more her newly discovered paradise became fragmented and fragile.

Not for the first time, she felt bits falling off her life. Suddenly the glorious colours of the flora, the fine white sand of the beach and the pristine sparkle of the ocean, became a mocking reminder of her isolation.

Jeffrey had reimposed himself into her consciousness and his presence made her feel guilt.

Wandering aimlessly in search of something to distract her thoughts, she came upon the chest freezer under its canopy of solar panels and, remembering Qito's boasted skill at preparing meals, lifted the lid to look inside.

There, arranged in neatly labelled plastic boxes, were all the meals they had so far enjoyed and several that were, as yet, untouched. So Qito, for all his worldly pre-eminence, had been prepared to let her believe he was a master chef, when all the meals had been prepared on the yacht and delivered to them frozen, needing only to be de-frosted.

Closing the lid, Helen felt the discovery somehow more profound, and less amusing, than it might have been in any other context.

Was deceit endemic to the male species, she wondered?

15

That afternoon Qito worked with greater intensity than ever before. He had, previously, broken off to comment on the cries of the birds and identified them for her – his knowledge of the flora and fauna of the island was impressive – but this afternoon he worked in total silence which, she felt, was creating a distance between them.

As she posed, she painfully considered just how she might face Jeffrey if Qito's confidence in him proved to be justified while, at the same time, resenting the confusion that the previously unconsidered possibility had brought. She had behaved mindlessly, she decided, and felt that retribution, should he take the trouble, would be quite painful.

Her lurking masochism, driven by guilt, roared into her head on a flight of fantasy. Standing under Qito's penetrating gaze she wished she could close down time and space so that she could immediately – this instant – confront Jeffrey with her suspicions so that he would have to either confirm or disprove them. Quite suddenly the prospective confrontation had taken on a quite exciting connotation – whichever way it went. The only immediate question her sexuality presented was what was she to do when, as she confidently expected he would, her mysterious fisherman lover reappeared?

Her mind told her one thing while her body urged quite another. The dilemma was still unresolved when, after a silent dinner – which reminded her of Qito's posturing as a resourceful chef – Qito took himself off to his bed.

Tonight she decided to take a bottle of the delicious heady wine down to the beach and there sat on her blanket and gazed out into the lagoon, her eyes keening for first sight of the lantern which marked the dinghy's progress. Uncertain of the passage of time – she wore no watch – she waited in vain for what seemed several hours before, wrapping herself in the blanket, she lay back on the sand and drifted off into the welcoming arms of a wine-induced drowse.

It was the birds' dawn chorus that woke her in time to witness a spectacular sunrise. She woke irritated and chilled and, spurning an early morning bathe, turned through the shrubs to the camp-site. For once she had risen before Qito and, feeling an urgent desire for coffee, found matches and started the propane gas cooker. She hesitated to fetch croissants from the freezer since this would indicate to Qito that she had discovered his secret but then did it anyway, popping them into the oven to crisp.

'What are you doing?'

Looking round she saw Qito had come out from the tent and was standing watching her. She was almost embarrassed to notice that his naked belly was adorned with a soaring erection. 'Making breakfast,' she told him, then, brimming with devilment, turned to fully face him and fixed her eyes on the exclamation mark at his groin. 'On the other hand, would you like me to do something about that?'

Qito frowned darkly at her and, turning away, moved some way into the bushes where she heard the splash of his early morning urination. 'There goes your hard-on!' she sang gaily after him. 'It's too late now!'

When a still-disapproving, but now detumescent, Qito returned, he found her already at the table eating a hot croissant and coffee. When he reached for the coffee pot she reproved him. 'First wash your hands,' she said as primly as she could manage.

'You're in a funny mood this morning,' he said acidly. 'What happened? Didn't your mysterious lover show up?'

'None of your business.'

Qito laughed and sat at the table and, ignoring her injunction, helped himself to the coffee. 'So he didn't! I probably frightened him off. Maybe he thought I was an angry husband or lover.'

She felt the urge to puncture the pleasure he was having at her expense so said: 'More likely *grandfather*!' but immediately regretted it when Qito, provoked, got up and walked away from her. Rising, she went after him to find him looking out across the lagoon. 'I'm sorry,' she said, putting a hand to his broad shoulder. 'You're right. He didn't come and I am irritable.'

Turning to her, his face wreathed in a smile as warm as the morning sun, he put out his strong arms, and she, feeling curiously self-conscious, went into his embrace. 'And I'm a silly old man,' he told her. 'You know just how silly? Seeing you with that man, I was jealous.'

Enveloped in a rush of warm affection she looked into his soulful eyes. 'And not only that,' she smiled, 'you're an old fraud!' In the face of Qito's offended expression she went on, 'You've not been cooking – you've been defrosting!'

'When did you find me out?' he asked with heavy mock contrition.

'Yesterday.'

Nodding, Qito pulled her back into the embrace. 'What we old men lack in virility we have to make up for with guile. Forgive me?' he asked.

Nodding into his shoulder, she murmured. 'We have to make allowances for a genius.'

Qito laughed and thrust her away. 'What was it you said: "Too late"? You were quite right! Twenty years too late. My God, that Jeffrey is a lucky man! Not only is she beautiful, a perfect model and knows what she wants but is also charitable to old men. Get thee from me, Satan's child!' he cried before grabbing up her hand and kissing it.

Together, hand in hand, she aware of a feeling of great privilege, they walked into the lagoon's water and indulgently washed each other down.

Later that afternoon, as she posed, she was consumed by the intensity which Qito brought to his work, and regretted that, while he looked at her, he saw only a shape worth putting to canvas. Having said he had been jealous of her fisherman and complimented her outrageously, she discovered a longing to seduce the great man. She imagined herself, some distant day, opening a newspaper to read of his passing and regretting not having taken the opportunity which currently presented itself. The incident in Jeffrey's penthouse she discounted, since that had been for Jeffrey's pleasure more than anyone else's. Standing there she determined that before this idyll ended she would make a memory of a shared moment with Qito.

It seemed that moment had come when, as the light began to fade, Qito called a halt and, coming to her, took one of her wrists firmly in hand to lead her to a glade of bamboo.

'What are you doing?' she asked as he took a vine, previously tied to one of the bamboos, and bending it down, tied her wrist to it.

'Taming a wild banshee,' he told her.

She protested further, but to no avail, when he tied her other wrist and, letting go of the springy bamboos, had her stretched helplessly between the two of them. About to protest that she had daydreamed something gentler and more intimate between them, she watched, silently aghast, as he started to move away. 'You can't leave me here like this!' she shouted after him. Unmoved, Qito sauntered away into the gathering night and didn't look back.

Her mind in tumult, it took her several moments to find the breath to scream further protest. Aware that the spaces between the trees were already darkening she had begun to feel real fear when, without warning, she felt herself grabbed from behind. The man, there was no doubt it was a man, put one arm about her breasts while the other sought out and penetrated her groin. Outraged and screaming, she tried to twist herself out of the unknown man's grasping arms.

'Be quiet,' said Jeffrey's voice in her ear.

Her body instantly stilled, her mind went into confused orbit. 'Where did you come from?' she gasped.

'Never mind that now. There are urgent things to be done to you.'

Even as she twisted in her bonds, trying to catch a glimpse of his face, she felt him probing, then penetrating her to unleash in her an outrush of frustration. Still she protested. 'No!' she cried. 'We have to talk!'

'Don't talk,' he murmured, his voice now harsh. 'Screw!'

Her writhing had dragged one of her loosely tied wrists free and she swung on the other still-tied wrist, to stumble and almost fall as Jeffrey continued to hold her, now bent almost double, and, mercilessly impaling her, took all the breath from her body and smothered the protests of her brain.

'Bastard!' she screamed.

'Filthy slut,' he answered her.

'I *hate* you!'

'You disgust me.'

Just then, at the expense of rope burns, she managed to free her second wrist and, with a violent thrashing movement, pulled herself away from the urgent liquid fire he had stoked deep inside her and turned to face him with fists bunched and anger flaring.

Her small victory was short-lived as, his face fired like some wild forest creature, he caught her up and, his weight bearing her to the ground, again penetrated between her defiant thighs. Pinned firmly now, she was consumed by the moment. All thoughts of betrayal and guilt fled from a mind overwhelmed by the sensations he was creating. Nothing mattered now other than to answer her bodily urge to surrender. Her legs wound around his heaving body, she dug her nails deep into his back, the better to urge him even deeper and more firmly into her.

'Yes!' she cried as naked lust forced her body to rise to meet his every thrust. As he savaged deep into her their cries rose into the night canopy, stilling those of the other night creatures who, it seemed, had paused to lend an indulgent ear to the human intruders so noisily locked together on the floor of their domain.

'Yes!' she screamed again as the now familiar surge laid siege to her breathless body as he led her to all-consuming completion.

After the mutuality of climax they lay in each other's arms, he still lodged deep in her, and the rasping of their desperate lungs fighting for breath was now the only sound in the quieted night, until she spoke. 'Annabel told me you were married.'

'Annabel lied,' he told her.

Immediately assailed by two conflicting reactions – relief and a flood of guilt at her precipitate 'revenge' – she groaned. 'Oh no!'

Jeffrey raised his head to look at her. 'You're disappointed?' he asked.

Everything she had done since fleeing from him flashed before her with lightning speed and explicit detail. 'Not with you. With me,' she murmured. 'Why would she lie about something like that?'

'Jealousy.'

'You had an affair with her?'

'No. It seems that for years she's been having an "affair" with me. Purely mental, I hasten to add. I sensed it but ignored it. I have a strict rule never to mix business with pleasure.'

'She just invented it?'

'Not entirely. I *was* married. We were students – I was in a state of depression. The whole thing was madness. The marriage barely outlasted the honeymoon before we both agreed it had all been a terrible mistake. We waited the statutory two years and got a no-fault divorce by mutual agreement.'

'And that's all?'

'That's all,' he answered flatly.

Feeling that 'madness' was the word to describe her own state of mind since running away from Paris, she fell into a morose silence.

'What's the matter?' he asked.

Pushing him from her she rose, only now aware that her back had been pressed into a patch of prickly thorns, and shook her head. 'There's things I have to tell you,' she murmured.

'Confessions?' he asked.

Only able to muster a nod in reply she turned away desolate in the knowledge that she had behaved badly – at the very least, foolishly – and terrified in case he would not forgive her. As they stumbled through the night towards the campsite she sought to divert her fear-filled mind. 'You still haven't told me how you got here.'

'Annabel confessed what she'd done and showed me the fax. I called Carla on the yacht, heard where you were, and took the next plane.'

Mention of Carla and the yacht made her realise that her idyll on the island was at an end. Attempting to make light of it she said: 'I suppose that means I'll have to put some clothes on,' but inwardly she felt she was losing a great deal more than that.

It was wildly impossible but she had a longing for things to stay just as they were – she left to wander primitively naked, visited at night by an undemanding lover, and leaving the complications of civilised relationships to others less enlightened.

Coming to the campsite she saw the yacht's crew had all but dismantled it, leaving little of the tranquil sanctuary she had known.

Tsai Lo, appearing out of the shadows, came forward with a broad smile, holding out a sarong for her to wind about her body. Looking into the girl's porcelain beauty she was reminded to add her name to the list of confessions she would have to make. Suddenly the thought of returning to the sophistication of the yacht overwhelmed her. Turning to Jeffrey, aware that her voice was tinged with desperation, she asked, 'Couldn't we stay on the island tonight? There's so much to talk about.'

'But they've taken everything away,' Jeffrey protested.

'It doesn't get cold at night. We could sleep on the beach.'

'You're nuts!' he told her, smiling. 'Besides the Captain's anxious about a hurricane warning and wants to sail immediately. We can talk on the yacht *and* sleep in a bed.'

Defeated, she allowed herself to be handed into the waiting launch and silently, morosely, even, watched the boat's growing wake stretching back to the island like some umbilical cord that must inevitably snap. The sense of impending loss caused a shiver to run through her.

Thinking her chilly, Jeffrey put his arm round her shoulders. 'I have a confession to make as well,' he said.

'You do?'

Jeffrey nodded. 'I find your interest in my marital status highly flattering.'

'Oh? Why?'

'Could it be that your thoughts have wandered in the same direction as mine?'

Feeling that he had broken into her mind and was rifling through her innermost thoughts, Helen reacted defensively. 'I don't know what you're talking about,' she told him, adding hastily, 'and I don't think I want to.' When his response was merely to chuckle she felt infuriated. 'Anyway – we have yet to talk.'

The launch was coming alongside the anchored yacht and she took the opportunity to distance herself from further discussion by standing up as if preparing to disembark.

Jeffrey didn't let her go that easily.

'What will we talk about? Carla and Tsai? Qito? Your fisherman?'

Shocked that he knew about even that, she was pleased to note he had left out the two pilots from the roll call. 'Among others,' she said tartly and got perverse pleasure at seeing the surprise on his face.

At that moment the launch crew turned to hand her to the lowered gangway and she stepped out of the small boat and climbed to the deck. Not waiting for Jeffrey, she made her way aft to the stairway that led down to the stateroom deck.

Coming into the stateroom she felt overwhelmed with a sense of claustrophobia. The walls seemed to be closing in on her. She felt an almost panic-stricken impulse to turn and run before it was too late. Too late for what, she had no idea. Could it be that after only three days without walls she had grown unaccustomed to being in an enclosed space?

When Jeffrey followed her into the stateroom she felt a spasm of resentment at his presumption. Staring at him as if at an intruder, she felt confused. 'Who told you about the fisherman?' she asked, even though it was blatantly obvious.

'Qito saw you.'

Perversely aware that she had him at a disadvantage, but not sure why, she insisted, 'Saw us doing what?'

'According to Qito you were enjoying yourself.'

'True.' The word exploded from her. 'And I hope you realise that it's all your fault!'

'*My* fault?'

'Certainly. If it wasn't for you I would still be a virtuous widow.' Seeing his stunned silence as an opportunity for a good exit, Helen turned on her heels and went into the bathroom, where she firmly locked the door.

Unwinding the sarong, which though light seemed suddenly constricting, she was about to turn on the shower when she caught sight of herself in the mirror and came to an astonished halt. She barely recognised the honey-coloured creature reflected there. Hair wild, eyes savage, breasts more prominent than ever above slimmed-down ribs and belly, even she could find herself exciting.

'You've changed,' she told herself.

When there came a knock on the door she assumed it must be Jeffrey and called a caustic 'Go away!' only to hear Tsai's voice.

'Miss Helen?' asked the melodious voice. 'Do you need anything?'

Crossing to the door, Helen looked beyond the smiling girl to see no sign of Jeffrey. 'Come in,' she told her. 'I feel like being indulged. You can wash my back.'

Tsai's eyes rounded with pleasure. 'You have such a beautiful colour,' the girl smiled, stripping herself of her cheongsam. 'Afterwards I will give you a beautiful massage. Yes?'

Standing under the shower with Tsai's expert hands soaping her back, she found it titillating to imagine Jeffrey's face, should he come upon them both just as they were now. So titillating that she found herself turning, without inhibition, to present her naked breasts to the soothing caress of Tsai's hands.

Very titillating, she decided.

When Jeffrey returned it was to find Helen stretched naked on the massage table and the subject of Tsai's expertise. Watching him reflected in a mirror above her head, she was amused to see him hesitate and, thinking himself unobserved, take a moment to admire the sleek lines of Tsai's body. Thinking she had given him more than enough time, she turned on to her back and pretended to see him for the first time. 'Jeffrey, you're just in time! There's a phrase running through my head and I can't remember where it came from – perhaps you'd know?'

Looking puzzled Jeffrey came a pace nearer the table and looked down on her. 'What phrase?'

'I don't know if I remember it exactly but it goes something like: "Brave are they that dare to do what others scarcely dare to dream." Do you know it?'

'No. I don't think I've heard it before.'

Sitting up, and for no good reason feeling extravagantly pleased with herself, she put out her arms to Jeffrey who, awkwardly, came to the side of the table and returned the embrace. 'It's true though, isn't it? We "dared to do", didn't we?'

'You make it sound as if it is over.'

'Not "over". Perhaps a little different.'

'In what way?'

Lying back on the massage bench, Helen allowed herself a long, deep reflective smile. 'Who knows?' she asked as she took Tsai's hands and led her to stand at her head then lay her hands on her breasts. 'Did you have something to tell me?' she asked a startled, completely engrossed Jeffrey.

'Yes,' he said, then seemed to hesitate as if his mind, centred on the sight of Tsai's hands moving over Helen's breasts, had wandered from the subject.

'What?'

'What?' he echoed as if looking at the two naked girls had completely distracted his thoughts.

'What is it you have to tell me?'

'Oh!' cried Jeffrey, flushing guiltily. 'Yes. The Captain's decided not to sail. Apparently, the hurricane is skirting the area just out to sea and he thinks it might be dangerous.' Jeffrey's voice was trailing away as his highly eroticised thoughts centred on Helen's openly naked body.

'So we could have spent the night on the island?'

'Sorry?' asked Jeffrey, as if he hadn't heard a word she had been saying.

Delighting in the distraction she and Tsai were providing, Helen laughed. 'Come here,' she said, waving to a place at the side of the bench where she could reach him. Jeffrey obediently moved to one side of the bench where, reaching out, Helen felt him standing erect under his linen trousers. 'Darling!' she cried, as if delighted by the discovery. 'Is that for me or for Tsai?'

Jeffrey flushed with embarrassment as Tsai failed to totally smother the giggle that had come to her throat. Jeffrey, totally distracted, looked from Tsai to Helen in confusion as she sought to unzip his trousers and bring his risen flesh into view. 'Helen!' he protested. 'We're expected for dinner!'

Her fist firmly encompassing him, she murmured, 'You didn't answer my question ...'

'What question?' Jeffrey asked, embarrassment giving edge to his voice.

'Is your cock hard in tribute to me or Tsai?'

'That's a ridiculous question!' Jeffrey protested.

'To us both, then?' she insisted.

Forcibly removing her hand, Jeffrey turned away, attempting to stuff himself back into his trousers, until Helen's ringing voice caused him to hesitate. 'I wouldn't do that if I were you, darling.'

Turning, Jeffrey looked startled. 'What are you talking about?'

'You have to be punished,' she said with a bright smile.

'Punished?' he asked. 'What for?'

Noting that he had asked only the reason for his impending 'sentence' without questioning the principle, Helen, much emboldened, went on: 'For spreading false information that deprived me of another night on the island.'

Jeffrey's expression froze as he stared at her while, apparently, searching for a suitable response. 'We'll discuss this later!' he said firmly and made a dash for the bedroom door. Delighted to see him retreating in confusion, Helen let her laugh follow him as he called from the bedroom. 'You'd better hurry up. Dinner will be waiting.'

Feeling that she had won an, as yet, unquantifiable victory, she lay back and looked up into Tsai's serious, slightly puzzled, face.

'I've definitely changed,' she told the puzzled girl.

16

That night dinner was a noticeably subdued affair. Helen, sensing that Jeffrey was wary of her, felt filled with a wholly new self-confidence, while Carla's unusually subdued mood and constant assessing glances, made Helen feel that she had, somehow, moved to centre stage in this glittering company. Martinez, the yacht's owner, paid particular attention to her every request and Qito was positively beaming every time he looked her way. Further confirmation that Carla saw her as a threat came from the total silence of Carla's 'creature', Jimmy, who reflected his 'mistress's' mood by sullenly avoiding eye contact with anybody.

'Qito tells me he has created a masterpiece,' Carla's voice, laced with ice, rang down the length of the stateroom table to Helen. 'You must have offered a great deal of "inspiration",' Carla added with barely disguised sarcasm.

Helen smiled sweetly. 'I don't know about that. I just did what I was told.'

Carla's response was heavy with threat. 'What a good little girl you must be,' she said.

'I do do my best whenever possible.'

'And so generous, too,' smiled Carla with all the warmth and affection of a cobra about to strike.

Jeffrey's voice, unusually hesitant, broke the silence that followed. 'Are we going to be permitted a sneak preview?' he asked.

'There is still work to do,' said Qito. 'Perhaps tomorrow night – after dinner.'

'How lovely!' cried Carla. 'We must make it an occasion.' Then, surprisingly turning to Martinez, she added: 'Musn't we, Carlos?'

Martinez looked a little uncomfortable before murmuring, 'If you insist, Carla.'

Carla nodded. 'I do,' before sipping on her wine and challenging Helen with a direct stare. 'I've already seen the result of Qito's devotional labour and come to *my* conclusion. You will all have the chance to play at critics for the evening – and, afterwards, come to your own verdicts,' before adding with a gay laugh, 'along with plaudits and punishment, of course.'

Since everyone at the table had immediately looked at her, Helen had no doubt to whom the last word had been intended. Under the flare of Carla's steady gaze she found herself confused by feelings of resentment which immediately rose only to be instantly swamped in a contrary emotion of excitement. Inwardly aware that her shiny new armour of confidence was being exposed as only paper thin, she looked to Jeffrey for comfort, only to see that he seemed to be, not only aware of, but amused by the conflict that Carla's words had created in her.

Quelled by Carla's display of petulance, Helen took the first opportunity she could of escaping onto the deck. A multitude of seductive perfumes wafted on the evening breeze, reminding her of the short idyll that now seemed to have been irretrievably lost. She could barely summon the will to turn to greet Jeffrey as he joined her at the ship's rail.

'What's wrong with you tonight?' he asked.

'With me?' she asked. 'What about Carla? Why is she being so bitchy to me?'

Putting a warming arm about her shoulders, Jeffrey laughed.

'That's obvious. She's eaten up with jealousy about your days alone with Qito. You should be flattered.'

'Well, I'm not and she's got no reason. Nothing happened between me and Qito on the island.'

Jeffrey smiled. 'I believe you. But you don't know what Qito's been saying. He takes a great deal of adolescent pleasure in seeing Carla provoked.'

'Then I'll put the record straight the first chance I get.'

'And spoil Qito's pleasure? Surely not?'

Helen turned to Jeffrey angrily. 'You saw and heard her in there. I was starting to worry in case she came at me with a knife!'

Jeffrey's scornful laugh made Helen turn away with an unsettling feeling of anger. Still bristling, she was suddenly alert.

Out to sea, obviously approaching the island, she saw the lonely bobbing light that marked the stern of her mysterious lover's dinghy.

Overwhelmed with a rush of warmth to the man's loyalty – he must surely have seen the moored yacht – she, unawares, spoke her unbidden thought out loud. 'He's come back!'

'Who has?' asked Jeffrey before going on to answer his own question. 'Your fisherman?'

Nodding, Helen pointed out the light on the moonlit sea. 'That's his boat.' She hadn't realised how silent and thoughtful Jeffrey had become until, turning to him, she asked. 'Why does he have that bright light hanging over the water like that?'

It seemed Jeffrey had to wrench his mind to her question before answering. 'To attract fish. The light excites them and brings them in close – like moths to a flame.'

Involuntarily, Helen found herself shuddering. 'Weird!' she murmured.

'What's weird?'

'To be standing on the deck of this sophisticated pleasure machine in sight of a primaeval game of life and death.'

Jeffrey was silent for a moment as both watched the light getting ever closer to the island. 'It seems fish aren't the only creatures he draws to his lamp.'

'What does that mean?'

'You want to go to him, don't you?'

Meaning to make a pretence at protest she turned to look directly at Jeffrey's serious face and suddenly read there a complete understanding of the other, darker, impulse which had risen in her. 'Yes,' she said, flatly. 'As a matter of fact, I do.'

'Then go,' said Jeffrey. 'I won't stop you.'

They were still making silent challenge and answer when Carla's voice cut through the night. 'But I will!' she said, coming to stand close to the startled Helen. 'One man – two men – aren't enough for you, huh? You want to play the slut for some seaborne peasant!'

Bridling, Helen demanded, 'What business is it of yours?'

Carla answered with an equally brittle tone. 'Jeffrey is my friend and Qito is my husband! I'll not allow you to insult either one.'

Startled to find herself angered but able to stand up to the formidable Carla, Helen flared back: 'If you're bothered by what might have happened between me and Qito on the island, you can relax. Nothing happened. But, in the second place, it's downright patronising of you to appoint yourself defender of either Qito or Jeffrey. They're both old enough to speak for themselves. In the third place, I don't give a damn what you think!'

The resonating silence that followed Helen's outburst was broken by a curiously disarming Carla. 'Our little mouse has grown fangs!' she cried in tones suggesting a delightful discovery. 'It's obvious that something must have happened on the island.' Reaching out a hand she laid it gently to Helen's face. 'However shall we tame this wildcat?' she asked of Jeffrey.

'I don't think I want her tamed,' he answered.

'Are you going to let her go ashore then?'

'That's her decision.'

'And will you take her back without conditions?'

'Yes.'

Smiling beneficently at Helen, Carla went on: 'How wonderful young love can be. And you, lovely child, how did you mean to get ashore?'

Looking out to the seductively moonlit island, lying less than a hundred metres from the yacht's anchorage, she turned back to Carla to speak defiantly, 'Swim, if I have to!'

Carla laughed with delight. 'I think you should. Life should never be too simple. And what of your return – what then?'

Puzzled, Helen asked, 'What do you mean?'

'All indulgence has a price. We shall have to punish you on your return, don't you agree?'

Looking into Jeffrey's face Helen could see the equivocation in his expression. Challenged and feeling that to retreat now would forever condemn her in his eyes to weakness, she braced herself to once more face Carla and, realising that Carla's threat merely added spice to the excitement, said, 'All right. I agree.'

'Lovely!' cried Carla and then, reaching forward, opened the single catch that held Helen's dress, leaving her naked. Helen kicked off her shoes and turned to the yacht's rail. 'Did you think I wouldn't dare?' she asked Jeffrey.

'Just remember to come back,' he called as Helen, waving, turned to face the ocean and made as perfect an arc as she could in diving into the sea.

Jeffrey watched her strike for the shore, leaving a glowing phosphorescence in her wake, and tried not to think of this as rejection.

'What a wonderful girl!' breathed Carla in genuine admiration as they both stood watching Helen, clearly visible in the silver moonlight.

Jeffrey was about to reply when the First Officer appeared at their side and, leaning forward, peered into the water. 'Did someone just dive over the side?'

'Yes. Helen did. Why?' asked Jeffrey.

'Because this afternoon we spotted a bull-nose shark in the lagoon!'

'Oh dear,' said Carla. 'Are they one of the dangerous kinds?'

'Vicious,' said the excited First Officer. 'More dangerous than the Great White. Can you see her?'

It was then, scanning the beach, that they saw Helen rise from the surf and trot gently along on the dry sand.'

'She made it!' breathed Jeffrey.

'She still has to get back,' Carla reminded him as the First Officer moved off.

Seeing a teasing light in Carla's eye, Jeffrey had a sudden insight. 'You knew, didn't you?'

Carla affected a casual air, 'I do believe that someone did mention that we shouldn't swim.' Not even bothering to disguise her total insincerity, she went on, 'It completely slipped my mind until that charming officer reminded me.'

'She might have been killed!' Jeffrey protested.

'What is life without, at least, a little excitement?' Carla asked. 'However, nothing was lost.'

'Yes, but what do I do now? I can't let her swim back in the morning, but suppose she decides to come back before then?'

Carla shrugged. 'It sounds to me as if you will have to maintain a whole night vigil.' Leaning in, Carla kissed Jeffrey firmly on the cheek. 'Pleasant thoughts,' she said, before turning away to the boat's interior.

Stooping to pick up Helen's shoes and dress from the deck, he turned with them in his hands to look out across the glistening waters of the lagoon and tried not to imagine what was happening behind the screening shrubbery. His mind in conflict, he tried to rationalise what he had done and imagine what might have happened had he objected to Helen going ashore. Her words, spoken just hours ago, resonated in his mind: 'Those that do . . .' fought for pre-eminence with another, half remembered, maxim: 'A man will never know what he truly owns until he gives it away.' The question remaining was – would he ever regain her?

Standing at the rail on this warm sub-tropical night, Jeffrey recognised that it was the most important question he would ever ask himself.

Rounding the promontory of rocks and shrubs that separated her from the beached boat, Helen hesitated. She could see the man in the light spilling from his stern lamp, looking one way and then the other along the beach, looking for her and wondering if she were still on the island or on the yacht. What, she wondered, had brought him back to the island when he must know it was, given the presence of the yacht in the lagoon, more than likely she would be on board. How could he have sensed that she might do exactly what she had done – thrown caution to the winds and come, eagerly, to his side?

In considering his motives she was also forced to question her own. If she were to believe Jeffrey's forthright denial of his being married then she, Helen, could no longer excuse herself on the grounds of inflicting punishment on him. The anger and frustration she had felt alone on the island with Qito was also no longer any kind of justification.

So she was left with pure lust. Lust for a totally unknown, silent man who came and went with the tides. In her dilemma she felt she was two separate personae. Her hungry body urged her forward but her mind whispered caution. The choices were there in stark contrast. The bright glare of the primitive gas lamp on his fishing boat was in front of her while, by turning her head, she could look back to the riding lights of the anchored yacht. She had also to ask herself why she had hesitated. How simple it would all have been, had the impulse that had caused her to dive from the yacht's deck been enough to carry her forward to the man's waiting arms. Rationality, she considered, was the ultimate passion killer. Either that, or the comparative chill of the waters had sobered her up somewhat. She had come to prolong the 'wild child' freedom of her days on the island but knew that it would be only for this one last night and as ephemeral as making a grab for a ghost.

Her indecision mounting to be almost physically painful, she had started to turn sadly away when there was a movement in the bushes to her immediate right. Looking there she saw the man's face gazing, expressionless, directly at her. For a moment they stood facing each other before Helen felt forced to speak.

Unsure even of which language the man spoke or understood, she tried communicating with the universal shake of the head. 'No,' she said, her voice shaky with indecision. 'I only came to say goodbye.'

If the man understood he showed no sign of it and came forward to face her directly. Looking at the fine definition of his muscular body, the quietly confident and totally impassive face, she wanted to turn and run from her own bodily urges.

'He knows about you. They all know about you,' she offered, and then as confusion engulfed her, pleaded, 'They're going to punish me if I stay.' Mentally she added: 'And even if I don't', and suddenly everything was excitingly clear to her. She had licence. All was possible – everything permissible. This magnificent man before her was to be had at a price and she had only to decide if the price was worth it.

The man, though so close she could feel the heat of his body, made no move to reach out for her and was making it clear that if there was to be a first move then it was going to have to come from her.

Perversely angered, as she always was by being made responsible for her own actions, and even while wishing he had resolved her dilemma by simply taking her, she reached out to take his ever-readied magnificence, first into her hands, and then, as it flickered and convulsed like a live creature, gently lowered her lips to him in supplication.

The man towering over her groaned his protest and reached to lift her to her feet and again she was forced to fight him off. 'No!' she told him as sternly as she could muster but, when he knelt, wrenching himself from her, and bore down on her shoulders, there was no protest that could be of any avail. Furiously she tried to roll clear of his grasp but it was hopeless. His sheer animal strength pinned her down, spread her and soared deep into her. Now able to tell herself that she had no other choice, Helen was able to surrender with dignity.

The man, suffering no such inhibition, went about seeking his own satisfaction and played her like the accessory to his own pleasure that she revelled in knowing she was. Her protests gave way to pleasured gasps and cries as he created turmoil in her, thankfully deadening all thought of right and wrong, as the sand played mattress to their heaving bodies.

Her body, writhing with satisfaction at finally getting its own way, hushed her mind, but it fought back with vivid images of Jeffrey – and Carla – as if they loomed over the writhing wanton bodies and smiled in satisfaction of the dreadful price they would demand for re-entry into rationality.

'I'm to be punished for this!' she gasped into the uncomprehending face of the man who ravaged her. 'Beg forgiveness!

Humiliate myself!' but even as the thoughts lashed her she knew they were only adding to the pace of her rising climax. Soon she was screaming in orgasm as the relentless man thrashed on inside her. On and on. No longer caring whether she was willing or not, he brought wave after wave of exquisite torment, until she felt she could stand it no more and started beating her closed fists against his stone-like chest. She had never felt more helpless as he effortlessly picked her up and, standing, still locked deep inside her, carried her into the lapping waters where her extreme vulnerability to the man was apparent. To quiet her highly vocal protests he simply bent her backwards until her head went underwater.

Panicked, she felt herself swallowing water even as the fire between her legs intensified. When he lifted her gasping from the water and allowed her to breathe, she used much of the breath to beg mercy, but he held her transfixed and pounded even deeper into her.

Sobbing, even as the fire within her grew more intense, she had a massive orgasm as she imagined herself fighting for her life where only his pleasure could save her. When he relented and waded them both back to shore, she was once more borne down onto the beach where the sand welcomed her by forming a perfectly shaped base to their final debauch. Still lodged deep inside her, she felt him surge, felt him throb and begin to move and, desperate to contain him this time, wound her legs about him, but to no avail. Once more he was pumping his warm seed onto her belly, leaving her feeling distraught and cheated.

Exhausted, she lay for a moment, eyes closed, and awaited his comforting embrace, but when, not feeling him close, she opened her eyes, he was already walking away towards his boat. 'Damn you!' she screamed after him. 'Go to hell!'

The man didn't bother to look back to her until, standing in his boat, his hand already on the rope that would raise the sail, he waved her to come forward. Not knowing where he might take her she came forward and climbed into the boat, looking up at him wide-eyed and feeling entirely bereft of free will.

The sail, once raised, immediately filled with the offshore breeze and the tiny dinghy moved smoothly forward into the night waters of the lagoon.

Looking round she saw, not without a pang of disappointment, that he was returning her to the yacht. Looking back she saw him pointing into the moon-silvered waters. 'Shark!' he said. 'Dangerous to swim.'

Suddenly terrified, Helen gazed down into the clear waters which she now saw as filled with menace. 'Sharks?' she asked the man, hollow voiced, and then swallowed hard as she saw him nod. Aware that only thin wooden planks separated her from a nightmare, she wished away the distance between the frail craft and the safety of the yacht.

As that extravagant craft loomed larger she saw this return as almost a metaphor for her own state of mind. Out here, distanced from civilisation, was a primitive and savage world while the yacht now took on the aspect of sanctuary and safety. Only her stomach quelled at the price she might be expected to pay for readmission.

When the boat nudged gently against the lowered gangway of the yacht, she scrambled for it half expecting the menacing shark to leap up in the tiny gap between the bobbing dinghy and the gangway. So intent was she to put distance between her and the monsters of the deep that by the time she turned to wish her mystery man farewell she saw his dinghy had already slid away and was headed for the gap in the reef.

She was startled to hear Jeffrey quietly calling to her and, turning, saw him leaning anxiously over the rail just above her head. 'I was watching for you,' he said, as he helped her up onto the decking. 'I meant to bring a boat for you when you were ready to come back. Did you know a shark was spotted in the lagoon this afternoon?'

Staring at him her mind was doing loops. Was this to be the only question he was going to ask? 'You knew?' she countered. 'You knew and didn't tell me?'

'I didn't know until after you'd reached the beach. I was worried as hell that you might try to swim back.'

Knowing that Jeffrey must have seen the fisherman, she felt embarrassed. 'I'm sorry,' she murmured. 'What I did was an act of madness.'

'The swim in shark-infested waters?' he asked.

She shook her head. 'Going at all. I'm sorry.'

Relieved to see the smile that lit his face, she went on. 'It's over now,' she murmured, as she went gratefully into his welcoming arms.

'Not quite,' he murmured. 'There's still your forfeit to pay.'

17

The discreet vibration of the ship in motion woke Helen. It was close to midday as she rose from the bed and drew back the blind that masked the long windows to look out onto the startling close passage of the water. Seeing the ocean at almost window level, and understanding that where she stood was actually below the sea level, reminded her of the shark in the lagoon, which changed her perception of the ocean from a thing of amorphous beauty into a viscous mass, masking the frightening savagery within its depths.

Pressing her head hard against the thick glass of the screening window she craned her head to look backwards, hoping to catch one last glimpse of the island. But there was nothing to be seen but the swell of the ocean as the yacht carved its disdainful way forward. Just for a moment she felt uneasily undecided which of John Milton's titles might best express her feelings – was it *Paradise Lost* or *Paradise Regained*? Only the day would tell.

As she showered and dressed, the intangible uneasiness she had felt on waking grew in her. There was a feeling of absence. Tsai had not come to attend her, she had seen nothing of Jeffrey and, as she emerged onto the main deck, she could almost imagine she was alone on the yacht. It was only the ever-attentive Korean stewards who welcomed her into the dining room that reassured her that the yacht had not become another *Marie Celeste.*

Having brought her a chilled, delicious melon, satayed

prawns and a green salad, she was still savouring the heavy white wine and craving coffee when a totally naked Tsai came padding silently to her side. 'You must come with me now,' the girl spoke in a voice so soft it had been almost a sigh.

'Where?' she asked.

'I must prepare you for this evening.'

Tsai's use of the word 'prepare' left little doubt about what she was to be prepared for. With the promise of excitement came also the darker shadows of doubt. 'Where's Jeffrey?' she asked of the girl.

Tsai shook her head in a gesture that might have been meant to convey that she didn't know or had been instructed not to say. Suddenly the earlier expectation of coffee had become a craving along with an alien urge to smoke a cigarette – a habit she had only experimented with in her early teens and then, she imagined, dismissed from her life. Now it was back, searing her tongue and coating her throat, unsummoned from wherever childish impulses are consigned. The reason became apparent when she reached for the table bell that would summon the stewards, and saw her hand shaking. Excitement, like warmed molasses, had seeped into her blood and was causing her heart to race along with her mind. 'I want some coffee,' she told the waiting girl.

Tsai again shook her head. 'All the men crew have been sent below and must not come out again until tomorrow.'

This news caused a convulsive shudder to pass from head to toe and, standing, Helen looked around the ship even more aware of the 'absence' she had sensed earlier. While the yacht clipped smartly through the ocean there was no sign of the ever-attentive deck crews. Pausing, uneasily aware of the unique isolation surrounding her, she felt the welcome onrush of helplessness. Knowing she could do little to protest at whatever might be about to be done to her, rendered her guiltless. Standing there, Tsai anxiously awaiting her reaction, she realised the care with which she had been prepared for this moment. It was as if Jeffrey had known from the outset that she was going to be presented with this test and had gently accustomed her to accept it when the time came. She turned to look into Tsai's porcelain face and finally smiled her acceptance of that which she was now convinced was inevitable. 'Let's go,' she said.

Beaming with relief, Tsai led the way from the dining room and down the stairway that led to the main stateroom deck. Confident that she was to be taken to her own cabin she was a little surprised when, at the base of the stairs, Tsai turned left instead of going straight on.

Tucked away, almost under the stairs, was another stateroom.

Tsai opened the door and stood aside to allow a now curious Helen to precede her.

Stepping into the darkened cabin the first word that came to Helen's mind was incongruity. The room was furnished more like a medieval chamber than a space on the modern hedonistic machine that was the yacht. Chains and leather lined every wall, while the whole place was lit with what, at first, seemed guttering candles but turned out to be cleverly disguised flickering lamps. None of these accoutrements to bizarre pleasure took her eye more keenly than the human element in the room. Strapped naked to a wooden cross was the yacht's owner – Martinez. His eyes, hugely rounded, were fixed on Helen as she stood staring at him but, she saw, his silence was explained by the leather thong that gagged his mouth.

Propelled forward by an instinct she recognised as having been instilled in her during her visit to Madame Victoria's, Helen came to stand immediately before the man with his deliciously desperate eyes. Between her and this man, with whom she had barely previously spoken, sprang an immediate affinity. The light sarong that was all she wore became constricting so, tugging at the knot that held the sarong, she loosened it and let it slip to the floor where Tsai immediately moved to pick it up. The widening of Martinez's eyes as he looked on her honey-coloured body was all the goad she needed to go further.

Looking directly into his eyes her hands sought out his hardening flesh. 'Have you been whipped?' she heard her huskily toned voice ask and, when she saw his nodded reply, felt enveloped in an intensity of excitement that scorched her body and threatened her soul. Reaching forward she kissed his gagged mouth, then his throat. An explosive grunt escaped his constrained mouth as her lips sought out the matted hair on his chest and nipped affectionately at his nipples.

All consciousness of another world – even of her surroundings, and the excited, cautionary, protests of Tsai – fled from her mind as her hands gave him pleasure, so paying tribute to their companionship of pain. Even as she worked and teased she understood that once, before finding total freedom on the island, she would never have dared do this without Jeffrey's prior sanction and she was engulfed in a soaring sense of triumph.

Standing before this helpless man she was her own arbiter, with no need of excuse or alibi to explain her self-indulgence. This too, she appreciated, had been gifted her by Jeffrey, but what followed, as Martinez erupted convulsively into her manipulating hands, came, unheralded, from some dark resource of her own mind.

Carefully conserving and guarding every drop of him in her hands, Helen rose and looking at Martinez squarely and without shame, directly into his eyes, offered up his cock's harvest to his lips. 'Clean them,' she told him. The act seemed to pleasure Martinez enormously. His eyes closed in sublime acceptance while his grunts were far from protests.

A kind of madness gripped Helen as shock-waves of arousal sought out every last nerve in her body. She trembled with excitement as she reminded herself that a man stood helpless, his eyes pleading for savagery. It was as if she could read his mind. How well she had been taught the joy of submission – of surrendering free-will to the whim of another. She knew that Martinez's mind would be racing with expectation of the surprise and shock of her inflicted pain. His silent demands begged not to be disappointed. Still looking directly into his eyes she found herself wondering by what avenue Martinez had come to this knowledge. She knew only too well her own guilt and her own needs and was, conversely, angered.

'Bring me a whip,' she murmured to the attendant Tsai.

For a moment Tsai hesitated and Helen knew the Chinese girl was about to protest but seeing Martinez's eyes lit with expectation she spoke again. 'Do it!' she insisted.

Tsai moved to the display of instruments pinned to the walls and, after a momentary pause, returned with a long pliable stick of many tails. The moment Helen's hands closed about the leather stem a surge of live power raced upwards from her closed fist to lay siege to her quaking body. At the same moment she was assailed by the knowledge that having come this far, having raised expectations, she must not disappoint and her confidence wavered. Needing sanction she spoke to Tsai. 'Loosen the gag,' she told the girl and was momentarily relieved of the oppression of his eyes, so full of pleading.

Gasping with the relief of his mouth's bondage, Martinez smiled on Helen. 'You are so beautiful, mistress.'

The title, spoken so fervently, shocked Helen. Was that how he saw her? A dominant woman able to deal with him as she chose? Standing there she knew her eyes were filled with fire but her mind was full of doubts. She felt she was to be tested by this man far more than she had ever been with Jeffrey.

For a moment she yearned for the simplicity of submission just as Martinez's eyes begged her now. She was to find the hesitation fatal as the doubts flooded in to quench the fires that had so recently been lit.

'I'm sorry,' she told Martinez. 'I cannot be your mistress.'

His eyes clouded with disappointment. Martinez pleaded, 'Please, mistress, I am helpless before you – you give me your pain.'

Turning away from the oppressive eyes, Helen shook her head. 'I cannot hurt you. I do not love you.'

A warm laugh startled Helen and, turning, she was in time to see Carla stepping through a door which had previously seemed merely a panel of mirror set into the wall. 'Well said!' Carla was smiling as she came forward to embrace the surprised Helen. 'Isn't it fortunate that I *do* love you?'

'Were you watching me?' Helen asked.

'Of course I was. Why else should I arrange your temptation?' Carla smiled. 'You fulfilled my every expectation. I have always maintained that the submissive mind, given time, makes the best master. Jeffrey disagreed but you have proved me right and him wrong. Congratulations.'

'Jeffrey saw?'

'Everything!' cried Carla then, leaving Helen to absorb this, Carla's eye lighted on Tsai. 'You, however, have disappointed me. Why were my orders not carried out?'

As Tsai stood trembling and incoherent, Helen stepped forward. 'What orders?'

Carla turned to Helen, her eyes lit with delight. 'But your punishment, darling. Tonight I shall prove to you just how highly I regard you. We shall, all of us, hear your confessions and then pass judgement. Even Carlos.' Carla smiled, moving to stroke the helpless man's face. 'Won't you, darling?' she asked before bringing a resounding slap to his cheek. 'Say you love me.'

'I love you,' murmured Martinez.

'Good!' Carla turned to Tsai. 'You will bring Helen before my tribunal at precisely seven tonight. She will be prepared as I ordered and you will also be required to present yourself as a penitent. I trust I am understood?'

Tsai dipped her head and let out a sigh of acknowledgement as Carla, bestowing a dazzling smile on them all, swept from the room.

Looking to Tsai, Helen found herself shaking. Whether it was fear or excitement was impossible to know. Within her were two quite separate emotions which were equally difficult to recognise. There was only one thing of which she could be sure. Tonight, whatever was to happen, would resolve her emotional conflict one way or the other. Shivering, she felt the breath of change settling about her like the first chill of winter.

Looking at the result of Tsai's skilful labours in the mirror, Helen felt a little bewildered. After Carla's departure from the peculiarly exotic stateroom Tsai had indicated that they should complete Helen's preparation for the coming evening's events in her own cabin, which was where they now stood.

Helen had imagined that her 'preparation' for Carla's punishment would result in her being dressed in something fetishistic and submissive – leather and, possibly, chains. The exotic make-up Tsai had applied had done nothing to diminish this expectation, and so it was with some surprise that she now looked into the mirror and saw herself dressed in a crisp, white peasant blouse and a knee-length skirt which flounced out from the waist. Barefoot and bare-legged, she looked like nothing so much as an Italian peasant girl about to attend a village dance.

'This is it?' she asked of Tsai.

Tsai nodded. 'It is Madame Carla's instructions precisely.'

It was unexpected but also subtly exciting. She wore nothing but the blouse and the skirt and so, although presentable, she also felt deliciously vulnerable. Adjusting the top she saw how its cotton laced neckline could be loosened and simply pulled down to reveal her breasts, while the skirt needed only to be lifted to leave her, essentially, naked.

Tsai, by contrast, looked severely formal in her white and gold oriental dress. Feeling her heart fluttering in her breast like an agitated live bird, Helen smiled. 'So . . .' she said, '. . . what happens next?'

'Mister Jeffrey will come to fetch you and escort you to the party,' Tsai hissed urgently. 'All the stewards are confined below so I must serve the evening meal.'

Remembering the veritable squad of stewards that normally attended the yacht's guests, Helen was surprised. 'All by yourself?'

With a secretive smile Tsai beamed, 'Not by myself alone. I shall have a French maid to assist me.'

Judging from the delighted light in Tsai's eye, Helen was able to judge that the French maid was also to be something of a surprise. Turning to look at the healthy peasant girl in the mirror she could also see that, thankfully, it was not to be her. 'Do we have a French maid on board?' she asked.

'Oh yes!' hissed an excited Tsai.

Sensing there were other intriguing elements yet to be revealed about the forthcoming night, Helen was about to insist on being told more about them when the stateroom door opened and a Caribbean pirate entered!

It took a moment for Helen to absorb that the tall figure dressed in an elaborately ruffled shirt, a thick black leather belt securing his wide-bottomed black trousers tucked into knee-high black boots, was Jeffrey, his face half disguised by the eye patch he wore over his left eye.

He looked magnificently threatening and Helen felt a comprehensive rush of excitement in looking at him.

Jeffrey dismissed Tsai from the room and then turned to the trembling Helen who, nervously excited, attempted to cover her rising excitement with an essayed humour. 'I might have guessed it was to be fancy dress,' she said on a nervous laugh.

Still silent, Jeffrey stood, hands on hips, in theatrical parody of a pantomime pirate but his voice bore no trace of humour as he spoke. 'Bare your breasts,' he told her.

Trembling with excitement at this peremptory order Helen challengingly held Jeffrey's gaze as she reached first one hand and then the other to slowly draw the crisp cotton top down to her waist. As she did so she realised that the half sleeves restricted her arm movement, so imposing a subtle bondage to the action. Her breasts naked, she squared her shoulders to present herself more flatteringly, all the while looking challengingly at him. The memory of everything this man had taught her to enjoy – things no other man had ever dared hint at – flooded in on her. All the dominant conflicts she had experienced standing before the helpless, submissive Martinez, fled before her overwhelming excitement at recovering the experience of surrender to Jeffrey.

His next words confirmed her most delightful fantasy. 'On your knees,' he said, his voice sure and certain.

Careful to flounce out the skirt to its fullest, Helen sank gracefully to her knees before the figure of the man her racing mind told her was, truly, a pirate confronting a captive princess. Raising her eyes to his as he came forward to stand over her kneeling, bare-breasted figure, she, unasked, raised her hands to place them on her head – a gesture which indicated her total submission. At the same time, she was consciously aware that it presented her breasts even more prominently.

'I had almost forgotten how beautiful you are,' he told her, his words flushing away any last residual restraint she might have nurtured.

'I am what you want me to be,' she murmured, feeling the anguish of their locked eyes.

Jeffrey smiled and came forward to take her head in his hand and press it against the groin of his trousers – where her cheek felt his excitement already stirring. 'You couldn't possibly know what I want of you,' he said through an excited growl.

'Anything,' she pledged urgently.

'Remember that,' he said, 'because tonight may be difficult for you.'

Moving her head so that she could look up at him towering over her, she whispered, 'If you're there, nothing is going to be difficult and nothing ...' she added, '... impossible.'

His face wreathed in a delighted smile, Jeffrey reached down to gently raise her from her kneeling position to stand expectantly before him. 'It's almost a shame to share you while I'm feeling like this. It seems ages since we last made love.' As he spoke he carefully rearranged the peasant blouse to cover her breasts.

Emboldened by this implicit declaration of love, she smiled. 'Is that what's to be done with me tonight? Am I to be "made love" to?' The flicker of doubt crossing his face only increased her excitement. 'I was led to believe I was to be punished.'

'Do you deserve to be punished?' Jeffrey asked.

Helen felt a lava-like rush of heat which emerged from her throat in one word. 'Terribly,' she murmured.

His voice throbbing, he asked, 'And you're mine?'

With a curious feeling that she, though dedicating herself to his will, had the initiative, she nodded before challenging him directly. 'I ask only that you don't disappoint me,' she murmured.

Helen watched him struggle between an obvious desire to take her where they stood and the promise of the unknown night ahead, before reluctantly and resignedly deciding to honour their hosts. 'They're waiting for us,' he said, ushering her to the door.

Together they moved silently through the curiously quiet but vibrantly alive ship, and mounted the stairs until they stood together for a moment on the threshold of the dining salon. From inside came the sound of sonorous music as Jeffrey took her by the shoulders and turned her towards him.

'Whatever happens tonight,' he said, 'remember I love you.'

His words encompassed her soul with the warm glow of security and the certain knowledge that tonight they would be making memories that would last them a lifetime. As they came into the dining salon she felt invulnerable. Nothing could harm her now.

18

Helen stepped into the heady atmosphere of the candle-lit salon to be immediately confronted by the turned back of a towering French maid. Standing over six foot in seven-inch platform heels, it wasn't until the startling apparition turned towards her in greeting that she discerned, somewhere under layers of make-up and sweeping fake eyelashes and moustache, the more familiar shape of Martinez. It was some moments before she understood she was being offered a glass of champagne from the silver tray in the 'maid's' hand. Taking the offered glass and almost laughing out loud at 'her' wobbly attempt at a curtsey, Martinez's bulk moved aside to reveal the much more sobering figure of Carla.

Her rounded figure was emphasised by a red and green leather basque drawn about an incredibly small waist from which stemmed rounded hips and thighs, making her legs incredibly long. A high leather collar about her throat was ablaze with an encrustation of diamonds and emeralds which dazzled in the candlelight as the devastating figure swayed forward to greet them. She was almost on them before Helen quailed at the sight of the riding crop which Carla was playfully slapping into the open palm of one hand.

'Jeffrey,' she mewed. 'You look so authentic! Absolutely terrifying!'

Helen might have used the same adjective to describe Carla as the famous eyes centred on her. 'And Helen! You look ravishing, my dear. Almost good enough to eat!'

As they exchanged cheek kisses Helen saw over Carla's shoulder the grinning figure of Qito, dressed in a vaguely Middle Eastern robe and turban that might have been meant to present him as a simulated sultan or as if he had been caught on his way to take a bath. Qito was there to take her hand to his lips the moment she was freed of Carla's embrace. 'Tonight is to be the first viewing of our collaboration,' Qito told her.

Having all but forgotten the real point of their isolation on the island, Helen's interest immediately quickened. 'I hope you're not disappointed?' she asked as he led her towards an easel which was still covered with a shroud of canvas. 'Can I take a peek?'

Qito shook his head. 'Later,' he said. 'For the moment we must not detract from Carla.'

Helen saw that Carla had assumed proprietorial rights over Jeffrey and was standing, arm in arm with him, talking to a flamboyant parody of Carmen Miranda, complete with fruit bowl headdress.

Momentarily unable to discern who might be under this extravagant disguise she turned to ask Qito.

'Jimmy!' he cried with delight. 'Don't tell me you've forgotten Carla's ever-present little hairdresser.'

'He makes a very authentic woman,' said Helen, adding, without thinking, 'Is he gay?'

Qito laughed. 'He's whatever Carla wants him to be.' Qito pulled her into a confidential whisper. 'I'm planning to throw him overboard later tonight and I'm counting on your assistance.'

At that moment they were distracted by the raised voice of Tsai. Helen turned to see the diminutive Tsai shrilly berating the French maid who had, it seemed, tottered once too often on his high heels and spilled a tray of drinks. 'Stupid!' Tsai was yelling at the trembling man who stood at least a foot higher than her. 'You are a very stupid maid and, if that happens again, I shall have to beat you most severely!'

Martinez had dropped to his knees before the seemingly furious Tsai and was begging her forgiveness as Helen turned to Qito. 'Can Tsai talk to him like that?'

'Tsai occupies a very special place on this boat. Tonight she speaks for Carla.'

There was a sudden explosion of energy from the direction of 'Carmen Miranda'. Jimmy was suddenly on his feet, waving his hips in an impersonation of the forties Latin singer/dancer, and, noisily rattling maracas, danced around the still-kneeling Martinez singing one of Carmen Miranda's best known songs. 'Aye-ayeaye I like you very much . . .' while Carla, joining in, added an incredible sexuality to the scene.

It was just then that Helen caught sight of Jeffrey's eyes. He had taken a chair, his long leather boots crossed one over the other, while his stare was fixed, eyes soft and unsmiling, on Carla in her fetishistic costume. The message in his eyes struck home to Helen with a clarity she found startling. Jeffrey, unguarded, wore the expression of a puppy being teased with a chocolate biscuit. That the 'biscuit' was Carla and not herself sent a stab of jealousy racing through her. Propelled forward by a determination to claim those eyes for herself, she came to stand directly before Jeffrey. As he looked on her, smiling, she spoke. 'Do you want her?' she asked.

'Carla?' he mused, as if he thought she might have meant 'Carmen Miranda'.

Nodding, Helen could only wonder why she was provoking a situation she wasn't sure she could handle. Was it possible she could extend her masochism to encompass watching Jeffrey with Carla? She wasn't sure. All she knew was that it was important that his eyes were on her and not Carla. Aware that she had placed herself in a ridiculous position she was grateful when, still sitting, he gestured her forward.

Standing over him, acutely conscious that he could no longer see the display behind her, she thrilled to feel his hands running up under her skirt to caress her thighs. 'There are many beautiful, highly desirable, women in the world and Carla is one of them. A man would have to be dead not to respond to her, but he would have to be a fool not to know what is truly important – and *you* are important to me.'

Helen was still trying to frame a response while cursing herself for the weakness his caressing hands were inducing in her, when she heard Carla's voice ringing out above the music. 'The painting, everybody, is about to be unveiled!'

'We'll talk later,' Jeffrey murmured as, standing, he put his arm about her waist and led her to the veiled canvas.

Carla's flaring eyes fixed on Helen in a way that caused her stomach to clench. 'We are privileged to be the first to see Qito's latest *oeuvre* – a work he has told me he considers among his best to date and, of course, inspired by the lovely Helen.'

The words, while sounding like compliments, carried, to Helen, a sub-text of threat in which she found a curious satisfaction.

'And here it is,' said Carla, dramatically throwing back the cover to reveal the canvas.

For a moment there was a stunned silence. Glowing out of the canvas was a riot of colour which momentarily stunned the senses and obscured the central figure of a woman, eyes wild and threatening as if proclaiming herself to be a creature of this world but somehow above it, challenging onlookers to gaze anywhere but at her eyes. The power Qito had created from colours and canvas was astonishing. This feral woman was both beautiful and terrifying.

'Great God!' cried Jeffrey into the silence. 'She is beautiful!'

Startled that Jeffrey should have spoken of her as if in the third person, Helen looked to see that he was transfixed by her image in precisely the same manner she had resented when he had, earlier, looked on Carla. There was a message in this but, for the moment, she found it difficult to decode from her own internal tumult.

As cries of congratulation and applause broke out, Helen turned back to see that Carla had come to stand directly before her. 'Congratulations,' Carla smiled as she leant forward and cupped Helen's chin in her hand to place an open-mouthed kiss on her lips. Leaning back, Carla looked directly into Helen's startled eyes. 'Any woman that can inspire Qito as you did deserves our thanks, but should also remember that those who play with the gods play a dangerous game. The world may see a creative work of genius wrought from paints and canvas but I see a tribute of love from my man to another woman. Such aspiration has a terrible price.' So saying, Carla released her hold on Helen's chin and turned away to join the small group, Jeffrey among them, about the easel.

Qito came to Helen's side. 'Did I do you justice?' he asked.

Astonished to find tears welling, Helen turned to him and put her arms about his neck. 'Carla hates me,' she blurted into his ear.

'Nonsense! That is simply a measure of how much she loves you,' Qito murmured back into her ear.

'I don't understand that,' Helen told him as she straightened from him.

'You will,' he promised.

Carla's voice rang out. 'Let's now enjoy our buffet supper!' she was saying.

As Qito, caught up in a flurry of congratulations, was

carried towards the buffet table, Helen was left standing alone floundering in a quandary of confusion, to which Qito's image of her only added. Jeffrey had unequivocally declared his love yet Carla's kiss still burned on her lips reviving memories of how totally she had surrendered to her in the scene with Tsai. She had earlier that day been tempted to dominate the willing Martinez and yet had melted into submission before Jeffrey. This flood of confusing signals left her feeling uncertain as to who or what she really was. When she told Qito she didn't understand, she had, she now realised, been voicing an uncertainty which went far beyond a simple response to her present dilemma. Remembering Qito's last words: 'You will,' she fervently hoped she might.

Jeffrey's voice, close in her ear, startled her from her own internal debate. 'Let's talk,' he said and, taking her arm, led her from the dining room onto the deck.

The warm, balmy air, stirring only lethargically in the night's breeze, calmed her as they paced the deck to come to look out over the swell of the ocean, silvered in the moonlight.

'The canvas is extraordinary,' Jeffrey was saying. 'Incredibly lyrical – totally unlike anything Qito has done before.'

With Jeffrey's words fluttering about her ears with the irrelevance of a moth about a flame, Helen found far more urgent topics to discuss. 'Do you really love me?' she asked. 'After all that I've done can you forgive me?'

'What *did* you do?' asked Jeffrey lightly. 'React impetuously to what Annabel told you? I can forgive that. I even find it a little flattering.'

'Flattering?'

'Yes. After all, it does show your feelings for me run deeper than just a passing affair.'

Surprised to hear that he hadn't yet appreciated that, Helen mused: 'I thought I'd already adequately demonstrated that ...'

As he turned to her, she rejoiced to see his eyes lit with pleasure. 'I had hoped so,' he said as he reached out to embrace her.

Nestling against his chest, Helen had never felt more safe in her life. Out of grief she had stumbled on a rocky, sometimes shocking road, but now felt she had come safely home to harbour. Raising her head she invited a kiss, which Jeffrey greedily accepted. Afterwards, they stayed close in each other's arms and allowed their mutual pleasure the silence it deserved until Jeffrey spoke – his voice so soft and quiet that she had to strain to hear him above the soughing sea sounds around them.

'When I was very small,' he whispered 'my parents took me on holiday with them to the Lake District. I can't remember a single thing about it except, on the drive back to London, they stopped off at a pub. I stayed in the back of the car half asleep until my mother came out to bring me a drink – probably orange juice or Coke, I don't remember – but the one thing I do remember is the sandwich she gave me. It was delicious. Cheese – no pickle – but that taste stayed on my palate for years. Even after college, even when my father died, I still remembered that sandwich.'

When Jeffrey broke off Helen looked at him and saw that he was deeply moved. She waited, sure he was about to confess something extremely important.

'It was the cheese, you see? Strong and tangy. It was the most delicious thing I'd ever tasted and I spent years trying to rediscover it. I must have tried almost every cheese there was in the world but the closest I ever came to it was a mature Cheddar. I searched every cheesemonger in London and everywhere I went trying to find that elusive something. I got close, but never quite found "it". There was something missing, you see? Something about that sandwich I had yet to identify.'

Jeffrey paused again while Helen listened, willing him to come to the point and desperately hoping that when he did she would understand why the telling of this anecdote was so important to him.

'Then one day – quite by accident – I found it! There, singing on my palate, was the taste I had remembered since I was four years old. Do you know what it was that I had been missing all those years?'

Helen remained silent as Jeffrey went on. 'A slice of onion!' Jeffrey cried triumphantly. 'For years I had tried all those variations of cheese and eaten onions but it had never occurred to me to put them together into the same sandwich. You see? Two very ordinary elements, under my nose for years, yet only when they came together did I realise they constituted something I had searched high and low to find. It was magical. I was four years old again, half asleep in the back of my father's car. Do you understand what I'm saying?'

Bewildered, Helen shook her head.

'I'm saying that you can spend your life looking for something – a smile, a light in someone's eyes, a voice or accent, and, somehow, although it may be close to what you are searching for, it isn't exactly what you want. Then, one day, someone comes along who just happens to mix two ordinary enough elements to make a dream come true. Now do you understand what I'm trying to say?'

'I think you're saying that I'm the onion in your cheese sandwich ...?'

'Exactly!' cried Jeffrey triumphantly. 'You are beautiful, intelligent and charming – but I've known all those qualities in other women. You bring something else – something elusive but not frightening or dauntingly other-worldly. Something unique that I can cherish. I saw it tonight, defined for me by Qito's canvas. Seeing you through his eyes I have no doubts. I love you,' he added simply. 'Is that enough?'

Renewing their kiss, Helen felt suddenly appalled at ever having mistrusted him, but equally there arose in her a furious need to be purged of this new guilt. 'Jeffrey, there are things I have to tell you ...'

Smiling, Jeffrey nuzzled her face. 'And you are going to,' he murmured. 'But I haven't forgotten you asked me not to disappoint you.'

Her loins suddenly in convulsion, Helen wondered at the shift Jeffrey could effect in her emotions. With barely a change of tone or even inflection he had wrenched her from the warm glow of affectionate embrace into quivering submission. Involuntarily, her arms had dropped from his, her back straightened and, as she looked into his still-warm eyes, she felt herself heating. She cursed her quavering voice as she spoke. 'You don't know every stupid thing I did.'

'Do I need to know?' he asked with quiet firmness.

'*I* need you to know,' she answered.

Nodding, Jeffrey moved away a pace before turning back to her. 'Do you love me?' he asked.

Helen nodded.

'Do you believe I love you?' he insisted.

Her throat, constricted with rising excitement, would only permit her to nod in reply.

'Bare your breasts,' he said in a voice so low that it was almost lost in the quiet sigh of the sea breeze.

Excitedly mute, she reached one quivering hand to her right shoulder to pull down the laced top while raising an elbow and awkwardly freeing it. Her eyes, blurred but firm, remained on his while she repeated the movement to her left side, then, her arms freed, she drew the blouse down, flinching as this tight bodice top flicked against her engorged nipples. Drawing back her shoulders to make better display of herself, she stood in silent challenge.

There was a tiny dull clink of metal as Jeffrey came forward and caught up her wrists. Glancing down she saw a handcuff clicking about one wrist and only then raised her eyes to his, half expecting that he would now turn her and so pinion her wrists behind her. As always, Jeffrey was to surprise her. Instead, she found herself facing the ship's rail and looking out at the silvered sea glistening under a huge tropical moon.

With one swift movement Jeffrey had hooked the other cuff about her wrists with the ship's rail in between. Tethered, she could not fully straighten and, as if following some natural law, found herself most comfortable by leaning slightly forward and resting her forearms on the varnished wooden rail. It was a posture which a distant observer might think of as simply relaxed but, to her just then, was the most exquisite form of bondage she could imagine.

When Jeffrey moved behind her she found she could no longer comfortably turn her head to watch him. When he came to embrace her, pressing himself hard against her, she gasped with urgent need of him to take her there and then. When his hands closed round her to cup her breasts and tease her raging nipples she gasped out her demands in the coarsest words she could summon.

'Not quite yet,' Jeffrey muttered through teeth clenched tight with excitement. 'You don't get off that lightly!'

Her heart racing, her breathing so deep it caused her bared torso to convulse, she cried out in frustration as his hands sought out the hem of the full skirt and drew it with agonising slowness up her thighs to be finally tucked into the waistband of the skirt, leaving her naked from the waist down. 'Please!'

she begged as her libido threatened to go into overload. 'For pity's sake take me!'

Jeffrey's voice was close and insistent in her ear. 'Have no fear,' he murmured, 'you are going to be ravished, and much more besides – but at a time, and by persons, of my choosing.'

'No!' she screamed. 'I want *you! Now!*'

His chuckle all but sent her into instant spasm. 'Do you really think you're in any position to make demands?' he asked, his hands caressing her as, her questing loins finding him pressing hard against her, she again sobbed out her need.

'All pleasure must be paid for. Pleasure past and pleasure to come both carry incredibly high price tags – and I would hate to *disappoint* you.'

Abruptly, Jeffrey stepped back from his tight embrace and her heated sex struck chill even against the sultry night air. Her mouth was already open – readying yet another plea – when his bare hand struck firmly against her exposed buttocks. The sting of the blow stayed in the one small area for only a moment before its heat flooded through her hungry body and all but consumed her. 'Yes!' she cried out across the empty ocean.

In answer his hand came down again – three more times in rapid succession – before he spoke. 'Tell me about your lover on the beach. Was he beautiful?'

Helen tried to force her mind to think – to concentrate – on what she might say, how best to say it, but she was in such confusion that only the truth seemed to have any validity. 'Yes!' she yelled defiantly.

Three sharp stinging slaps of his hand followed in quick succession and she rejoiced that the currency of her guilt was now established.

'Tell me everything,' Jeffrey insisted into her ear.

'Yes!' she cried. 'He would appear – just be there – at night ...' She broke off as she received three more rapid slaps. Her breath now difficult to control, she went on. 'He was brutal, we never made love – we just screwed!'

The slaps this time stung as her already roused flesh became more sensitive with each successive blow.

'He was huge – his cock was enormous ...'

Slap – slap – slap.

'He would tease me with it. Hold back and then plunge so deep he would hurt me.'

Jeffrey's hand rose and fell and he was forced to put his free hand out to grip her tightly as her body sought to escape the implacable rise and fall of his hand.

Recovering, grateful when he left his hand resting on her inflamed flesh and drew away the heated pain, she gasped: 'Then he would make me wait. Make me beg. I loved it! I loved his savage pain!'

This outburst earnt her six blows and it took her a moment to recover before inviting more of his punishment. 'But when he came he would pull out. He would never come in me – never let me feel everything!'

Three more, the most intense yet, seared into her convulsing flesh.

'His hot sperm would shoot on my belly, on my breasts and into my mouth ...'

Wildly out of control Helen could feel only the heat of the blows which now rained down in quick succession. As each landed she heard herself greeting it exultantly and demanding more – and harder.

'And you ... ?' asked Jeffrey. 'Did you come?'

'Yes! Gloriously! Wonderfully!'

'Like this?' he demanded as his probing fingers first spread her and then plunged deeply into her, all but lifting her off her feet.

'Yes!' she screamed in defiance.

Jeffrey's probing became more violent, more vicious and for one distracted moment she thought he might be about to plunge his entire bunched fist into her.

Instead, as she writhed on the fleshy spike he had made of his fingers, he reached with one finger of his other hand and expertly sought out her risen fleshy clitoris. His touch was like that of a trigger to a detonator. Totally out of control, uncaring who heard, she proclaimed her orgasm in a scream that went forth like sheet lightning into the calm blackness of the night.

Her knees buckling to come into painful contact with the lower rung of the deck rail, she recovered in time to realise that Jeffrey was moving away and leaving her there. 'No!' she called out desperately. 'Don't leave me here! Not like this!' Twisting herself awkwardly against the rail she could see him stepping from the deck into the saloon. 'There's more!' she called vainly into the night.

By turning herself to stand, still firmly pinioned by the wrists, the other way, she found she could follow Jeffrey's progress as he made his way through to the library where she saw Carla rising from a couch to greet him. She could hear nothing of what was said through the thick armoured glass of the deck windows and could only guess that they were discussing her. Seeing Carla's laugh and quick embrace of Jeffrey only increased her feeling of isolation and vulnerability. His chastisement had excited her beyond measure and the fire of it, though dampened by his absence, still worried away at her hungry loins. When she saw Carla, magnificent still in her fetishistic leathers, move to leave the library, she knew immediately where she would next appear.

She was not to be disappointed. Carla stepped out onto the deck and came towards the quailing Helen, smiling and making deliberate display of the riding crop laid across one open palm. 'Well now ...' mused Carla '... it seems this is my turn.'

Biting back an urge to plead, Helen stared fixedly into Carla's dancing eyes. 'Face front!' Carla suddenly snapped, adding as Helen turned to obey by staring out into the moonlit sea, 'Spread your legs!'

Immediately, helplessly, liquid, Helen did as she was ordered and mentally braced herself for a sterner test than any Jeffrey had inflicted.

'Four days, was it?' Carla asked so quietly that she might almost have been speaking only to herself. 'Four days and three nights? Is that the sum of the time you spent alone with my husband?'

Helen, unable to do more, nodded then flinched as she felt the first of Carla's contacts. Expecting a cut from the whip it took her a moment to realise that what she felt was merely Carla's hand reaching out to caress her inflamed flesh.

'And, in that time, how many times did you screw him?'

'None! We never did anything on the island.'

'Too busy with your fisherman, then?' asked Carla.

'Yes! He exhausted me.'

'And you never gave a thought to what Qito might be feeling?'

'I did. Yes, I did, but he was too intent on his work. He's a serious man. He took me there to paint and that's all he did.'

Ignoring the last of her answer, Carla insisted she concentrate on what, to her, was the most important business at hand. 'So he never thought about you as a woman – what about you? Did you not want him between your greedy legs?'

For a moment Helen, remembering the one moment when she had invited Qito to respond to her, hesitated. To answer truthfully she knew would invite pain against which she had no defence. When Carla, impatient for an answer, cut a stinging blow aimed with expert evenness across both buttocks, she cried out. 'Yes, I wanted him. I wanted him to fuck me!'

Carla's voice sounded almost affectionate. 'The truth at last!' she murmured triumphantly. 'Tell me, could you love him?'

'I admire him. I could worship him. I don't know if I could love him.'

'And me?' asked Carla.

The inference of the question escaped Helen for one startled moment and even more when Carla reached out and, cupping her face in one strong hand, turned her head to face directly into her own. 'Could you love me?' she breathed so close that Helen felt the sting of her breath against her opened mouth.

'Yes,' she murmured, astonished at her own realisation.

Carla's lips opened to reveal strong white teeth set into a beatific smile. 'And what more do you have to tell me about you and Qito?'

Trembling in the face of Carla's relentless pressure Helen reached for the truth as if it were a lifeline. 'I sucked his cock,' she murmured quietly. 'I had to. Jeffrey was there and told me to.'

Still close, Carla's smile became even more serpentine. 'What a good little girl you are,' she hissed. 'So young and beautiful – and *so* obedient!'

Breaking from the intimate closeness, Carla stepped back

a pace and Helen, bracing herself, faced forward once more to look on the placid swelling of the passing sea.

'What do you suppose happens to good little girls who indulge themselves at another woman's expense?' Carla asked.

'I don't know,' breathed Helen.

'Yes you do,' Carla insisted. 'They get punished, don't they?'

Eyes closed, Helen waited, unable to bring herself to beg for what she knew was inevitable. 'Answer me,' snapped Carla.

'Yes!' screamed Helen.

Carla's tone was immediately conciliatory. 'Of course they do,' she said with satisfaction. 'Now you will have to help me ...' She paused as Helen urged her outraged brain to ignore the searing heat at her buttocks and prepare to make answer to Carla. 'I was always so terrible at arithmetic,' Carla was saying. 'Let me see ... you did say it was *four* days to which must be added three nights – which, of course, count double. How many does that make? Four, three and three?'

'Ten,' managed Helen through gritted teeth.

'Ten?' asked Carla as if savouring the number on her palate. 'Plus an allowance of, shall we say, *five* for your unfortunate lapse into enforced fellatio? Would you think that fair?'

With a flare of spirited defiance Helen snapped back, 'You're going to do it anyway so why don't you just get on with it?'

Delighted, and after a carefully judged intimidatory pause, Carla asked, 'How many does that make in total?'

The tension on Helen's expectant body caused a shuddering rebellion to sweep through her and, setting her teeth, she gave no reply. 'Well,' Carla sighed. 'If you're not prepared to help me with the calculations I shall just have to guess when to stop.'

Pausing again as if waiting for an answer which, defiantly, never came, Carla went on. 'I intend that you shall have your punishment in groups of five. After each group there will be a pause during which you may recover and then, after thanking me for my indulgence, ask me to proceed. Do you understand?'

With Carla's hand lovingly caressing her buttocks and her entire body visibly shaking, Helen could not force any reply from between her tight-set teeth.

'I'm waiting,' murmured Carla.

With flaring anger at this torment, Helen spat out, 'For what?'

'Your permission to begin, of course!'

Her voice wild, Helen snarled: 'Bitch!' only to hear the cry becoming a wailing scream as, without pause or pity, the lash descended. The first five strokes were so swiftly given that they overwhelmed her, taking away Helen's power to voice her indignation. As the heat spread across her buttocks, Carla's cooling hand, placed caressingly on her, felt like a benevolence.

Head bent, each sobbing breath drawn noisily through flaring nostrils, Helen fought for control as her brain raced to rationalise what was being done to her. Yes, she had behaved foolishly towards Jeffrey and welcomed his punishment as a purging of sin. But what of Carla? What hurt had she inflicted on her? So why then should she submit to this punishment? The only possible answer was in Carla's pleasure. For some reason this sent Helen's daunted spirits flying. She had wanted Qito's pleasure for his fame and to make a memory. She was astonished to find she wanted Carla's pain for the same reason.

'Well?' insisted Carla.

Raising her fallen head from her chest Helen took a deep

breath and knew the response expected of her. 'I thank you for your indulgence and am ready to receive more.'

'Well said!' called a delighted Carla and, into the grim and painful interval that followed, she allowed only Helen's anguished voice to be heard.

Once more bowed into recovery Helen was startled to hear Carla speak. 'Ah! I see we have attracted an audience.'

Helen turned to see that Jeffrey, surrounded by the ludicrous 'Carmen Miranda' figure and Martinez, had, drinks in hand, come to see the show. Only Qito was absent.

Deluged with humiliation, Helen sought out Jeffrey's eyes. Smiling, he came forward and, taking her chin delicately in his hand, placed a light kiss on her lips. 'Be brave, my darling,' he told her before turning away from the plea in her eyes.

From behind the assembled group came Tsai, eyes on Helen before turning to Carla. 'Let me take her punishment,' said the girl.

'How delightful!' cried Carla. 'That you should, on so short an acquaintance, be willing to sacrifice yourself.' Carla paused. 'I leave the decision to you all,' she said. 'Shall Tsai be whipped in Helen's place?'

The first to answer was Helen. 'No!' she screamed.

Carla's surprised eyes rounded on her. 'What do we have here? Can this truly be love at first sight? What more has a woman to give than that she should be whipped in another's place? Such nobility deserves reward.' Carla paused as if searching her mind for the one touch that would exquisitely fit the moment. Her eyes falling on the 'French maid', she beckoned Martinez forward. 'You may serve our noble friend with the sweetness of your tongue. On your knees before her!'

Martinez scrambled down onto his knees and worked his way through Helen's legs to kneel up, and like an excited puppy, reach with his fingers to spread Helen's labia and wait on Carla's orders.

'His pleasure combining with my pain – sweet and sour!' cried a delighted Carla, addressing herself to the anxious Tsai. 'Fitting, don't you think?'

Helen, once more facing forward, heard what sounded suspiciously like a sob from Tsai and, in confusion, wondered what was in the Chinese girl's mind. There was little time for further thought as Carla's voice rapped an order to Martinez. 'You may begin,' she told the kneeling man.

Helen flinched as his searching tongue probed deeply into her but, even as the pleasure began, she felt the barrage of five swift strokes scorch into her. Her knees giving way under her she, simultaneously, found a steadying grip between her legs from Martinez who still fervently delved for pleasure, while she felt hands softer than Carla's, caress and soothe the fiery pain that marked her flesh. Realising the soothing hands must belong to Tsai she leant forward and, giving herself up to the pleasure-sparks being struck at her, decided to get the remaining five strokes done with as soon as possible.

'Thank you, Carla, for your indulgences and I am now ready for more,' but even as she braced herself against the coming pain she heard Jeffrey intervene.

'How much has she had already?' he asked.

'Ten of fifteen.' Carla's voice was challenging.

Helen heard a slight shuffle of feet as people repositioned themselves. She wondered what was going on as she felt Jeffrey's hand on her, examining the site of the thrashing. If Helen had hoped Jeffrey might be about to intervene his next words dashed all such hopes. 'You haven't cut her skin,' he said as if surprised. 'Truly an expert.'

'I aim to give satisfaction.' Carla's voice was filled with amusement. 'May I continue?'

Helen, strained for the sound of Jeffrey's voice. Remembering she had already recited her designated chant, she braced herself and cursed the pain that was her due until her eye caught something that, in that moment of trauma, seemed magical. Far out in the silvered night she saw a bright light bobbing on the water! For a moment she fantasised her beach lover sailing to her rescue but, as she strained to make out the boat marked by the light, she saw others appear, bobbing like so many fireflies on the swelling ocean. An armada coming to her rescue? Realising her mind was racing towards the fanciful she was brought abruptly back to the present by the smarting of the riding stick. Her voice raised in vain protest she found her eyes were staying open despite the pain, and fixed on those bobbing lights which seemed to be speeding closer. So intense was her concentration that she absorbed this final beating with ease.

Feeling the heat was soothed from her by Tsai's soft hands she became aware once more of the compensatory pleasures being fired by Martinez's tongue as he continued to work doggedly, even frenziedly, between her thighs.

Carla's voice jolted her back to the present. 'Well?' she demanded.

Ignoring her, Helen kept her eyes on the fishing boats which, for a moment, seemed to be speeding towards them side on, until she rationalised the distance between them was being closed not by their motion but the speed of the yacht. Would they pass between them, she wondered. Would fishermen have binoculars or telescopes which, even now, might be fixed on her? Memories of her adolescent Peeping Tom flooded in on her as she pulled her torso upright and prepared herself for the combination of whatever was to come next.

Jimmy's voice screeched out in sudden surprise. 'Hey, look!

There's a fishing fleet out there! We're going right through them!'

Helen smiled to herself as she imagined her own recent thoughts now flooding through Jeffrey's mind. 'Well?' she demanded over her shoulder. 'What are you waiting for?'

Her defiance received quick answer as she heard Jeffrey demand that he be given the riding crop. 'Turn her!' he snapped and it was Jimmy, having discarded his ludicrous fruit bowl headdress, that came forward with the key to the handcuffs and, leaning over the rail, unlocked them.

Turned, Helen found herself looking directly into Jeffrey's livid face and had no doubt about his intention as he murmured an angry: 'Bitch!' into her boldly challenging face. 'Hands on your head,' he told her.

With as much dignity as she could muster Helen slowly raised her hands and, with infinite care, placed them on her head while at the same time impudently thrusting her breasts forward from the waist so that they reached to the tip of the stick. Her eyes alight, she made plain that she was daring him to do his worst.

Jeffrey seemed to hesitate. 'Those boats are very close now,' he murmured. 'So you suppose "he" is out there and can see you?'

'I hope so,' Helen replied, her defiant spirit soaring.

'Hold her upright!' Jeffrey ordered, and Helen felt Martinez rising from his kneeling position to take her about the waist and pull her hard against his own body. She had barely time to register that Martinez was pressing his own full arousal against her before all such thoughts were driven away by the resulting four stripes of the crop. Summoning every last ounce of will that could be scavenged from her outraged body, she raised her head. As Martinez's hold on her relaxed, she smiled directly into Jeffrey's dumbfounded face. 'Thank you,' she said, keeping her voice firm and managed.

Jeffrey hesitated a moment, seemingly disconcerted by her response, before reaching forward to catch her, lifting her into his arms and carrying her like a bride swiftly from the scene.

Down through the boat and directly into the stateroom Helen found herself being unceremoniously dumped on the bed. Resentfully she tried getting up into a sitting position, her bottom still on fire. 'Bastard!' she screamed at him.

Jeffrey, his 'pirate' costume thrown to the four corners of the cabin, advanced on her, furiously aroused. 'Slut!' he seethed as he caught her up, spread her and penetrated her as she continued to scream protest while pummelling the solidity of his heaving body with her closed fists.

Silencing her with a hand across her mouth, Jeffrey spat his words into her face. 'I've marked you! You're mine! Understand? Nobody else's!'

Despite her rising orgasm Helen managed to keep her anger going even when it was obvious to them both that it had been reduced to pretence. Rising to meet his every cruel thrust, she greeted his aggression just as she had welcomed the expiation of Carla's whip. Nothing mattered but the combustion at their thighs. When Jeffrey explosively exhausted himself she moaned in protest. The fires dampened, they lay in each other's arms, recovering their breath and knowing that they had in each other a relationship fired in the kiln of forgiveness.

They lay in astonished silence for some moments, listening to each other's breathing, until, driven by an urgent need for full confession Helen thought of the inflight episode of which she had yet to tell Jeffrey.

'There's something more you have to know before you forgive me ...'

Jeffrey raised himself slightly on the bed and looked

tenderly down into her widened, apprehensive eyes. 'There's nothing more I need to know,' he murmured. 'Nothing! Except . . .'

'What?'

'Do you want to be with me?'

'Yes,' she said.

'Permanently?' he insisted.

'Yes.'

19

A blast from a car horn half roused Helen from a deep velvety sleep and, annoyed at the intrusion of traffic, she had turned over to return to it when realisation dawned. A car horn? In the middle of the ocean?

Instantly alert she sat up, noted Jeffrey's absence, and went to the long side window to open the slatted blinds. She found herself looking at the feet of people passing along a quayside. They were in harbour!

Excited to know just where they might have fetched up she would have hurried on deck to find out, but first there were urgent preliminaries to be taken care of in the bathroom.

It was there she caught a vision of herself in the mirror.

The sight of her battle 'honours' brought about an ineffable surge of energy. Filled with the need to share her excitement with Jeffrey she positively raced into the shower then dried herself, wincing as the towel passed over her bruised buttocks, brushed out her hair, grabbed up a sarong and was in the act of reaching for the stateroom door when it startled her by opening, seemingly, of its own will.

Looking up she saw a beaming Jeffrey standing. 'Great news,' he told her.

Feeling her entire body alive and open to experience she reacted sourly to his obvious excitement. 'Don't I get a good morning kiss?' she asked.

Smiling broadly he caught her up and their kiss added further fuel to the smoulder in her belly. Overwhelmed with an urgent need she took his hand, intending to lead him to the bed, but he, infuriating her, pulled himself free. 'Don't you want to hear my news?'

'Can't I hear it later?'

'No. Now. We have to pack.'

'Where are we going?'

'Los Angeles,' he said, his excitement bursting forth. 'One of the investigators I hired has turned up a witness there.'

Helen became almost angry to have this reminder of her guilt thrust at her. Since meeting Jeffrey, especially since Paris, she had concentrated her anger and then guilt on him and their relationship. To be reminded of her previous, greater guilt in the context of her lustful mood was devastating. 'Must you bring that up now?' she wailed sitting heavily on the bed and mourning the loss of her earlier mood.

'Absolutely!' cried Jeffrey. 'If half what my man reported is true it will change everything.'

Helen looked up at Jeffrey and felt a great gulf opening between them, just as she had over dinner that night in Paris. 'Do you want everything to change?' she asked.

'Not between us – of course not. What I want is to lift this burden of guilt from you.'

'And how will you do that?'

'By going to Los Angeles and talking to this man. He's a student at UCLA.'

'And what does he know about anything?'

'That's what I want you to hear. First hand. From him.' Taking her by the arm Jeffrey insisted she stand up. 'We haven't much time. I've chartered a private jet that'll have us there in six hours. We're three hours ahead of them in time zone terms so, if you hurry, we'll be there in time to talk to him tonight.'

Looking at him Helen felt a sense of foreboding. Life had already cruelly demonstrated how one cruel trick of Nature could destroy an apparently seamless happiness and she feared any new intrusive element coming between her and Jeffrey. 'Do you think this really is a good idea?' she asked plaintively.

Normally excited by surprise, Helen, instead, felt sulkily depressed by this abrupt change of pace. Their goodbyes to those left behind on the yacht had been warm enough but Helen felt a deep sense of loss at leaving Qito and Carla and also the tearful Tsai. The luxuriously appointed interior of the aircraft had eight armchairs – they were far too grand to be described as 'seats' – grouped in two facing sets of four which the stewardess, not without a sly smile, indicated could be converted into two huge king-sized beds, then turned to demonstrate the video and music as if they were to be grouped, along with the beds, as further potentials for in-flight entertainment. After telling them they were cleared for immediate take-off she made a discreet withdrawal.

'Pretty girl,' commented Jeffrey as the twin engines rose to screaming pitch and the extravagant machine began to move.

Helen's tone was more acid than she had intended as she answered, 'No doubt she would happily demonstrate the beds for you.'

'Something wrong?' asked Jeffrey with much injured innocence in his voice.

'Nothing,' said Helen shortly and turned to stare out of the window as the jet raced along the tarmac and lifted into the skies.

Shutting Jeffrey out by feigning sleep she cursed her present mood. She was in flight with a man who had declared his love for her and wanted nothing more than to bring her peace of mind and she couldn't understand why she resented him as if he were an intrusive stranger. Finally, just before genuine sleep overtook her, she understood. He was wrenching her from the refuge of forgetfulness that had made these past weeks possible and was now forcing her to face the root of her guilt.

Fearful of what might come from such a confrontation she knew for certain that, whatever the outcome, nothing would ever be the same again.

True to Jeffrey's prediction the plane made it to Los Angeles by 4 pm local time, landing not in the sprawl of LA International but at Burbank in the San Fernando Valley. As they transferred, with very little formality, from the jet to the long black limousine waiting for them, Jeffrey explained that the traffic in Los Angeles was chaotic and made Burbank handier to the UCLA campus at Westwood, than the downtown LAX.

Wesley Pike was a rangy young man, standing six feet four and blinking at Helen through pebble glasses that made his eyes look as if they were in a permanent state of surprise. 'You don't recognise me, do you?' he asked as they met in the discreetly quiet Boulevard Café in Westwood.

Shaking her head Helen sat in the offered chair and felt a bewildering unreality settle about her. That morning she had woken on a yacht alongside the quay in Guadeloupe; nine or so hours later she had been transported across a continent and felt her mind had been lost somewhere in transit.

'I was one of the dive leaders that day,' Wesley was saying. 'Jesus – what a day! The worst of my life.' Helen watched the raw-boned young man shifting his gaze randomly between herself and Jeffrey before addressing her directly. 'They lied to you,' he said.

'Exactly what happened?' asked Jeffrey.

Wesley shifted uneasily in his seat and looked almost grateful to be interrupted by the girl that came to take their order. Uninterested in the food Helen settled for coffee while Wesley, his appetite belying his thin build, ordered several complicated sandwiches which seemed, to Helen, to take ages to detail.

Finally turning back to the point Wesley went on. 'I was working at the dive school only to make some money during the summer, you understand?'

'Get to the point,' Jeffrey urged.

'Right! Well that day we had a rush of business. Too many people – too little equipment. The boss told me to check out some of the older stuff and see what could be used to meet the shortfall. I found a couple of usable items but we were still a couple of sets short and I told him there was no way we could stretch. He took over from me and pulled out this old air tank – a real museum piece – you know, steel and all, which they don't make any more – today's air tanks are aluminium. Anyway, they told me to issue it. I protested that there were signs of corrosion around the valve but he told me he'd used worse in the past and if I wanted to keep working there I'd better do as he asked.' Wesley paused and glanced at Helen. 'Sadly, your husband got the short straw.'

Helen, feeling slightly sick, stayed silent as Jeffrey pressed for more detail. 'They knowingly gave him a faulty air tank?'

Wesley looked even more uncomfortable. 'Well . . . yes, but . . .'

'But what?'

'Corrosion usually works from the inside out which makes it hard to see . . .'

'So how did you know it was there?'

'From the general state of the tank and the valve. It hadn't been maintained in God knows how long. You could say I was making an educated guess.'

'But if you could, they could, too. They should have known?'

Wesley nodded. 'They should never have issued that tank.'

'So what do you think happened down there?'

'I *know* what happened. Anybody with half an eye could see what happened.'

'Which was what?'

'The tank must have been knocked against something on the wreck they were diving on. The knock caused the tank valve to blow off . . .' Wesley glanced awkwardly at Helen '. . . it crushed the back of his skull.'

Helen felt as if a great weight was crushing her as she sat there and when Jeffrey reached out a hand to hers she held on to it as if to a lifeline.

'So he died instantly?'

Wesley nodded. 'The story about him getting trapped and his air running out – they made that up to try and get off the hook. They thought a law suit for negligence would bankrupt them so they told me and everyone else to keep their mouths shut.' Welsey's huge eyes peered at Helen. 'I'm sorry, ma'am, but it's been bothering me ever since. I'm glad to, finally, tell the truth.'

Jeffrey was relentless. 'And the truth is that nobody – not Helen – or anyone else on God's earth could have made any difference by being there?'

Wesley shook his head. 'The only difference it would have made would have been that this lady – excuse me ma'am – would have seen her husband die.'

'And you'll sign an *affidavit* to that effect?'

Wesley was still nodding agreement when Helen shot to her feet. 'No!' she cried. 'Please – just get me out of here!'

Wesley, looking confused, got to his feet as Jeffrey put an arm round the distressed Helen and, telling Wesley he would be in touch the next day, led Helen from the café and into the waiting limousine.

Sobbing uncontrollably Helen sat huddled in the capacious rear of the car and she heard Jeffrey directing the driver to the Bel Air Hotel.

Gathering every last ounce of strength left in her Helen, unwilling to look directly at him, spoke. 'Jeffrey ... I want a separate room tonight.'

Jeffrey renewed his comforting embrace. 'Is that a good idea, darling? You really want to be alone?'

'I *won't* be alone,' she told him in set, determined, tones. 'There's things I have to tell Kenneth.'

Jeffrey nodded his understanding and sat back in his seat as they rode to the hotel in silence.

Helen usually preferred the fast facility of the shower to the bath but, this night, felt in need of a long contemplative soak.

Eyes closed, she consciously prepared herself for the night ahead. She had never subscribed to any formal religions – finding worthy values in them all, she lived in an ethical supermarket – taking this item from there and that from another place and vaguely imagining herself one day arriving at a spiritual check-out, fully provided for what may lie ahead.

Her belief in the spiritual survival after death was based more on optimism than conviction – an attitude she thought totally rational since atheism – a total rejection of all gods and the hereafter – required a bravery she didn't possess. The atheists were brave since, if *they* were proved wrong, they had much more to lose than the mistaken believer.

What, then, did she hope for in the coming night's communion?

Her belief in the survival of the spirit after death being tenuous, her one firm conviction was in the spirituality of the living and that spiritual survival, as much during life as after death, if any, depended on the discovery of the true self, and it was that which she sought tonight.

When she was at a pre-pubertal age and still prepared to believe 'grown-ups' were the font of all wisdom, she had been much affected by a remark made to her by Aunt May. Visits from Aunt May, considered by her mother to be of the 'shameful' side of the family, were rare but one day, walking a wintry Eastbourne promenade, Aunt May had uttered words that, these many years later, were still locked into her consciousness. Aunt May had said: 'To get by in life you have to lie. Everybody does it. Tell them what's good for them to know, tell them any damn thing you want but never, *never* lie to yourself. Do that and you're lost!'

Aunt May lay with her tonight in this Bel Air bathroom. She may not, this night, summon the shade of Kenneth, but was convinced she could, with application, find herself.

Determined to confront herself in the best possible light Helen rose from the bath and, after drying herself, oiled her body, applied some lip-gloss and a touch of mascara, brushed out her hair and went naked into the darkened bedroom and spread herself, offering up every orifice, on the top covers of the bed.

Unable to immediately face the agony of Kenneth's death she, with a conscious sense of cowardice, began with Millie's telephone call.

'You'll have to start going out sometime. Either that or join a religious order.'

It had been the appalling prospect of facing a positive

philosophical choice, as much as anything, that had led her to Millie's pre-Christmas party and the meeting with Jeffrey.

Jeffrey, she now saw, was a man carrying almost as much guilt as herself. Could it have been the mutual need of expiation that had established their first bonding?

Both had unconsciously recognised the other's need; Jeffrey had given her the physical pain with which she had sought to obliterate – or, as she now recognised, disguise – the spiritual catharsis of loss.

That Kenneth had gone and she remained were facts beyond denial. Kenneth, she reasoned, had the certainty of death while she was left with the bewilderment of life. Kenneth had gone where she could not follow and all the grieving in the world would not change that so, in one sense, the choice was simple. Life or death.

Since there was no life without the living of it, it would seem she had simply to accept the facts and go forward bravely. Which brought her to what might be the crux – who, or what, was she?

Aunt May's homily haunted her as she reviewed the people and events of the past weeks. To which of them had she shown her true self?

First, foremost and central to everything, there was Jeffrey. She had no doubt in her mind that she had stood spiritually naked before him and that his judgement mattered the most to her since it was, among all living people, the most informed.

At that time of their meeting she had been spiritually numb and ready to greet any feeling or stimulation as better than the emotional void into which Kenneth's death had plunged her.

Jeffrey had served her need instead of exploiting it.

More, he had assiduously sought out Wesley Pike and shown her that her guilt was baseless. In doing that he risked the core of their relationship. So what had motivated him? He had already spoken of love but where lay the border between love and lust?

Was it marked by shame?

Where lay the boundary between what was done in lust and given in love? Were both indistinguishable to a dispassionate observer from Outer Space, marked on the one hand by the shame of lust and on the other by exaltation of love? If so, had she felt shame?

Most certainly not before Jeffrey. With Qito? With Madame Victoria, with Carla ...? This last gave her pause. The image of Carla excited her beyond reason. With Carla she had discovered that lust recognises no gender frontier. Everything she had done since meeting Jeffrey had been directed by him until her precipitous flight from Paris.

The two pilots on the plane, the nervous novice stewardess, her joyous submission to Carla and the excitement of Tsai. The fisherman on the island. These had been lust-led ideas of her own but they did not shame her, so where now lay that elusive no man's land between lust and love?

Lust simply demanded gratification while love took its time and brought with it the onus of trust. Could Jeffrey trust her? Did those excursions from his trust make her unworthy of his love? If so, why then had he forgiven her?

She was confused by an inextricable link between the image of the flaring, exciting Carla, exulting in the joy of sexual domination, and Jeffrey. Where was the connection?

It was then that she drew a crystalline clear image of Jeffrey's eyes as he had looked on Carla. At the time she had jealously considered that, in that moment at least, he had desired Carla before herself. Now, quite suddenly, the pattern was resolved and she knew exactly what Jeffrey, but more importantly, she, wanted of herself.

It was as if a great weight had been lifted from her as she understood that while Jeffrey had relieved her of an oppressive guilt, his own remained.

She now knew that, relieved of her own guilt, she had within her hands the power to grant him the gift of shame!

The coming day could not now dawn too soon.

20

At Helen's insistence she and Jeffrey met the following morning on the neutral ground of the hotel's coffee shop.

Jeffrey, smiling anxiously, rose to greet her as she made her deliberately delayed entrance. He waited warily as she consciously took her time over ordering her breakfast, but couldn't contain himself the moment the waitress had left them. 'Well?' he asked. 'Did you come to any conclusions?'

'Several,' she said lightly. 'I had a good long talk with myself and feel confident that I now know what I want.'

'Do your plans include me?'

Helen felt her spirits soar. She knew precisely what agonies Jeffrey must have suffered in the night and found herself content to continue teasing him. 'Possibly,' she finally allowed.

Jeffrey visibly flinched. 'Just "possibly"?'

'Perhaps "conditionally" would have been a better word.'

Anxiously nodding he insisted, 'So what do I have to do?'

At that moment the waitress returned with piled plates of toast, scrambled eggs and overflowing glasses of the juices she had ordered. Helen, sitting back, considered the interruption perfectly timed and let Jeffrey watch with frustration as she deliberately fussed over the cream and sugar pots.

Finally, she relented enough to allow herself to smile brightly into his apprehensive face. 'The first thing you have to know is that I've changed.'

'Changed . . . ?'

'Very much so.'

'In what way?'

'Difficult to define,' she said, consciously enigmatic.

'Try,' he urged.

'No. It's impossible to put into words.'

'Then how am I to find out?'

'In time.'

'How long a time? For Christ's sake, Helen, the past night has been a purgatory for me. I did some thinking too. I love you. Also I want to marry you.'

'Which "me"?' she asked. 'The compliant little sex-slave? If so I'm afraid you might be disappointed.'

'I *never* thought of you like that,' he protested. 'I never *treated* you like that. I thought what I was doing was providing the shock treatment you needed.'

Nodding, she allowed him his point. 'And you did it remarkably well, but there are questions arising.'

'Anything you want to know about me . . . anything.'

'There is one point – the answer to which could be crucial.' She looked directly into his eyes and made an interval of silence as she bit greedily into her buttered toast. Carefully dabbing the crumbs from her lips, she went on: 'How did you come to know Madame Victoria?'

Jeffrey's expression went from astonishment to caution as he absorbed this most unexpected question. 'I don't understand . . .' he murmured defensively.

'My understanding of that estimable establishment was that it catered to men seeking a certain form of physical domination. I was merely curious as to how you came to be such a welcome guest there.'

Watching him closely Helen was, for a moment, afraid Jeffrey was about to retreat into blustering denial and was pleased when her faith in his honesty was justified by seeing him relax, for the first time that morning, and smile.

'You've found me out,' he finally said.

'Have I?' she asked, pretending uncertainty. 'In what way – *exactly*?'

'I'll answer you the same way you answered me: It's difficult to put into words.'

Sitting back into the banquette Helen allowed him to bathe in the brilliance of her smile. 'Then it seems we are left with the necessity of practical demonstration.'

'What does that mean – *exactly*?'

'Do you remember the first time you took me to your place?' Seeing Jeffrey warily silent, she went on. 'We were lying under the sun lamps in the conservatory. You said you wanted to worship me?' She waited until she had Jeffrey's answering nod before adding, 'Well, I now intend you shall have your chance.'

After a moment of considered silence Jeffrey nodded. 'There's nothing in the world I want more than that chance.'

'Good!' she said breezily. 'In that case I shall need the morning alone. I have some shopping to do. What do you say to us meeting back here in time for lunch?'

'Can't I come with you?' he pleaded.

'No,' she said firmly.

Nodding, Jeffrey rose with her. 'Whatever it is you want,' he said anxiously, 'they can deliver to the hotel and charge it to my account.'

'Thank you,' she smiled, allowed him a cheek-pecking kiss and was turning away when he caught her.

'You didn't answer when I asked you to marry me.'

'We've time to discuss that, surely,' she smiled.

'No we haven't. I wanted us to get married today.'

'Today? Is that possible?'

'Not in California, but in Nevada we could. I was hoping we'd take a plane to Las Vegas. They leave every half hour.'

'Then there's no need to decide before lunch is there?' she asked. 'Meanwhile I have my shopping to do.'

Jeffrey nodded before her pussy-cat smile. 'You certainly seem to have your priorities straightened out.'

'Along with much else – as you will shortly discover. Until lunch, darling ...' she called as she moved away from Jeffrey's imploring – and undeniably tempting – gaze.

Lunch was a meal taken in fraught silence. The boxes containing Helen's various purchases arrived one after the other and Jeffrey was constantly interrupted by requests for his signature.

One of the names of the stores to which Helen had given her custom caught his eye. 'Leather Bound?' he asked, looking up from the debit slip to her challenging eyes.

Helen dismissed his concern with a shrug of her shoulders. 'A whim of mine,' she smiled.

Jeffrey had signed and then picked at the meal in which neither was particularly interested. 'So when am I to know what's expected of me?' he finally asked.

'I'm surprised you haven't already guessed,' she answered in deliberately syrupy tones.

'My imagination is running riot but I haven't dared to come to any conclusion.'

Deciding that the time had come to relent a little she reached across the table to take his hand and asked, 'Do the words: "Love, honour and *obey*" have any meaning for you?'

'They do,' he answered throatily. 'The question is: who is to obey whom?'

'If you haven't understood that ...' she said '... then you haven't been listening.'

It seemed Jeffrey was having difficulty with his throat as he asked: 'When am I to be allowed to "understand"?'

Rising from the table Helen motioned him to stay where he was. 'I shall be in my room. One hour from now you may call me there.' Smiling, she leant down and kissed his cheek. 'Bye, darling,' she called as she breezily turned away.

Jeffrey stood naked in the very centre of Helen's room and knew that he was in the only place in the entire world he wished to be.

Helen's instructions on the telephone had been crystal clear.

'In fifteen minutes you will come to my room. The door will be ajar. Just inside the door you will find a small lobby where you may strip. Naked you will go forward into the room and wait for me. Be warned that I shall consider anything less than a manifestly full arousal a personal insult.'

The latter part of her instruction had worried Jeffrey but, in the event, he awaited her knowing that he had never before known such an overwhelming excitement. His anticipation of what might be to come was heightened by the transformation Helen had wrought in the hotel room. The furnishings and fixtures were almost identical to those of his own room but Helen had managed to completely alter the ambience.

With the afternoon sun completely eliminated by the heavy drapes the room's only illumination came from two candles – widely dispersed – which rendered a solemn ritualistic air.

His nerves, already tense and jangling, were sent into a state of near panic when he heard her voice cut through the dimly lit room.

'Don't turn,' she rapped. 'Stay exactly as you are until I tell you otherwise.'

Rigid now Jeffrey waited, every fibre vibrant with anticipation. His ears tingling with the soft sounds of movement behind him and his nose filled with the heavy musky perfume she wore, Jeffrey inwardly begged for some sight of her.

When next she spoke she was close to his shoulder. 'I intend asking much of you,' she sighed into his ear. 'A great deal more than you ever demanded of me. Do you understand?'

His throat closed, Jeffrey could only nod.

'You will find that a woman can be far more pitiless than any man would know how to be.' Jeffrey heard the slight sounds of Helen moving away from him and tensely waited until she spoke again. 'In a moment you will turn and see the results of my morning's shopping. It is on your reaction that our entire future depends. If you understand – nod.'

Jeffrey's immediate assenting nod sent Helen's confidence soaring. In truth she was almost as nervous as Jeffrey was excited and had to take a very deep breath before speaking again. 'You may now turn and look at me,' she said softly.

Hesitating a moment as he fervently prayed that he was not about to be disappointed or made ridiculous, Jeffrey turned and thought he saw, not Helen but a vision conjured out of his most fervent imaginings.

She stood tall in six-inch heels of closely fitted black leather boots and fishnets supported by eight garter straps suspended from the base of a scarlet leather basque. It was cut high over her hips, and rose over a tightly cinched waist to the breasts which were barely covered by a frill of black lace. About her throat was a collar, such as he had last seen on Carla, while on her face she wore a half-mask above which her hair was swept upwards to be caught by a glittering Spanish comb.

Aware that he was simply staring dumbfounded while Helen challengingly waited for his reaction, he allowed his weakened legs to speak for him as he sank to a kneeling position before her.

With a light delighted laugh Helen came forward to loom over him, legs spread, and letting him see the leather riding stick she had in her hands. Her question was superfluous but she insisted anyway. 'Do you approve?' she asked.

For answer Jeffrey let out a gurgle of excitement as he leant forward to kiss her boots.

'I take it you do,' she told him, turning away in a deliberately dismissive gesture only too aware of the electric shock-waves travelling up her arm, emanating from her tight grip about the riding stick. 'Get on your feet,' she told him and didn't turn to look at him until the tiny sounds of his moving to obey subsided.

Still with her back turned, she spoke again. 'I shall not tie you for your whipping since to do so would be to imply that I might be afraid of your reaction.' Now turning to him, relieved to see he was even more aroused than previously, she went on. 'I am not,' she told him as she advanced on his now trembling figure. 'However, now and for the last time you have the opportunity to dissent and leave. There will be no further opportunities for you so to do, so I suggest you give your answer very careful consideration.'

Finding voice for the first time since coming into her presence, Jeffrey spoke with assertive force. 'You're more than I hoped – everything I ever dreamt about.'

Finding his answer pleasing, she smiled. 'And everything that went before was simply instruction in what you really wanted?'

Jeffrey nodded. 'As I said earlier – you have found me out.'

Elated, it was Helen's turn for the affirmative nod. 'I trust you will find I proved an apt and attentive pupil.'

'Do you still want to marry me?' Helen asked as she lay on the bed while Jeffrey, obeying her instructions, furrowed with his tongue between her thighs.

'More than ever,' he breathed.

'Very well,' she said. 'You have my permission to make the arrangements.'

An air taxi brought them to a Las Vegas already brazenly lit by its night neon. The ceremony, with a minimum of attention to fussy detail, was conducted in a place called the 'Wee Kirk o' the Heather' after which the happy couple retired to the honeymoon suite of a ludicrously over-decorated Casino Hotel.

There, Helen confronted her new husband.

'Tonight you will do something – in full view of all the diners in the club restaurant – which you and I have never before dared. I want your sworn oath that you will not disappoint me – no matter what.'

His throat working nervously, Jeffrey felt bold enough to protest. 'There's no question that I'll do whatever you tell me,' he breathed. 'But I would ask you to remember that the people that come to Las Vegas are not as sophisticated as in some cities. There might be trouble if it's too explicit.'

Helen smiled. 'It is *very* extreme.' she smiled. 'But you will obey – no matter what?'

Filled with apprehension he felt he had no other option but to agree.

Together, he dressed in a black-tie tuxedo, she in a flowing, newly purchased evening gown, they made a striking entrance into the almost-filled-to-capacity club room. Conducted to a table which seemed to have been carved from a jungle clearing, they were seated and served aperitifs.

Enjoying making him wait, Helen sipped at her drink and commented on the big-band dance music playing in the background. 'The orchestra is very good, don't you think?' she asked of the tense Jeffrey.

'Excellent,' he said.

Helen sat back and appeared to be devoting her attention entirely to the music for some time before speaking again. 'It's time, darling,' she said. 'Time to test how far you dare to trust me.'

Even in the roseate glow of the table lamp Helen saw how suddenly he paled. 'Look,' he said as he rose to accompany her towards the dance floor. 'I'm going to go through with it no matter what – just bear in mind what I said. These people are not the sophisticated kind we might meet in Paris or London.'

Pausing on the edge of the sparsely populated dance floor Helen smiled. 'But you will do whatever it is I ask of you?'

Nervously, Jeffrey nodded. 'What is it I have to do?' he asked, his words made almost inaudible by apprehension.

'As I told you – something you and I have never done before. Can't you imagine what that might be?'

Shaking his head Jeffrey prepared himself for the worst.

'What you are going to do – now, instantly, and before all these people – without regard to the consequences is . . .' she let the sentence hang for some moments and enjoyed his stricken anticipation before going on '. . . *dance* with me.'

And dance they did.

LOOK OUT FOR THE BLACK LACE 15TH ANNIVERSARY SPECIAL EDITIONS. COLLECT ALL 10 TITLES IN THE SERIES!

All books priced £7.99 in the UK. Please note publication dates apply to the UK only. For other territories, please contact your retailer.

Published in March 2008

CASSANDRA'S CONFLICT
Fredrica Alleyn
ISBN 978 0 352 34186 0

A house in Hampstead. Present-day. Behind a façade of cultured respectability lies a world of decadent indulgence and dark eroticism. Cassandra's sheltered life is transformed when she gets employed as governess to the Baron's children. He draws her into games where lust can feed on the erotic charge of submission. Games where only he knows the rules and where unusual pleasures can flourish.

Published in April 2008

GEMINI HEAT
Portia Da Costa
ISBN 978 0 352 34187 7

As the metropolis sizzles in the freak early summer temperatures, identical twin sisters Deana and Delia Ferraro are cooking up a heat wave of their own. Surrounded by an atmosphere of relentless humidity, Deana and Delia find themselves rivals for the attentions of Jackson de Guile – an exotic, wealthy entrepreneur and master of power dynamics – who draws them both into a web of luxurious debauchery.

Their erotic encounters become increasingly bizarre as the twins vie for the rewards that pleasuring him brings them – tainted rewards which only serve to confuse their perceptions of the limits of sexual experience.

Published in May 2008

BLACK ORCHID
Roxanne Carr
ISBN 978 0 352 34188 4

At the Black Orchid Club, adventurous women who yearn for the pleasures of exotic, even kinky sex can quench their desires in discreet and luxurious surroundings. Having tasted the fulfilment of unique and powerful lusts, one such adventurous woman learns what happens when the need for limitless indulgence becomes an addiction.

Published in June 2008

FORBIDDEN FRUIT
Susie Raymond
ISBN 978 0 352 34189 1

The last thing sexy thirty-something Beth expected was to get involved with a much younger man. But when she finds him spying on her in the dressing room at work she embarks on an erotic journey with the straining youth, teaching him and teasing him as she leads him through myriad sensuous exercises at her stylish modern home. As their lascivious games become more and more intense, Beth soon begins to realise that she is the one being awakened to a new world of desire – and that hers is the mind quickly becoming consumed with lust.

Published in July 2008

JULIET RISING
Cleo Cordell
ISBN 978 0 352 34192 1

Nothing is more important to Reynard than winning the favours of the bright and wilful Juliet, a pupil at Madame Nicol's exclusive but strict 18th century ladies' academy. Her captivating beauty tinged with a hint of cruelty soon has Reynard willing to do anything to win her approval. But Juliet's methods have little effect on Andreas, the real object of her lustful obsessions. Unable to bend him to her will, she is forced to watch him lavish his manly talents on her fellow pupils. That is, until she agrees to change her stuck-up, stubborn ways and become an eager erotic participant.

Published in August 2008

ODALISQUE

Fleur Reynolds

ISBN 978 0 352 34193 8

Set against a backdrop of sophisticated elegance, a tale of family intrigue, forbidden passions and depraved secrets unfolds. Beautiful but scheming, successful designer Auralie plots to bring about the downfall of her virtuous cousin, Jeanine. Recently widowed, but still young and glamorous, Jeanine finds her passions being rekindled by Auralie's husband. But she is playing into Auralie's hands – vindictive hands that drag Jeanine into a world of erotic depravity. Why are the cousins locked into this sexual feud? And what is the purpose of Jeanine's mysterious Confessor, and his sordid underground sect?

Published in September 2008

THE STALLION

Georgina Brown

ISBN 978 0 352 34199 0

The world of showjumping is as steamy as it is competitive. Ambitious young rider Penny Bennett enters into a wager with her oldest rival and friend, Ariadne, to win her thoroughbred stallion, guaranteed to bring Penny money and success. But first she must attain the sponsorship and very personal attention of showjumping's biggest impresario, Alister Beaumont.

Beaumont's riding school, however, is not all it seems. There's the weird relationship between Alister and his cigar-smoking sister. And the bizarre clothes they want Penny to wear. But in this atmosphere of unbridled kinkiness, Penny is determined not only to win the wager but to discover the truth about Beaumont's strange hobbies.

Published in October 2008

THE DEVIL AND THE DEEP BLUE SEA
Cheryl Mildenhall
ISBN 978 0 352 34200 3

When Hillary and her girlfriends rent a country house for their summer vacation, it is a pleasant surprise to find that its secretive and kinky owner – Darius Harwood – seems to be the most desirable man in the locale. That is, before Hillary meets Haldane, the blonde and beautifully proportioned Norwegian sailor who works nearby. Intrigued by the sexual allure of two very different men, Hillary can't resist exploring the possibilities on offer. But these opportunities for misbehaviour quickly lead her into a tricky situation for which a difficult decision has to be made.

Published in November 2008

THE NINETY DAYS OF GENEVIEVE
Lucinda Carrington
ISBN 978 0 352 34201 0

A ninety-day sex contract wasn't exactly what Genevieve Loften had in mind when she began business negotiations with the arrogant and attractive James Sinclair. As a career move she wanted to go along with it; the pay-off was potentially huge.

However, she didn't imagine that he would make her the star performer in a series of increasingly kinky and exotic fantasies. Thrown into a world of sexual misadventure, Genevieve learns how to balance her high-pressure career with the twilight world of fetishism and debauchery.

ALSO LOOK OUT FOR

THE NEW BLACK LACE BOOK OF WOMEN'S SEXUAL FANTASIES
Edited and compiled by Mitzi Szereto
ISBN 978 0 352 34172 3

The second anthology of detailed sexual fantasies contributed by women from all over the world. The book is a result of a year's research by an expert on erotic writing and gives a fascinating insight into the rich diversity of the female sexual imagination.

Black Lace Booklist

Information is correct at time of printing. To avoid disappointment, check availability before ordering. Go to www.black-lace-books.com.
All books are priced £7.99 unless another price is given.

BLACK LACE BOOKS WITH A CONTEMPORARY SETTING

❑ THE ANGELS' SHARE Maya Hess	ISBN 978 0 352 34043 6	
❑ ASKING FOR TROUBLE Kristina Lloyd	ISBN 978 0 352 33362 9	
❑ BLACK LIPSTICK KISSES Monica Belle	ISBN 978 0 352 33885 3	£6.99
❑ THE BLUE GUIDE Carrie Williams	ISBN 978 0 352 34132 7	
❑ THE BOSS Monica Belle	ISBN 978 0 352 34088 7	
❑ BOUND IN BLUE Monica Belle	ISBN 978 0 352 34012 2	
❑ CAMPAIGN HEAT Gabrielle Marcola	ISBN 978 0 352 33941 6	
❑ CAT SCRATCH FEVER Sophie Mouette	ISBN 978 0 352 34021 4	
❑ CIRCUS EXCITE Nikki Magennis	ISBN 978 0 352 34033 7	
❑ CLUB CRÈME Primula Bond	ISBN 978 0 352 33907 2	£6.99
❑ CONFESSIONAL Judith Roycroft	ISBN 978 0 352 33421 3	
❑ CONTINUUM Portia Da Costa	ISBN 978 0 352 33120 5	
❑ DANGEROUS CONSEQUENCES Pamela Rochford	ISBN 978 0 352 33185 4	
❑ DARK DESIGNS Madelynne Ellis	ISBN 978 0 352 34075 7	
❑ THE DEVIL INSIDE Portia Da Costa	ISBN 978 0 352 32993 6	
❑ EQUAL OPPORTUNITIES Mathilde Madden	ISBN 978 0 352 34070 2	
❑ FIRE AND ICE Laura Hamilton	ISBN 978 0 352 33486 2	
❑ GONE WILD Maria Eppie	ISBN 978 0 352 33670 5	
❑ HOTBED Portia Da Costa	ISBN 978 0 352 33614 9	
❑ IN PURSUIT OF ANNA Natasha Rostova	ISBN 978 0 352 34060 3	
❑ IN THE FLESH Emma Holly	ISBN 978 0 352 34117 4	
❑ LEARNING TO LOVE IT Alison Tyler	ISBN 978 0 352 33535 7	
❑ MAD ABOUT THE BOY Mathilde Madden	ISBN 978 0 352 34001 6	
❑ MAKE YOU A MAN Anna Clare	ISBN 978 0 352 34006 1	
❑ MAN HUNT Cathleen Ross	ISBN 978 0 352 33583 8	
❑ THE MASTER OF SHILDEN Lucinda Carrington	ISBN 978 0 352 33140 3	
❑ MIXED DOUBLES Zoe le Verdier	ISBN 978 0 352 33312 4	£6.99
❑ MIXED SIGNALS Anna Clare	ISBN 978 0 352 33889 1	£6.99
❑ MS BEHAVIOUR Mini Lee	ISBN 978 0 352 33962 1	

❑ PACKING HEAT Karina Moore ISBN 978 0 352 33356 8 £6.99
❑ PAGAN HEAT Monica Belle ISBN 978 0 352 33974 4
❑ PEEP SHOW Mathilde Madden ISBN 978 0 352 33924 9
❑ THE POWER GAME Carrera Devonshire ISBN 978 0 352 33990 4
❑ THE PRIVATE UNDOING OF A PUBLIC SERVANT Leonie Martel ISBN 978 0 352 34066 5
❑ RUDE AWAKENING Pamela Kyle ISBN 978 0 352 33036 9
❑ SAUCE FOR THE GOOSE Mary Rose Maxwell ISBN 978 0 352 33492 3
❑ SPLIT Kristina Lloyd ISBN 978 0 352 34154 9
❑ STELLA DOES HOLLYWOOD Stella Black ISBN 978 0 352 33588 3
❑ THE STRANGER Portia Da Costa ISBN 978 0 352 33211 0
❑ SUITE SEVENTEEN Portia Da Costa ISBN 978 0 352 34109 9
❑ TONGUE IN CHEEK Tabitha Flyte ISBN 978 0 352 33484 8
❑ THE TOP OF HER GAME Emma Holly ISBN 978 0 352 34116 7
❑ UNNATURAL SELECTION Alaine Hood ISBN 978 0 352 33963 8
❑ VELVET GLOVE Emma Holly ISBN 978 0 352 34115 0
❑ VILLAGE OF SECRETS Mercedes Kelly ISBN 978 0 352 33344 5
❑ WILD BY NATURE Monica Belle ISBN 978 0 352 33915 7 £6.99
❑ WILD CARD Madeline Moore ISBN 978 0 352 34038 2
❑ WING OF MADNESS Mae Nixon ISBN 978 0 352 34099 3

BLACK LACE BOOKS WITH AN HISTORICAL SETTING

❑ THE BARBARIAN GEISHA Charlotte Royal ISBN 978 0 352 33267 7
❑ BARBARIAN PRIZE Deanna Ashford ISBN 978 0 352 34017 7
❑ THE CAPTIVATION Natasha Rostova ISBN 978 0 352 33234 9
❑ DARKER THAN LOVE Kristina Lloyd ISBN 978 0 352 33279 0
❑ WILD KINGDOM Deanna Ashford ISBN 978 0 352 33549 4
❑ DIVINE TORMENT Janine Ashbless ISBN 978 0 352 33719 1
❑ FRENCH MANNERS Olivia Christie ISBN 978 0 352 33214 1
❑ LORD WRAXALL'S FANCY Anna Lieff Saxby ISBN 978 0 352 33080 2
❑ NICOLE'S REVENGE Lisette Allen ISBN 978 0 352 32984 4
❑ THE SENSES BEJEWELLED Cleo Cordell ISBN 978 0 352 32904 2 £6.99
❑ THE SOCIETY OF SIN Sian Lacey Taylder ISBN 978 0 352 34080 1
❑ TEMPLAR PRIZE Deanna Ashford ISBN 978 0 352 34137 2
❑ UNDRESSING THE DEVIL Angel Strand ISBN 978 0 352 33938 6

BLACK LACE BOOKS WITH A PARANORMAL THEME

❑ BRIGHT FIRE Maya Hess	ISBN 978 0 352 34104 4
❑ BURNING BRIGHT Janine Ashbless	ISBN 978 0 352 34085 6
❑ CRUEL ENCHANTMENT Janine Ashbless	ISBN 978 0 352 33483 1
❑ FLOOD Anna Clare	ISBN 978 0 352 34094 8
❑ GOTHIC BLUE Portia Da Costa	ISBN 978 0 352 33075 8
❑ THE PRIDE Edie Bingham	ISBN 978 0 352 33997 3
❑ THE SILVER COLLAR Mathilde Madden	ISBN 978 0 352 34141 9
❑ THE TEN VISIONS Olivia Knight	ISBN 978 0 352 34119 8

BLACK LACE ANTHOLOGIES

❑ BLACK LACE QUICKIES 1 Various	ISBN 978 0 352 34126 6	£2.99
❑ BLACK LACE QUICKIES 2 Various	ISBN 978 0 352 34127 3	£2.99
❑ BLACK LACE QUICKIES 3 Various	ISBN 978 0 352 34128 0	£2.99
❑ BLACK LACE QUICKIES 4 Various	ISBN 978 0 352 34129 7	£2.99
❑ BLACK LACE QUICKIES 5 Various	ISBN 978 0 352 34130 3	£2.99
❑ BLACK LACE QUICKIES 6 Various	ISBN 978 0 352 34133 4	£2.99
❑ BLACK LACE QUICKIES 7 Various	ISBN 978 0 352 34146 4	£2.99
❑ BLACK LACE QUICKIES 8 Various	ISBN 978 0 352 34147 1	£2.99
❑ BLACK LACE QUICKIES 9 Various	ISBN 978 0 352 34155 6	£2.99
❑ MORE WICKED WORDS Various	ISBN 978 0 352 33487 9	£6.99
❑ WICKED WORDS 3 Various	ISBN 978 0 352 33522 7	£6.99
❑ WICKED WORDS 4 Various	ISBN 978 0 352 33603 3	£6.99
❑ WICKED WORDS 5 Various	ISBN 978 0 352 33642 2	£6.99
❑ WICKED WORDS 6 Various	ISBN 978 0 352 33690 3	£6.99
❑ WICKED WORDS 7 Various	ISBN 978 0 352 33743 6	£6.99
❑ WICKED WORDS 8 Various	ISBN 978 0 352 33787 0	£6.99
❑ WICKED WORDS 9 Various	ISBN 978 0 352 33860 0	
❑ WICKED WORDS 10 Various	ISBN 978 0 352 33893 8	
❑ THE BEST OF BLACK LACE 2 Various	ISBN 978 0 352 33718 4	
❑ WICKED WORDS: SEX IN THE OFFICE Various	ISBN 978 0 352 33944 7	
❑ WICKED WORDS: SEX AT THE SPORTS CLUB Various	ISBN 978 0 352 33991 1	
❑ WICKED WORDS: SEX ON HOLIDAY Various	ISBN 978 0 352 33961 4	
❑ WICKED WORDS: SEX IN UNIFORM Various	ISBN 978 0 352 34002 3	
❑ WICKED WORDS: SEX IN THE KITCHEN Various	ISBN 978 0 352 34018 4	
❑ WICKED WORDS: SEX ON THE MOVE Various	ISBN 978 0 352 34034 4	
❑ WICKED WORDS: SEX AND MUSIC Various	ISBN 978 0 352 34061 0	

- ❑ WICKED WORDS: SEX AND SHOPPING Various — ISBN 978 0 352 34076 4
- ❑ SEX IN PUBLIC Various — ISBN 978 0 352 34089 4
- ❑ SEX WITH STRANGERS Various — ISBN 978 0 352 34105 1
- ❑ LOVE ON THE DARK SIDE Various — ISBN 978 0 352 34132 7
- ❑ LUST BITES Various — ISBN 978 0 352 34153 2

BLACK LACE NON-FICTION

- ❑ THE BLACK LACE BOOK OF WOMEN'S SEXUAL FANTASIES — ISBN 978 0 352 33793 1 — £6.99
  Edited by Kerri Sharp

To find out the latest information about Black Lace titles, check out the website: www.black-lace-books.com or send for a booklist with complete synopses by writing to:

Black Lace Booklist, Virgin Books Ltd
Random House,
20 Vauxhall Bridge Road,
London SW1V 2SA

Please include an SAE of decent size. Please note only British stamps are valid.

Our privacy policy
We will not disclose information you supply us to any other parties. We will not disclose any information which identifies you personally to any person without your express consent.

From time to time we may send out information about Black Lace books and special offers. Please tick here if you do not wish to receive Black Lace information. ❑

Please send me the books I have ticked above.

Name ....

Address ....

....

....

....

Post Code ....

Send to: Virgin Books Cash Sales,
Random House, 20 Vauxhall Bridge Road,
London SW1V 2SA.

US customers: for prices and details of how to order books for delivery by mail, call 888-330-8477.

Please enclose a cheque or postal order, made payable to Virgin Books Ltd, to the value of the books you have ordered plus postage and packing costs as follows:

UK and BFPO – £1.00 for the first book, 50p for each subsequent book.

Overseas (including Republic of Ireland) – £2.00 for the first book, £1.00 for each subsequent book.

If you would prefer to pay by VISA, ACCESS/MASTERCARD, DINERS CLUB, AMEX or SWITCH, please write your card number and expiry date here:

....

....

Signature

Please allow up to 28 days for delivery.